DEATH ON BULL PATH

CARRIE DOYLE

Poisoned Pen
PRESS

Published by Poisoned Pen Press, an imprint of Sourcebooks
P.O. Box 4410, Naperville, Illinois 60567-4410
(630) 961-3900
sourcebooks.com

Originally published as *Death on Bull Path* in 2016 in the United States
by Dunemere Books. This edition issued based on the paperback edition
published in 2018 in the United States by Dunemere Books.

Library of Congress Cataloging-in-Publication Data

Names: Doyle, Carrie, author.
Title: Death on bull path / Carrie Doyle.
Description: Naperville, Illinois : Poisoned Pen Press, [2021] | Series:
   Hamptons murder mysteries ; book 4 | First published in 2016 in the
   United States by Dunemere Books.
Identifiers: LCCN 2020027654 (paperback) | (epub)
Subjects: GSAFD: Mystery fiction.
Classification: LCC PS3604.O95473 4334 2021 (print) | LCC PS3604.O95473
   (ebook) | DDC 813/.6--dc23
LC record available at https://lccn.loc.gov/2020027654

Printed and bound in Canada.
MBP 10 9 8 7 6 5 4 3 2 1

Prologue

NO ONE REMEMBERED THE WOMAN. IF PRESSED, THERE WAS A vague acknowledgment that there had been another person there—a warm body toward whom the men sometimes directed their attention—but an inquiry into a description of her features produced blank stares and head-scratching. Furthermore, a request to describe her demeanor—Scared? Angry? Excited?—was impossible for the observers to answer. The woman had been absorbed into the shadows of the bar and left no lingering impression.

It was the two men everyone had noticed. They were loud, garrulous, and flashy. They had arrived after dinner service had ended, and it was clear that this was not their first stop on the bar circuit. Shots followed by chasers were downed over the course of two hours. Multiple high fives and champagne toasts were witnessed. Each man made several trips to the bathroom and returned rubbing his nose. As there was no waitress on duty that late on a Sunday, the men took turns approaching the bar and placing their drink orders, while their female companion remained seated in the darkened corner of their banquette. The men were up and down, unable to be still, and clearly there to party, but no one would ever be able to recall if the woman had been having a good time that night.

Sunday nights at the Windmill Inn are generally subdued. The same is true for all of East Hampton, even in the summer—but this was Labor Day weekend. It was the bitter end of a sun-choked and glorious summer, and now there was a chill in the air and the leaves were slightly crisping before their descent to the ground.

The ocean was a bit choppier, and seasonal rentals were wrapping up; everyone wanted that last gasp—to eke out the final thrills of summer before returning to the city and stone-cold reality.

Shane Boskin and Gary DiAngelo wanted more than the last gasp. They wanted to milk this weekend for everything it had to offer. Although Shane was dark and Gary fair, the two men were similar: they were both in their midthirties, strong and fit, Wall Street guys. They were clad alike in button-down shirts, khaki pants, fleece vests bearing the emblem of the hedge funds they worked for, and both with very expensive watches on their wrists (this being the unspoken uniform of men in their position). They were attractive, but that impression was generated not by the perfection of their facial features but rather by the identical swagger and confidence that gave them both a powerful charisma.

After several last calls, the men reluctantly left. Their female companion had slipped out just before Jesse, the bartender, came over the first time and asked the men to settle their bill. It took a protracted ten minutes for the men to finish their drinks and slap down their Amex Black Cards. After assuring Jesse that they had an Uber waiting and would not be getting behind the wheel, they departed. Shane grabbed a handful of rosemary-spiced mixed nuts on his way out, something Jesse would later recall because it was only as Shane plunged his hand into the nut dish that Jesse first noticed the glint of the wedding band. Gary had his cell phone pasted to his ear as he sauntered out. The lone fragment of conversation that Jesse overheard was Gary inviting someone "back to the house to party." Both men, and presumably their companion, disappeared into the night.

It was a couple of hours later when 911 received the call.

1

ANTONIA BINGHAM PAUSED AT THE THRESHOLD OF HER INN TO
make sure she was not tracking in any sand with her shoes. She
had completed her morning walk along Georgica Beach, proceeding as far as Wainscott, before doing a one-eighty to return home.
She now felt completely energized and her pockets were filled
with bounty: the ocean-smoothed slivers of sea glass that she had
discovered near the shore. After a busy summer season, she was
ready to slow down, take better care of herself, and burrow into
fall. Although off-season meant a reduction of guests at the inn
and therefore less income, fall symbolized new beginnings and a
freshness that she relished. Besides, she was eager to have time to
catch up on all of the repairs and paperwork that she had neglected
for three months. An added bonus was that autumn was butter-
nut squash season! Antonia couldn't wait to start trying out new
recipes in the kitchen. Her mouth watered just thinking of maple-
glazed squash dotted with chunks of Gorgonzola, toasted walnuts,
and thin, almost transparent, ribbons of prosciutto.

"Antonia, Sergeant Flanagan is here to see you," chirped
Connie from the front desk as she checked out a departing couple
from Texas.

"Thanks, Connie. Where can I find him?"

"He's in your office."

Antonia's already pink cheeks reddened. "My office? Oh fid-
dlesticks, it's a mess! I wish you'd put him in the parlor!"

Connie's laugh was lighthearted. She had a cheerful disposition and an easygoing attitude that made her a perfect fit for the reception desk. "I know. I tried, but he said he wanted someplace less public."

Antonia patted her lustrous but windblown black waves into a semblance of order and shrugged. "Oh well, I suppose he's seen my office before."

Antonia was not alarmed that a police officer awaited her. Unfortunately, she had been involved in a few murder cases in recent months—thankfully as a crime *solver* rather than a suspect (or victim)—and she assumed that the sergeant needed to dot the *i*'s in one or another of her statements.

As she moved along the hall of her antique Georgian-style inn—the three-story shingled structure was built in 1840—she ruminated over how much her attitude toward cops had changed in recent years. After a terrible marriage to a police officer in California, she had been left with little trust in and pretty much total disdain for anyone in law enforcement. She couldn't forgive her ex-husband's colleagues for turning a blind eye to the violence and suffering he had inflicted upon her and her family. Fortunately she had found that the police officers in East Hampton were different. She was even starting to develop a wary faith in them, particularly Sergeant Flanagan, who, if she was completely honest, had given her a few outs when she had meddled in things when she shouldn't have. True, he thought her a giant pain in the rear, but she knew that he had a grudging respect for her.

"You know, you're allowed to sit when you wait for me," teased Antonia as she entered her overflowing office.

The seasoned cop in his well-pressed uniform turned and gave her a wry look. He had dark, close-cropped hair, was extremely fit, and always stood erect like a soldier, as if sitting somehow compromised his authority.

"There's nowhere to sit."

"Oh, nonsense," said Antonia, scurrying to remove a pile of folders from the guest chair that stood opposite her desk. "You could have moved these, or you could have parked it in my seat."

"There are a lot of risks in my job, but a visit to your office is the most hazardous."

"Ha, ha, is that police humor?" asked Antonia as she plopped in her chair.

"Does police humor exist?" asked Sergeant Flanagan, looking down at her with a raised brow.

"Well, Sergeant Flanagan, I think this is the most banter we've had in our entire acquaintance." Antonia smiled.

Flanagan brushed away some invisible dust from the seat opposite Antonia and sat down precariously. "Sadly, it has to end here. I have some questions for you."

Much to Antonia's delight, she noticed that Soyla, who worked in the inn's restaurant, had left a plate of freshly baked blueberry mini muffins and a teapot of steeping Earl Grey on a corner of Antonia's full desk. Those morning walks always made Antonia hungry! She held up the plate and offered it to the sergeant, but he demurred with a wave of his hand. *It must be how he stays so fit,* thought Antonia as she took a bite of the still-warm treat. What kind of a person turns down freshly baked blueberry muffins? And the berries were local and in season too—plump and sweet as they burst in her mouth. It took an extraordinary amount of self-control for him to refuse them, Antonia concluded. Something she was sorely lacking.

"So what's up?" asked Antonia after she had swallowed her third bite. "Is this about Susie Whitaker?"

Antonia had recently helped solve a cold case involving the

murder of a sixteen year-old girl back in the 1990s. It had been very tragic, but thankfully the killer was now behind bars.

"Actually, no," Sergeant Flanagan responded. "It's about a double homicide that occurred in the Northwest Woods last night."

Antonia nearly choked on her breakfast. "*What? Another* murder?"

"*Double* murder," Sergeant Flanagan corrected. "I am unable to divulge much information about the victims, pending notification to their families, so I need to ensure your utmost discretion. What we know so far, through an Uber receipt we found in one of the victim's wallets, is that he was at the Windmill Inn last night. Perhaps both of the victims were."

"*Here?*" gasped Antonia. "Oh my goodness, were they staying here?" This would be terrible for business.

"I don't know, you tell me." Sergeant Flanagan held up a color copy of two driver's licenses: Shane Adam Boskin and Gary Vincent DiAngelo.

Antonia squinted but neither looked familiar, nor did the names ring any bells.

"Let me check the reservation log."

Antonia clicked onto the computer in front of her and scanned the room list. No one with either of those names had been registered at the inn. She even did a search for past reservations but found nothing.

"They didn't stay here, at least under those names. Let me check the dinner reservations list and see if they ate here."

She clicked over to another file, but again neither name appeared. "They might have been eating here, but as guests of someone else who made the reservation. Otherwise, perhaps they were at the bar? We haven't gone through receipts yet from last night. But I can check with Jesse the bartender and Glen our maître d.'"

"Are they here now?"

"Actually, Glen should be."

"Let's go see him."

"Those guys? Yeah, I saw them," said Glen, who was squinting at the picture that Sergeant Flanagan held. They had found Glen seated at a leather booth in the restaurant going through the previous night's receipts. "Let me guess—they got into a bar fight after they left."

"Worse than that," said Sergeant Flanagan. "They're dead."

This got Glen's full attention. "What?"

"Murdered," interjected Antonia.

"No way, that's horrible." When he spoke candidly, Glen's strong Long Island accent was in full bloom, so words like "horrible" were pronounced more like "HAW-rubble." "What happened?"

"Tell me what they were doing here," said Sergeant Flanagan, ignoring Glen's question.

A lock of Glen's thickly gelled hair fell in front of his eyes, and he quickly swept it away. "They came in toward the end of the night, to the bar. It was obvious they'd already been out drinking and this was just a pit stop. I didn't pay much attention to them when they came in because the restaurant was slammed, but they got louder and louder the more they drank, and I told Jesse to cut them off and make sure they had a ride home."

"Were they talking to anyone else?"

"I didn't really notice. But I think they had a girl with them."

"A girl?" asked Antonia.

Sergeant Flanagan turned and gave her an irritated look. "Miss

Bingham, please allow me to do the questioning. You're only here in case you can add to the discussion."

"Fair enough," said Antonia. She sat down in the booth across from Glen in a form of capitulation, while Sergeant Flanagan remained standing.

"Not a girl, a woman," Glen clarified.

"What did she look like?" asked Sergeant Flanagan, whipping out his brown leather notebook and a pen.

"You know…I'm not sure. Brown hair? Wait, maybe blond."

"Which is it?"

"I'm not sure, I can't say definitely. Don't put me on a witness stand!" said Glen holding up his hands in a surrender pose.

"Clearly, at the rate we are going, I won't. Can you tell me her approximate age?"

"Um, twenties? Thirties?"

"Anything you can specifically remember about how she dressed?"

"I really didn't see her."

"Would you be able to identify her voice?"

"What, like, if she's at the restaurant?"

"No. In a 911 call."

"She made the 911 call?" Antonia asked with interest.

Sergeant Flanagan shot her a look of warning. Antonia slid her fingers across her lips as if she were zipping her mouth closed.

"I don't know. I doubt it. You should ask Jesse, he probably could tell you more."

"I will talk to him. But in the meantime, is there anything you can add? Was anyone else seated around them that engaged with them?"

"I don't think so."

"Anyone strange at the bar?"

Glen rubbed his chin distractedly. He was very well groomed with angular features and long eyelashes, causing female customers of all ages to flirt with him. He in turn would flirt back, which always secured him extra tips. He was the perfect point person for the restaurant, although he was incredibly high maintenance and constantly needed Antonia's commendations and commiserations.

"There was one big guy... I don't know if he was strange..."

"Oh? What was it about him?" asked the sergeant.

"I'm not sure... It's something I wouldn't have thought twice about, but now that you're asking, it was kind of weird. He was sitting alone at the bar, and he seemed very tense, you know, he had a nervous energy about him, like he wasn't there to have fun and he wasn't there to get drunk, he was just...there. And then someone bumped into the back of his chair by accident and he got really triggered and yelled to back the you-know-what off. It was really out of nowhere, and we're not that kind of place."

"Was it one of the victims that bumped into him?"

"No. No, actually it was a woman. And her boyfriend then got triggered also and said, like, 'What's your problem? It was an accident; she was just getting her coat on,' and the big guy looked angry, but then Jesse and I defused the situation and the couple left."

"What did the big guy look like?"

"You know, big. I'm tall but he was like six foot four. Had a big head. Probably late twenties. He looked like a dumb football player."

"Did it seem like he was doing business at the bar?"

"What do you mean, like selling drugs?"

At this Antonia chimed in and stated firmly, "No one sells drugs in my inn."

"We've *never* had that problem here," said Glen in an offended tone. "We keep a clean house."

"Do you have credit card receipts for this guy?"

Glen shook his head. "He paid cash. I remember that because not that many people do these days. I always make a joke, like hold up the bill and say 'what is this?' when people pay, because, you know, money is going extinct."

"When did he leave?"

Glen looked up at the ceiling. "You know what, I think he was one of the last to go. It was the victims and their lady friend and this guy at the end. They all left around the same time. But I can't be certain. You can ask Jesse; he may remember more."

"No way, those guys are dead?" Jesse mused in disbelief half an hour later. He clutched the photocopy of their licenses in his hand and shook his head.

"What can you tell me about them?" continued Sergeant Flanagan.

Antonia had called Jesse and asked him to come into work right away, and he had arrived somewhat bleary-eyed and sleepy, clad in a T-shirt and jeans, his hair going in all different directions. He was a recent college graduate who was working only for the season, before he moved out west in October and got what he referred to as a "real job." Antonia was sorry to see him go, as he was easy-going and, if she were to be totally honest, also easy on the eyes. She was certain that's why her bar business had gone up by 10 percent this summer and seemed to have been discovered by young twentysomethings.

"Those guys had been partying. They were pretty lit by the time they got here."

"What were they drinking?" asked the sergeant.

"We don't serve people if we think they've had too much," interjected Antonia.

Sergeant Flanagan turned toward her. "Thanks, Miss Bingham. I'll take it from here. Why don't you leave us for now."

"What? But it's my inn."

"And it's my case. So, thank you."

Reluctantly, Antonia wandered into the kitchen feeling like her inner snoop was wounded. The immaculate kitchen was quiet. It was still too early for the staff to have arrived to prep dinner, and Soyla had taken a break after the breakfast service. Antonia opened the refrigerator for what she liked to think was inspiration, but was possibly just a snack, and scanned the contents.

Earlier, when they were waiting for Jesse to arrive, Antonia had been able to press Sergeant Flanagan into giving her more information, insisting that it might jog her memory for anything related to the case. They both knew that was a load of hooey, but for some reason, the sergeant relented and filled her in (perhaps because she also overheard him on the cell confirming with a colleague that the families had been notified). He gave her a brief rundown.

The police had received a 911 call from a woman in distress, who said that she had been a guest at a house on Bull Path and when she returned from using the powder room she found that the two men she was with had been stabbed in the hot tub. She wasn't sure if they were dead because she had fled the house and was running in the woods, scared that the killer would pursue her. She didn't give her name and the call ended abruptly. And in answer to Antonia's follow-up questions, the sergeant informed her that the phone the woman had used was owned by Shane Boskin, which is why they couldn't "just trace the call." It had not yet been retrieved, and the woman had not yet come forward, and they were searching for her. No, they couldn't be sure she wasn't the killer, but that's why they needed to locate her. Yes, it was a violent crime, the police officer confirmed, which prompted Antonia to muse that all crimes were violent in their own way, weren't they? After that comment, the sergeant clammed up, perhaps regretting that he had even given Antonia a little window into the investigation.

Antonia was offended that her sleuthing skills were rejected, but the truth was, she had other things to worry about. Time to let the police do their jobs.

"This is a good thing. I need to stay away from murder," said Antonia out loud to the empty kitchen.

"Excuse me?" a male voiced queried.

Antonia turned around abruptly, like a naughty child who had been caught stealing cookies. She slammed the refrigerator door shut and stared at the man who had come through the back door.

"Nick!"

"I'm back, baby."

2

SHE FELT SUDDENLY SHY.

Antonia had not seen Nick Darrow since…well, since he had embraced her a few weeks earlier on what had become the best day of her life. And now he stood in her kitchen, this famous tall, dark, and handsome movie star clad in a dark-blue button-down and khakis, with his hair just a bit too long around the ears, smiling at her. And she could only feel a rush of random discombobulated thoughts: that his front incisor slightly overlapped the tooth next to it but the flaw only added to his charm; that it was the wisdom behind his eyes—the knowledge, the experience, the wariness—that made them more penetrating; that he was here, in her kitchen. He was here, in her kitchen!

"When did you get back?" she croaked.

"Last night," he said, not moving.

She swallowed, embarrassed but attempting to be casual. "So, um, how long are you in town for?"

His smile grew larger. "Aren't you going to kiss me hello?"

All she could think of was her current appearance and how it was a total failure. She had on a blue scoop-neck shirt that perhaps clung to her curves a little too tightly but had been appropriate for a "sporty" beach walk and black leggings that her friend Genevieve had coerced her to buy but were tighter than anything she would normally allow near her body. Her dark wavy hair was loose and hung down around her shoulders and would probably benefit from the swirl of a brush. She wished she could press a button, stop time, run upstairs, shower, and put on a perfectly sexy-casual outfit that a top fashion designer had made specifically for her. But that was just a wish. Now was reality.

"Of course, hi, welcome back," she said and walked over to Nick and gave him the type of hug you give an older uncle with a beard.

Nick appeared amused. "It's okay, I don't bite."

Antonia sighed. "I know. Sorry. It's just…well, I feel weird. Here you are. What happened before you left…I know we have been writing all these fun letters to each other while you were away…"

"Fun?"

"Okay, well, you know what I mean. Interesting, informative missives…"

"How about sexy and romantic?"

"Don't torture me," Antonia said, crossing her arms in front of her chest.

"Haven't you enjoyed my letters?" asked Nick.

"Of course…but now, it's like, what now? I have been thinking a lot. I know you said you were, well, not with your wife anymore, but I don't want to be a home-wrecker. You are, after all, married."

There it was. The elephant in the room. Nick was married to Melanie Wells, one of the most renowned actresses around, although more for her beauty and ability to look fantastic in any outfit than for her acting skills.

"I told you, Melanie and I are done."

"I still am not sure I'm okay with that… Do I have any role in this?"

Nick shook his head. "Once again, we've been over this. Melanie and I have had problems for years… You more than anyone know that."

"I guess I just feel bad…"

"Don't feel bad. To be honest, this had nothing to do with you. You're just my rebound."

"Thanks." She grimaced.

"I'm kidding. Look"—he put both of his hands on Antonia's shoulders—"Melanie wants out also. She's the one who asked *me* for a divorce. I think she has someone else she wants to be with. The reason I'm back in town is that I had to go to New York to meet with my lawyer. We both just hashed out a separation agreement. It is signed, sealed, and delivered. Melanie and I are over. My main priority now is our son, Finn, of course. But I also want to make you a priority."

He gave her a look that made her stomach drop. Could it really be true? It was so scary to see a glimmer of the most delirious happiness and know that it was within reach if she moved toward it.

"I just want to make sure that I'm not..."

He pressed down hard on her shoulders, as if the intensity would erase her silly thoughts. "You had nothing to do with the split, but you are the happy ending."

Was it possible? she wondered.

"Now kiss me," he commanded.

This would be their first *real* kiss. She knew that when she kissed him now, tangibly, the past kiss that they had shared—the kiss of her dreams—would instantly vanish and she would set a new course for her romantic destiny. The moment she and Nick had shared a few weeks ago, a moment she had only dreamed of in her wildest fantasies, had been so incredible that she wondered if it had happened at all. It was too good to be true. But now, if she kissed him, it would all be true and with truth comes reality. Was she prepared for that?

The answer was yes.

After their embrace, Nick gazed at her. "So now, tell me what was all this talk about murder again? I thought we were over it."

"Ah yes, so did I."

Nick had left shortly after their reunion with the agreement that they would meet for dinner the following evening at the 1770 House, another hotel just down the road from Antonia's Windmill Inn. Despite herself, Antonia had bristled when Nick suggested they dine there. Of course the food at 1770 House was fantastic and revered, and Antonia liked to remind herself that there was room for several inns and great restaurants in East Hampton, but she was only human and did suffer from uncontrollable pangs of professional jealousy. She wanted to be all "kumbaya" and support everyone, but a satanic little voice inside her head would sometimes question: *Really, Antonia? In the offseason? In January? There are that many people who want to come stay at white-shingled historic inns with award-winning restaurants?* But she did her best to silence it.

And the reality was that she would be dining with Nick Darrow tomorrow! (He had even suggested getting together this evening, but as it was the last day of Labor Day weekend, it was better to stick close to home and troubleshoot. Also, it wasn't so bad to play a little hard to get.) Tomorrow they would be together. And to hell with the fact that it was at a rival inn and she was supposed to be at her own inn cooking in the kitchen! Life was too short. Yes, life was indeed too short, a fact she was reminded of yet again when her frenemy Larry Lipper showed up at the inn just after lunch.

"Come on, Bingham, let's do it," he commanded.

She had been informing Marty, Kendra, and Soyla—her kitchen staff—about the evening specials when Larry Lipper burst into the kitchen.

"Do what?" Antonia asked with irritation.

"We gotta go."

"Where?"

"The crime scene," said Larry with exasperation. "We're back in business, baby."

It was odd to Antonia that, in the past few hours, two different men had called her "baby." The effect on her in each occasion couldn't have been more different. When Nick Darrow said it, it took her breath away. When Larry Lipper, the homunculus crime reporter for the *East Hampton Star*, who had an ego as big as the ocean and was completely void of tact, social conventions, and manners in general, said it, she felt, well, repulsed. She would never be Larry's baby, but she was Nick's!

"You are out of your mind on so many levels if you think I'm accompanying you to a crime scene."

"But you're my in," he protested.

Antonia could hear her executive chef, Marty, muttering obscenities to her sous chef, Kendra, behind her, and frankly she couldn't blame him.

"Excuse me a minute," she said, turning to her staff. "I have to take care of a problem. A very small, miniscule problem." Antonia motioned to Larry before taking him by the elbow and escorting him out to the dining room of the restaurant.

"Larry, listen, you can't come barging into my place of work all the time," Antonia admonished.

"Bingham, baby, don't forget who started this love affair

between us in the first place. You're the one who came to my office and threw yourself at me all those months ago. Begging for my attention. And now, what?"

"Don't call me baby."

He rolled his eyes. "Let's, for once, forgo the song and dance. We both know we are two peas in a pod when it comes to crime and solving it."

"I don't want to be in any pod with you. Not to mention I couldn't fit in your pod."

"Semantics from a foodie, I love it," said Larry. "But listen, I really do need your assistance. I need a Pepper Potts to my Iron Man. I know you know about those two hedgies who were offed after coming here. I want to take a gander at the crime scene but obviously the fuzz is blocking me. That's where you come in. The next-door neighbor to the share house where these *titans* of the business world were offed is none other than Iris Maple. I know she's a gal pal of yours from the East Hampton Library Author's Night committee, and seeing as she won't let me into her backyard for a bird's-eye view, I'm hoping she will let her little philanthropic buddy in, with a plus one."

"Larry...that's not a good idea."

"Why not? We all have a job to do, and mine is to keep our thousands of subscribers informed on the minute-to-minute details of this homicide."

"I think the police would say otherwise."

Larry shrugged. "Whatever. Look, you and I both are better at solving crime than they are. Haven't we closed three cases together? And let's be real. There is a homicidal maniac on the loose. Isn't it better if everyone comes together to catch the killer as soon as possible? We have to be all vigilante about this one, Bingham. You don't know who could be next."

If there was one thing in her life that she hated, it was agreeing with Larry Lipper. Well, that was not entirely true. She also hated the fact that when someone said murder these days, she felt an inexplicable force in her body that commanded her to investigate. What was that all about?

She sighed deeply. "Okay, a small peek can't hurt anyone."

"That's my girl," said Larry, slapping her on the back.

"I'm *not* your girl."

3

ONE OF THE BENEFITS OF LIVING IN EAST HAMPTON IS THAT there are various pockets of the town with entirely different landscapes. The Windmill Inn is located in the center of the picturesque village, on the corner of Windmill Way and Main Street, also known as Route 27, which is the main conduit that runs through all of the Hamptons. The inn is nestled in the center of the quaint New England–style village, just a stone's throw from all of the village's important historic, shingled buildings; its large cemetery; town pond; and most of its stores and churches. Spreading beyond the center of town, south of the highway, are the broad, spacious white sand beaches along the Atlantic Ocean; the manicured yards and pristine hedges enclosing estates; and links-style golf courses that would look at home in Scotland. North of the highway are the open farmlands where bounty such as potatoes and corn are harvested, the pebbly embankments along the bay, and the acres of dense and scrubby woodlands where the trees outnumber people and cast thick shade across the land.

It was the latter area where the double murder had occurred. A few blocks after making a right off Route 114 onto Stephen Hands Path by Dayton's farm stand, Larry's car was abruptly plunged into shadows. Despite the sunny day, the tall trees in the Northwest Woods blotted the sky, and there was only patchy illumination. Antonia was always amazed at how a short drive from one area of East Hampton to another could completely transport her into another panorama.

At the point of the Northwest Woods is Gardiner's Bay that connects Sag Harbor, Shelter Island, Gardiner's Island, and the north side of the town of East Hampton to the Long Island Sound. The surrounding area, which was originally called "Northwest Meddow," has documentation going back to 1653, four years after the original settlers arrived in East Hampton. It was the region's earliest port, and during the seventeenth century, it was bustling with trade. Items such as whale oil, furs, cattle, tools, and sheep were exported, while goodies such as rum, cocoa, indigo, spices, and mahogany were imported. For 150 years, the backdrop was very different than it is now: at the time, it boasted large farms, a mill, a school, a fish factory, and a shipbuilding business and was the center of commercial business in the town. But the settlement ended in 1885, primarily because the port at Sag Harbor, which had a deep-water harbor that could accommodate much larger vessels, exceeded it. In addition, the Northwest Harbor silted up. Since the abandonment of the original settlement, the region had returned to what it had been, and that was wilderness. In the decades since 1885, a forest began to grow—comprised mostly of oak trees but also with a pinch of dogwood, sassafras, and gray birch—and it is now a dense woods.

"Here we go again, Bingham. You and me, justice warriors, off to stop crime. They should give us medals," said Larry.

Antonia didn't even bother responding. Larry reached across Antonia, grazing her breasts with his arm (probably not by accident) before he flipped open the glove compartment and pulled out a giant pack of red licorice.

"Help yourself," he offered after taking a few pieces for himself.

"No thanks."

"Your loss."

"I'm sure," murmured Antonia, as she gazed distractedly out the window. She was still digesting the news that Nick Darrow had returned and was officially a free man. Something in her mind couldn't comprehend it on any level. It was too good to be true, and she was always wary of things too good to be true. But maybe she was just being a pessimist. Maybe it was okay for her to be completely happy?

"What's going on with you, Bingham? You seem out of it."

Antonia flipped back to reality. "No, just thinking about the murder. I can't believe those guys were at my inn last night and now they're dead."

"Not just dead but hacked to death, from what I understand. Stabbed repeatedly."

"How is that possible? I understand that they were big men. Wouldn't they have been able to fight off a killer?"

"There were no defensive wounds."

Antonia turned toward Larry in astonishment. "What do you mean?"

"My guy on the inside—and obviously don't hound me to tell you, because a good reporter will never reveal his sources—he tells me that there were no wounds on their hands. The police are thinking someone drugged these guys and with something more than just your run-of-the-mill roofie. Something that totally disabled them and allowed the killer to chop them up."

"That sounds horrible and gruesome."

"Yup. And there were multiple stab wounds indicating a lot of rage on the killer's part. Total overkill."

"Do they think it was the woman who called 911?" asked Antonia. "If she was with them all night, she certainly had time to roofie them."

"It would explain why she didn't stick around for the cops to come."

"Yup."

"I wonder why she wanted those guys dead," said Antonia. "It had to have been premeditated."

"Antonia!" said Iris Maple, opening her front door wider. "Thank goodness it's you. So nice to see a familiar face. Did you hear what happened next door? Now I have police everywhere and people knocking at my door..."

She ceased speaking and tensed as soon as she saw Larry Lipper lurking behind Antonia.

"Is this...man...with you?" she inquired coldly.

"Sadly, yes," said Antonia. "I think you two may have gotten off to a bad start. Larry Lipper is a reporter for the *Star*."

"I know, he informed me," said Iris, peering over her large glasses with disdain. She was in her seventies and had been a school librarian. Central casting could not have done a better job placing her in that role. She was currently in a completely no-nonsense stage of her life (although it may have been every stage in her life) and therefore impatient with people who annoyed her.

"Yes, well, Larry has actually helped solve so many recent crimes in East Hampton..."

"I thought that's why we had the police," said Iris curtly.

"They're incompetent," Larry burst out. "Look, I'm sorry if before I kind of didn't take my time explaining the situation to you..."

"Didn't take your time? You rushed into my house and made a beeline for my back patio without so much as an invitation."

Antonia gave Larry a disapproving look.

"Okay, sorry about that. I was excited. Two more dead bodies. Do you know what this will do for circulation?"

Antonia jumped in to clarify. "What he means, Iris, is that he is committed to assisting our police force in finding the killer. Larry cares deeply about our community and wants to ensure the safety of our citizens. If he acted impertinently, I can assure you that he is extremely sorry."

Antonia nudged Larry.

"Yes, yes, I'm very sorry," he said reluctantly. "Look, I can be like a dog, heading full force on the scent of a killer, but I do it in the name of justice."

"Well, it was very unsettling, particularly after what happened." Iris bristled.

"Yes, I'm sure," said Antonia. "I can only imagine how you felt. Were you home last night?"

"Of course I was, Antonia. Where else would I be?"

"Right."

"Did you hear anything?" probed Larry.

Iris sighed. "I suppose you may as well come in." She moved slightly and somewhat grudgingly aside to allow them into her house. "Then I can tell you what you want to know so you can be on your merry way and I can find some peace."

"Thank you," said Antonia.

"Ah, you're not one of those people," groaned Larry.

Antonia followed the direction of his gaze, which had landed on a floor mat with a collection of shoes and slippers under the front hall console.

"Do you want us to take off our shoes?" Antonia asked politely.

Iris sighed. "I am one of those people. I prefer it when people take off their dirty shoes. I loathe thinking of people traipsing around town in their footwear and then soiling my house. There are slippers there for your convenience," she added before leaving them to it.

"I'm sure nothing will fit my feet," said Larry smugly. "I have giant feet."

"I doubt that," said Antonia.

"And you know what they say about giant feet," he said, leaning in. "It means—"

"Please, spare me," Antonia replied dismissively. She slid her feet into a pair of fuzzy cotton slippers and waited while Larry, under protest, took off his shoes and donned a pair, lewdly whispering the end of his joke anyway. "Giant shoes..."

Antonia rolled her eyes at his fuggy breath in her ear. "I see you found a pair that's too big for even your giant masculine feet."

"These are clown shoes, clearly part of a costume. This whole 'don't bring dirt into my house' thing is a joke."

"House rules," said Antonia with a shrug, enjoying his discomfort.

"Old lady rules," fumed Larry, as he clomped away in the rubber-soled slippers.

The house was neatly kept and pleasant, as Antonia would have expected from Iris Maple. Iris had simple cropped hair, wore little to no makeup, and always made an effort to wear smart ensembles (skirt suits in summer, pantsuits in winter) with conservative accessories and jewelry.

Antonia and Larry were ushered from the front hall into the carpeted living room, which had a cathedral ceiling, large picture windows facing the backyard, and walls the color of Irish butter. A white sofa and two armchairs upholstered in a floral pattern were clustered next to a fireplace that although stacked with wood, appeared more ornamental than useful. Flanking the fireplace were bookshelves holding a small assortment of books (Antonia thought a librarian's house would be overrun with tomes, but perhaps Iris was only a borrower) in addition to tasteful bronze figurines and some simple wood carvings.

Larry scanned the room before muttering, "Old-ladyish."

Antonia shot him a warning glance.

"Won't you sit down," urged Iris. "Would you like a Diet Coke?"

"What, no tea?" said Larry.

"I don't have any tea," said Iris tersely. "And I wouldn't have taken you for a tea drinker."

"No, but I took *you* for one," he said.

Antonia decided to take the lead. "Can you tell us what you heard last night?"

"It's still such a shock. I'm very distraught. I'm sure this was a crime of passion, or whatever it's called. I hate the idea of mayhem in my neighborhood. It could have been me—some stranger wandering in here…"

"Very scary," concurred Antonia.

"This is what happens when the neighborhood gets compromised." Iris smoothed her skirt. "I can tell you that ever since that developer built the garish McMansion next to me, my quality of life has suffered. I used to have the loveliest neighbors, but they retired and moved down south, and then this odious man purchased their charming house, knocked it down, and erected the monstrosity. It is simply too large for the parcel of land that it sits on. And although I made sure to warn him that he better not be building a share house or one of those dreadful Airbnbs, that is exactly what he did. Now I have people coming and going all the time, people who have no consideration for their neighbors and just come here to party. It's tiresome." Iris sniffed in disapproval.

"I can only imagine. I would be very frustrated," commiserated Antonia.

"Did you ever get a chance to meet the guys who were killed?" asked Larry. He pulled out a notebook and began scribbling notes.

Iris shook her head. "No. I heard them, of course. They were here the entire month of August. Before that, I believe it was a family. Lots of noisy childish giggles and then splashes in the pool. I'm at my wit's end."

"And these guys were noisy?"

"Party after party. You can't believe it. I was just talking with my neighbor about it the other day. She lives behind the monstrosity—that's what we refer to it as—and her bedroom windows look right in. She hasn't gotten a decent night's sleep in years, and it's a shame."

"Last night, did you hear screams?" asked Larry.

"There's always screaming and music blaring out of that place! You can't imagine the chaos!" Iris's nostrils flared, and her cheeks bloomed pink for a moment then quickly subsided.

"Did you hear anything after you went to bed?" asked Antonia.

Iris sniffed and tossed her short hair. "Courtesy of the share house, I now sleep with a sound machine in my room, with the windows closed and the air-conditioning on. It is not ideal—the noise still penetrates even the most stringent devices. That's why I was able to hear the sirens. Then, shortly after the sirens, the police came to my door to check on me and search around the house."

"Did they find anything?"

"Not to my knowledge." Iris looked anxious.

"How frustrating," agreed Antonia.

"You cannot imagine. It makes it very hard to enjoy my retirement."

"What can you tell me about these guys?" asked Larry.

"They were obnoxiously loud. Coming in and out all hours of the night, car doors slamming, scream-talking, hyena-like laughter. This weekend I had back-to-back dinner dates at friends' homes, fortunately, therefore I didn't have to listen to the squeals emanating from their hot tub."

Larry flicked his notebook closed. "So, in other words, you got nothing."

Iris looked at him disdainfully. "I certainly did not give you the impression that I had information on this…this event."

"No, but one always hopes," said Larry, standing up and peering out the window. "Listen, mind if we poke around the backyard?"

Iris sighed deeply, as if agreement was a monumental concession on her part. "All right. But please do not step on my flower beds if you snoop around the fence. And I will lock the deadbolt when you go outside. It's just not safe. I plan on staying at my friend's house until this killer is caught. Please knock when you want to come back in."

"Will do," said Antonia.

"Can we have our shoes back, or do we need to wear slippers on your lawn?" asked Larry petulantly.

"You can have your shoes back," replied Iris with the authority she most certainly used when she worked in a school library.

"A cranky old broad," said Larry, as soon as he and Antonia were out back and Iris had locked the door.

"She's rattled. Her neighbors were killed! Not to mention you're not exactly Mr. Manners."

"Whatever. No time for pleasantries, Bingham. Time to make headlines."

The backyard was about an eighth of an acre, and was enclosed by an ugly wire fence. A variety of evergreen bushes, plants, and trees were planted in front of the barrier in an effort to camouflage it, and there were neat little rows of petunias winding around the yard. Antonia and Larry stepped off the wooden deck, which hosted an outdoor dining set—one table, with an umbrella planted squarely in the middle, and four chairs—painted a winter green. There was also a covered grill with the necessary accoutrements dangling on hooks off the side (spatula, fork, brush) and a bench full of small terracotta planters that appeared to hold various herbs. They made their way over to the right edge of the property, which abutted the house where the murders had taken place. Larry immediately stepped into the dark soil and smashed a row of flowers in his effort to get a better look at the house.

"Larry, you promised!"

He shrugged. "The only flowers that matter right now are the ones on the caskets."

Antonia rolled her eyes and then turned toward the neighbor's yard. Iris Maple had been correct in her assessment of the house next door: it was enormous and way too big for the lot. The giant shingled structure loomed over the slight strip of backyard where the builder had squeezed in a hot tub and lap pool. There was nary a wasted inch of grass. *How could this be up to code?* Antonia wondered. East Hampton had once been strict about the proportion of house size to the land, but in recent years it seemed that there had been a lot of variances granted. Construction and real estate were the main industries in town, and not only were most of the local voters somehow affiliated with them, but most of the local government was as well.

There were several law enforcement officers walking around the backyard, assessing the crime. Antonia saw a few faces she recognized and several she did not. Yellow crime scene tape loosely enclosed the hot tub, and there was visible blood spatter along the surrounding slate and a large puddle of it by the deck chairs. The smell of chlorine and blood curled into her nostrils, and she turned her head away in horror.

"Ugh, Larry, this is too gruesome for me."

Larry was scribbling away in his notebook as he continued to glance back at the scene. He was loving every minute of it, probably counting the blood spatters. "Come on, Bingham, this is the good part."

"No, Larry, this is the *sad* part. I need to get out of here."

Antonia felt as if she couldn't breathe. She stepped back and hastily made her way back to the back door. She knocked vigorously, and Iris Maple let her in.

"Are you okay, Antonia? You look quite pale."

"I just need to get back home. Thanks, Iris."

Iris shot her a quizzical look as Antonia continued through the house to the front door, dirty shoes and all. She burst outside and walked to the edge of the driveway, where she bent over and gasped for air. Larry came rushing out after her.

"Bingham, you okay? Trying to cook up some drama?" He had a teasing voice but she could hear the concern in it. He came up and patted her on the back awkwardly.

"I just need a second." Antonia felt like her head was swimming. She wasn't sure why she had reacted so badly, but she found the scene so disturbing, she had to get away. Iris Maple came out with a glass of water, which she drank. Both Iris and Larry watched her with concern until she stood up.

"I'm okay," she said finally. "I just want to go."

"Oh my God!" exclaimed Larry, his eyes wide. "I can't friggin' believe it!"

"Don't overreact, please," said Antonia with irritation.

"No, look!"

Both Antonia and Iris swiveled their heads in the direction that Larry pointed.

A young woman was stumbling out of the woods, half running, half hobbling. She looked like a creature that came back to life in a horror movie. Her hair was askew, mud and leaves clung to her dress, her eyes were wild. She was clad in a skimpy, spaghetti-strap black dress and only wore one shoe—a gold high heel—and appeared unaware of it. She was disoriented and confused.

"I think I need help," she announced in a wobbly voice.

4

ANTONIA AND IRIS HAD BEEN ABLE TO COAX THE YOUNG WOMAN into Iris's house and settle her in the armchair, where she tucked her legs underneath her and curled into the corner. She was whimpering slightly, her eyes darting around the room, giving the impression of a small animal cornered by its predator. Antonia had asked Larry to collect one of the policemen from next door, but he had refused.

"Once they get here, this broad will clam up and I won't get to hear firsthand what happened," he explained. "I need a quote."

"Larry, you are sick. She needs medical attention."

He scanned the young woman. "She needs a shower but looks fine to me."

Antonia didn't have time to argue with him. Instead she rubbed the young woman's back in an effort to calm her down while Iris went to the kitchen for a glass of water (which apparently was her cure-all).

"What's your name?" asked Antonia.

"Lauren," the woman said haltingly. "Lauren Wayne."

Although Lauren's appearance was in complete disarray, on closer inspection Antonia could tell she was a pretty girl. She was in her midtwenties, stood about five feet six inches and had long, dark hair and bright, hazel eyes that were currently smeared with eyeliner and mascara flakes. Her skin was tanned a deep bronze, her complexion clear. There was something vaguely Native American in her appearance. She had a small butterfly tattoo on her ankle and wore delicate gold hoops in her ears.

"What happened?" asked Larry.

"I don't...I don't remember," Lauren said, shaking her head.

"It's okay, just relax," cooed Antonia.

"Were you the one who called 911?" Larry pressed.

"911?" Lauren mused with confusion. "What?"

Antonia touched Larry's arm and whispered in his ear. "Larry, I think we need to back off."

Before Larry could answer Iris returned with the water. "Here, dear, drink this."

Lauren gratefully took the glass and had a few sips. Antonia noticed that she had cuts on the palms of her hands and scratches along her arms.

"Iris, do you have any antibiotic cream? Lauren looks a little scraped up."

"Sure, I'll get some," said Iris.

Lauren turned and examined her arms as if seeing them for the first time.

"Do they hurt?" asked Antonia.

She shook her head. Iris returned with a spray and began cleaning off Lauren's cuts. Lauren glanced around the room. "Where am I?"

"You're on Bull Path," said Antonia reassuringly.

"Bull Path?" Lauren inquired with skepticism. "Where is that? How did I get here?"

"What's the last thing you remember?" asked Larry.

Lauren took a deep breath and stared at the painting over the mantel, as if it held the answers. She spoke slowly and haltingly. "I was at Dawn's... We were watching a movie...then I don't remember anything until I woke up in the woods. My head was throbbing, my phone was gone, and I kept walking until I saw you."

"What about the guys?" asked Larry gruffly.

"What guys?" repeated Lauren.

"The victims."

Lauren's eyes became wide. "Victims? Victims of what?"

"Larry," said Antonia, trying to take his arm and steer him away.

Larry ignored her, flexed his biceps, and refused to budge. "Did you meet them at their house for a little party? Maybe things became a little too heady, you partied too hard?"

"I honestly don't know what you're talking about," she said weakly.

"Who's Dawn?" he asked.

"She's my friend. Is she here?"

Antonia shook her head. "I don't think so."

"I don't understand how I got here... We were watching a movie—"

"Which movie?" Larry interrupted.

"It was...it was a Matt Damon movie. You know, an action one. I can't think of the name right now..."

"Okay, and then how did you hook up with the guys?" he asked.

"What guys? I was at Dawn's, and then I woke up in the woods. I have no idea what happened."

"What's Dawn's last name, and where does she live?" he asked.

"Costa. She lives in Napeague."

"Larry, we should call her," said Antonia.

"Hang on," warned Larry. He turned back to Lauren. "Do you know a Gary DiAngelo and Shane Boskin?"

A flicker of horror passed over Lauren's face. Her eyes widened, and she looked pale. Antonia saw her bottom lip tremble slightly.

Instead of answering his question, Lauren stood up shakily.

She took a few wobbly steps before using the back of the chair to steady herself. "I need to lie down."

Iris and Antonia sprang into action, escorting Lauren to the sofa where they assisted her into a reclining position. Iris covered her with a mohair throw and tucked it in beneath her. Antonia adjusted the pillow under Lauren's head.

"I'll get a cool compress," said Iris.

"And I'll get the police," said Antonia firmly. It was time to let the professionals take over.

"I just have a few more questions," said Larry as he strolled over to Lauren.

"No you don't," admonished Antonia.

"How do you know Gary and Shane?" he persevered.

Lauren clenched her eyes shut and shook her head.

"Larry, stop," said Antonia.

Larry glowered and said in his worst stage whisper. "She may be a killer. I need to find out."

"A killer?" asked Lauren, struggling to sit up. "What? I'm going to be sick…"

And with that, Lauren passed out.

Larry was pouting on the ride home.

"Why did you have to go get the cops? Buzzkill."

"I'm not going through this again," said Antonia. "Besides, you obtained your quote, you have an exclusive interview with the witness, and I even saw you sneak a photograph of Lauren with your iPhone. I think your editor will be very content."

He shrugged. "Maybe. But I needed more time."

"It was the right thing to do," said Antonia confidently.

"Oh, don't be all righteous on me. You and I both know that you wanted to hear what she had to say. Sure, you may have said several times for the record that we should go get the cops, but your efforts were half-hearted. You are no different from me."

"I'm not sure what you're talking about." Antonia sniffed.

"Don't deny it, Bingham. You live for this stuff. You're forty years old; you should know that by now."

"Excuse me, but I am *thirty-six*. And only recently."

"Closer to forty than thirty."

Antonia decided to change the subject. "What's the plan now?"

"I'm dropping you off at your inn and I'm heading to Napeague to track down Dawn Costa."

"What do you think about Lauren?"

"Killer," said Larry with certainty.

"Really? How can you be so sure? She seemed kind of believable…like she really didn't remember anything."

"She'll plea temporary insanity if they are able to arrest her. She was laying groundwork…amnesia, feeling sick. Bottom line is, who else? We know the victims were hanging with a chick. She was in the woods, and she definitely knew the vics. Did you see her eyes when I mentioned their names? She freaked out."

"Maybe I should go with you to talk to her friend, Dawn."

"Ha! So you can pull me away just when things are getting good? No chance."

Antonia frowned. Larry gave her a sideways glance.

"Look, if you want to be helpful, Bingham, what you can do is, as soon as I drop you off, scan social media and see if Lauren and Dawn have Instagram or Facebook pages—which I am certain they do and are chock-full of selfies—and show their pictures to your staff. See if either of them was the girl with the victims last night."

"Okay. But you have to promise to let me know what happens with Dawn."

"Scout's honor."

"You were never a scout."

"I know."

There was a swell of activity when Antonia climbed up the front steps of the inn after Larry had dropped her off. Couples were seated in the Adirondack chairs on the front porch, imbibing drinks and taking in the view of the town pond, where two swans were preening for their audience. A young family was by the bike rack situating themselves on the complimentary cobalt Huffys that the inn provided to guests. There were people returning from the beach, preparing to head to town for lunch, while others were setting off for the beach with a basket of packed goodies. It was the Monday of Labor Day weekend, essentially the last day of summer to most people, and everyone was trying to maximize it. These were Antonia's favorite moments of being an innkeeper, when everything seemed to hum along nicely and everyone was happy.

She stopped by her office before returning to the kitchen to oversee dinner prep. Marty grunted and remarked sassily, "Look what the cat dragged in." He was deep in deboning chops, while Kendra was stirring sauces and Soyla was chopping herbs. Although Antonia was the executive chef, the kitchen staff was so adept that they could manage without her. She loved nothing more than immersing herself in cooking, but she definitely had some issues with focus and was easily distracted.

The fact was, Larry was correct: Antonia did enjoy investigative detective work. She loved learning peoples' stories and what made them tick; it was one of the things that drew her to innkeeping. She was in constant contact with people coming and going, guests from all over. It made Antonia feel more integrated in the world. Therefore, Antonia was eager to learn more about Lauren Wayne. She quickly left the kitchen (in good hands) and went to her office. After a scan of the small pile of messages that Connie had left her, she clicked on her laptop and went to Facebook first. Antonia wasn't a member, and in fact was something of a Luddite in general, eschewing everything techie and internet-related if possible, but curiosity had her in its grip and there was no stopping her now. She sincerely hoped that if she typed in Lauren's name, she would discover her account.

Lauren Wayne, as can be expected about someone of her age and demographic, did indeed have a Facebook page. In her profile picture, she was dressed in a tiny turquoise bikini blowing out candles on a birthday cake. There was also a background shot that was much larger, where she was with a large group of young women who were wearing sunglasses and drinking tropical drinks on chaise lounges somewhere. Antonia wondered if any of them were Lauren's friend Dawn, although according to Facebook, Lauren had 1,790 friends, so the odds might be slim. There must have been some sort of privacy protection on Lauren's page because Antonia was unable to scroll down and view other posts or pictures. She decided to type in "Dawn Costa." Facebook immediately indicated that were three Dawn

Costas, but one appeared to be in her fifties and the other listed her home state as Alaska, so Antonia clicked on the third.

The Dawn Costa that Antonia found was a midtwenties blond with arched eyebrows that were darker than her hair and a wry expression on her small mouth. She had a beauty mark—a mole—just above her lip, the same place where that supermodel had it. Like Lauren, she wore a bikini in her profile picture and had curves in all the right places as well as pencil-thin legs. She also had a tattoo, but this one was of some sort of Chinese symbol on her upper arm. Antonia wondered why the younger generation was so obsessed with tattoos. Tattoos were now as common as pierced ears, especially in the restaurant industry. She didn't have anything against them personally, but she had never been tempted to acquire one. If she couldn't even commit to a bumper sticker on her car, why in the heck would she want to brand herself with some symbol for life? I mean, it was silly. Would Lauren drive a car with a butterfly on it or Dawn with a Chinese symbol? Probably not; they would think it was tacky. But no problem putting it on their body and wearing it for the next sixty years.

There was a knock at the door before Jonathan, the manager of the inn, popped his head in.

"Sorry to interrupt, Antonia," he said in his florid English accent. For all Antonia knew, Jonathan could be from the roughest neighborhood in all of the United Kingdom, but to her he sounded like the king of England. She had hired him because of his effortless elegance, and he had proven to be an unflappable and meticulous manager of the inn. She liked that he was always well-appointed in neatly pressed shirts and a blazer and tie no matter the weather, and he wore distinguished horn-rimmed glasses over his long-lashed eyes. His hair was but a memory, but he was still youthful and an appealing gatekeeper to the Windmill Inn.

"What's up?" asked Antonia.

"Connie sent over a call to my office. A woman was trying to make a room reservation for this evening, and Connie said there was nothing available. The woman became quite upset and said that she was en route to town because her husband had been killed and she had nowhere else to stay tonight."

"Oh dear, what was her name?"

Jonathan glanced at a notepad he held in his hand. "Cindy Boskin?"

"She must be the wife of Shane Boskin. The man who was murdered last night…"

"I gathered. Very sad."

"We have nothing available?"

"Well, the Texans did check out today, but we have a couple coming in tomorrow. They had asked for an early check-in as they are arriving at JFK airport from France, and I had granted it."

"Hmmm…"

"It would normally be a hard no, but I brought it to you due to the circumstances."

"Right. Well, maybe you can call Mrs. Boskin back and say we have something until early tomorrow. We can then comp the couple from France a lunch or dinner for their troubles? I feel it's the right thing to do."

"Absolutely. I'll call her back."

He was about to depart, but Antonia stopped him. "Jonathan, have we ever seen this woman before?"

She turned her computer screen around and showed him

Dawn Costa's Facebook profile. Jonathan moved closer to the desk and squinted.

"Oh, Miss Costa, yes. She's in Room Eight."

"Wait, what?" Antonia was confused.

"She's been our guest this weekend. She's due to check out tomorrow."

"She's a guest here at the Windmill Inn?"

Jonathan gave her a quizzical look. "Yes. Is there a problem?"

"I hope not. It's just strange… Do you know if she's here now?"

"I'm not sure. I haven't seen her this morning."

Antonia stood up. "I need to find her."

"Is everything okay?"

"I hope so. Come with me."

Antonia zipped out of her office with Jonathan following closely behind. There was a small antique elevator in the inn, but as it moved at a glacial pace, Antonia chose to take the stairs. (And honestly, there were only three floors, so she didn't have far to go.) Room Eight was on the top floor and faced the back garden. Antonia walked across the carpeted hallway and knocked on the door firmly. There was no answer.

"I suppose she's gone out," said Jonathan.

"Hello, Miss Costa? It's Antonia Bingham, the innkeeper."

Antonia was tempted to enter, but really she had no cause for alarm. Or did she?

"I can run down and ask Connie if she's seen her today?" offered Jonathan. "I will also check with housekeeping. They must have come by to service the room."

"That would be great, thanks."

When Jonathan departed, Antonia leaned her ear against the door and knocked again. "Sorry to bother you… Are you in there?"

She could hear the cars outside flooding past on Route 27 and the birds chirping in the branches. Cackles of laughter from guests making use of the patio terrace outdoors floated upwards. Antonia didn't hear any sound or movement from the bedroom. Her eyes fluttered around the hallway, past the framed gold mirror that stood on the landing. Underneath the mirror was a skirted console that hosted a bowl of lemons and a small bouillotte lamp. Antonia noticed that the cord was unplugged and the light was off. This could happen with antique lamps: the cords became frayed and often slunk out of the sockets. Antonia walked over and plugged it back in. The light sputtered on and the hall became illuminated. She returned to the door and, hearing no movement, was about to abort and return downstairs when she heard a noise, more like a thud, from inside the guest room.

"Dawn, are you there?"

Antonia twisted the antique brass doorknob. It was vintage, one that could have appeared to be original, although when Antonia bought the inn, it was in such a state of disarray and disrepair that she had been forced to refurbish everything from scratch. This particular doorknob was discovered after weeks of scouring antique stores and the internet to find one that was appropriate to the era. She jingled the handle, but the door was locked.

"Dawn?"

Antonia pressed her ear closer to the door. Once again there was a noise, and although she wasn't certain, it sounded like a muffled voice. Antonia pulled the master set of keys out of her pocket and flipped through to find the key to Room Eight. It was unorthodox, but she had to trust her instincts, and something told her that trouble was afoot. Once she opened the door, her worst fears were confirmed.

5

Room Eight was one of the inn's more charming rooms, airy and robin's egg blue, with a pitched ceiling and a breeze that fluttered through the starched curtains flanking the large, bright windows. A queen-size canopy bed anchored the room, and a tufted upholstered bench bordered its base. Between the two western-facing windows, an antique American chest of drawers was situated, atop of which was a Chinese vase that held freshly cut hydrangeas. Discreet gold-framed watercolors depicting beach scenes by local artists adorned the walls. There was a door next to the closet that connected to Room Seven, but it was locked on both sides, as was the case when different guests occupied each space. It was always pleasant for Antonia to step into this mini-oasis and admire the bang-up job she had done in decorating, but today she was distracted by Dawn Costa, who was slumped in a fetal position in the corner, with her arms and legs tied with rope and her mouth gagged with a handkerchief.

"Oh no!" exclaimed Antonia, running to Dawn. She immediately pulled the gag out of Dawn's mouth, thus releasing gasps and chokes from the young woman.

"Are you okay? Are you hurt?" asked Antonia.

Dawn nodded frantically. "I'm not hurt...I just...ooh."

At this moment Jonathan returned to impart the news that Connie had not seen Dawn this morning, and his face turned to horror when he discovered the scene in front of him. He rushed over to help Antonia untie the ropes, which were mercifully loose enough to remove quickly.

"What happened?" asked Antonia. "Who did this to you?"

"I…I don't know," Dawn responded, her voice raspy. "I was asleep, and then I woke up and I was tied up like this. I tried to scream, but no one could hear me with the gag in my mouth."

"Let's get you up," said Jonathan.

Antonia and Jonathan helped Dawn to the bed. She wore a thin lavender nightshirt with matching shorts, and Antonia ascertained she must have been quite chilled after a night on the floor, so she wrapped the duvet around her. Dawn idly rubbed her wrists in the spot where the ropes had been tied.

"Did you see anyone?" asked Antonia, glancing around the room as if someone were lurking in the corners.

"No. I went to bed around twelve, and I remember I thought I was sort of dreaming that someone was in the room, and then I fell back asleep and woke up tied up."

"How awful!" Jonathan commiserated. "I hope he didn't hurt you…"

"No, I'm fine. They must have drugged me or something, because I slept right through it all. Gosh…what time is it?"

Jonathan looked at his watch. "It's almost four."

"Wow, they really knocked me out."

"What do you think they wanted?" asked Antonia.

"Nothing's missing," said Dawn.

"How do you know?" asked Antonia. She gave the girl a curious gaze.

Dawn blinked several times. "I feel a little weak," she said, deflecting the question.

"Hang on a second."

Antonia, having learned from Iris Maple that one must present water in this situation, went and filled up a glass of water from the sink in the bathroom. As the tap flowed, she glanced at Dawn's cosmetics and toiletries, which were littered on the counter. There was a hairbrush, face cream, moisturizer, sunblock, deodorant, a clear bag of makeup by designer brands, and toothpaste. And curiously, there were two toothbrushes. Antonia hesitated, before taking her finger and touching the brushes of each one. They were both damp.

"Here, drink this. You'll feel better," said Antonia, offering Dawn the glass of tepid water.

"Thanks," said Dawn, gulping it down. Antonia noticed that Dawn kept her eyes on them as she drank.

"Antonia, we must call the police," said Jonathan. "It doesn't appear as if the room was ransacked, but we need to report this at once."

"Yes, of course. Why don't you head downstairs and do that? Also, check with Connie and see if any other guests reported anything suspicious."

"Sure," said Jonathan.

"Wait…do you really think we should call the police?" asked Dawn, holding out her hand to stop Jonathan.

"Of course!" He bristled. "We have to find out who did this to you. They should be arrested!"

"I suppose…" Dawn hesitated. "I just think it's better if we let it go."

Jonathan shot Antonia a quizzical look.

"Let it go?" Jonathan echoed. "But you are a victim of a crime…"

"I know…I just don't want to make a big deal."

"Is there a reason you don't want us to call the police, Dawn?" Antonia asked softly.

Dawn cocked her head to the side but didn't answer.

"Do you know who did this to you?" Antonia pressed more purposefully.

Dawn stared at Antonia evenly. Despite the recent ordeal she had suffered—being bound and gagged apparently for hours—her eyes seemed void of any fear or tension. In fact, Antonia found her entire demeanor to be somewhat suspect. Of course people react to trauma in different ways and there is no correct response…yet, there was a sense of calm in Dawn that Antonia found disconcerting.

"No," Dawn said. "I don't know."

"Was anyone else staying here in the room with you?" asked Antonia.

Dawn glanced around the room, eyes darting from corner to corner as if a trace of someone might be left behind. "No, just me."

"Have you had visitors since you have been with us?"

"What do you mean?"

"I mean, has anyone else been in this room with you?"

"Well, housekeeping came in last night…"

"That's not what I mean," Antonia said, cutting her off. "Have you had guests up to the room?"

If Dawn was taken aback by her stern inquisition, Jonathan seemed downright put out by it. He kept giving Antonia sideways looks as if to implore her to stop. But as she was his boss, he had to remain silent.

"I'd rather not say," said Dawn finally.

Antonia was surprised by her answer. "All right, well, perhaps you would rather talk to the police. Jonathan, why don't you head down to call them?"

"I don't want to make trouble," said Dawn.

"It's really no trouble," said Antonia.

"While I'm down there, can I bring you anything? You must be hungry. Something to drink?" asked Jonathan solicitously.

"I'd love a coffee, please," said Dawn.

"Certainly."

Jonathan moved toward the door.

"Wait!" Dawn yelled.

Both Antonia and Jonathan froze and turned their attention to Dawn.

"Can you make it a cappuccino instead?"

Jonathan nodded.

When he had left, Antonia took the edge of her shirt and covered her hands, picking up the ropes from the floor. She didn't want to leave any additional fingerprints and compromise the scene. She could just imagine the tongue-lashing she would get from Sergeant Flanagan. Actually, it wouldn't be a verbal attack, that wasn't his style, just quiet disapproval. That was even worse. She gingerly put the rope on top of the dresser. Next to the bed, there was a pile of glossy magazines askew, the freebies that were dumped on every storefront and driveway in the summer. Antonia set about neatening them. She wasn't quite sure what to say to Dawn Costa and somehow thought it better if she allowed the girl to do the talking.

"This is so weird… I've never been accosted before," said Dawn. She picked up some pillows and punched them into fluffy submission before placing them behind her back and leaning daintily to lounge in the bed. "It feels very *Law & Order*."

Dawn's mood was ebullient and relaxed, which put Antonia further on her guard.

"I'm sure it's surreal," said Antonia. "Is there anyone you want me to call?"

Dawn pushed her blond hair behind her ears. "I guess I'll call my parents...but maybe not."

"You have nothing to be embarrassed about. You were a victim."

"Yeah, I suppose. It's not really a big deal."

"What are you talking about? I take this very seriously."

"Yeah, well, I guess I have post-traumatic stress syndrome. I just would rather leave them out of it. I'm fine."

"Do you want me to call them?"

"No, thanks."

Antonia subtly glanced at Dawn's wrists. There were no marks or compressions where the rope had tied them. In fact, the ropes had been very easy to remove. Dawn noticed Antonia staring at her arms and plunged them underneath the duvet. Antonia changed tack.

"Are you from around here, Dawn?" asked Antonia with an arched eyebrow.

"New Jersey."

"Ah, so was this your first time in the Hamptons?"

In order to feign nonchalance, Antonia turned and idly rearranged the hydrangeas in their vase. She would have liked to continue to straighten up the room, but she didn't want to end up eliminating any clues if this was a crime scene. But she wasn't quite sure it was.

"I've been to the Hamptons before," said Dawn. "I love it."

"Do you have friends out here?"

"Yeah, I know a lot of people. We tend to hang in Montauk. It's a chill scene."

Antonia wondered if she should even broach the topic of Lauren Wayne and Lauren's mention that Dawn had a house in Napeague, which abutted Montauk. It wasn't Antonia's business to snoop—that was better left to the police—and yet... Well, an attack at the inn would be bad for business, and if this girl was somehow less than truthful, it was better to nip it in the bud.

"Do you have a house here?" asked Antonia, turning to stare Dawn straight in the eye.

"A house here? Why do you ask that? I mean, would I stay in the inn if I had a house?" Dawn blinked several times.

"I don't know, would you?"

"That sounds weird."

"Does it? Lots of people come to stay here, you know, to get away from it all for a weekend, even if they have houses here," said Antonia, attempting to appear lighthearted and casual.

"I don't own a house here," said Dawn.

Darn, that was not the question, thought Antonia. It could be all semantics; Dawn may *rent* a house here but not own it. But Antonia didn't want the girl to think she was out to get her. She was about to drop it, but the little devil on her shoulder told her to plunder on.

"Ever rent?"

Dawn gave Antonia a cautious look. A small frown appeared in her plump lips. She sighed deeply and leaned back into her pillows. "I think I'm feeling a little sick, you know, from what happened."

Antonia hesitated. Finally she spoke. "I can imagine. I'm so sorry. Do you want some Tylenol?"

Antonia moved toward the bathroom. Dawn traced her movements with a wary gaze.

"No, that's okay," said Dawn. "Actually, you know, you can go. I can wait here for the police."

"Don't be silly! I'm sure you don't want to be alone. I mean, after what happened."

"The person who did this to me probably left by now."

"I hope so!" said Antonia. "Actually, the good news is we have cameras around the inn, so when the police come, we can go through the tapes and track down whoever did this to you. I think we can catch them pretty quickly."

"Cameras?"

"Yes, what's great is that technology is so advanced today that you can't even tell they are cameras. They are these little slivers—just small rectangles that you mount around the walls, they look like outlets, and they house tiny cameras. So convenient!"

Antonia was lying through her teeth. She knew things like that existed and had made a mental note to purchase these small devices for the inn, but as of now, the only cameras they had were for the front hall and back garden, which might not prove at all useful in identifying Dawn's attacker. Or *alleged* attacker.

"I didn't know the Windmill Inn was so high-tech," said Dawn. Her voice betrayed tension.

"Oh yes, that's us."

They stared at each other. Antonia wasn't certain if Dawn could tell she was bluffing, but she didn't flinch. Dawn appeared to be contemplating her next move. Suddenly, she burst into tears. Not just tears but scream cries.

"Okay, I did know my attacker…"

Antonia moved toward her and said gently, "You did?"

Dawn nodded her head vigorously. "I think…I think it was my friend…well, she *was* my friend. She's been stalking me—that's why I'm staying in a hotel. I don't want her to find me."

"What's the friend's name?" asked Antonia.

Dawn's sobs grew louder, and she began to wail. She had her head in her hands so Antonia could not see her face. "Her name is Lauren…Lauren Wayne. And she's crazy!"

6

WHEN THE POLICE ARRIVED, ANTONIA WAS REQUESTED TO evacuate Room Eight so they could question Dawn alone. Antonia had done so reluctantly. She was tempted to press her ear to the door (after all, she owned the joint, she had every right to eavesdrop, didn't she?) but as she was worried Sergeant Flanagan might not look kindly on this, she decided against it. Her plan was to endear herself to the police in an effort to gain information. If she were overly accommodating, they would have to throw her a bone, wouldn't they? She immediately asked Soyla for a plate of sandwiches, a tray of cookies, and an urn of coffee to be made ready for them when they finished. Meanwhile, not wanting to entirely escape the action, Antonia had beelined to her friend Joseph's apartment, which was located down the hall from Room Eight.

Joseph Fowler was a renowned writer of historical fiction who had moved into the inn a couple of years prior, after the death of his beloved wife, Margaret. In that time period, he had become a combination of best friend, father figure, and sounding board for Antonia. He was in his early sixties, with a full head of silver hair, sparkling eyes that conveyed wisdom and compassion, and chiseled features that included a straight nose and strong jaw. He was elegant in every sense of the word, from his manners and conversation abilities to his dress, which was a uniform of gold-cuffed blazers, pressed shirts, and charming bow ties. In fact, Joseph had a fan club. There was a large group of similarly aged women (as well as some older and younger) who flocked to the inn at teatime in hopes that they could nab Joseph for a chat.

A bout of polio at an early age had left Joseph mostly confined to a scooter, although he was able to walk with crutches when the need arose. He did, however, once suffer a dangerous fall at his house that went undiscovered for hours, which was what prompted the move into the inn. Antonia looked after Joseph as much as he looked after her, and they shared a moment every day to catch up with each other on what was transpiring in their lives.

"There's something fishy about this girl Dawn," concluded Antonia after she had filled Joseph in on all the details of the past day.

Joseph nodded. "It sounds like there are several holes in her story. Would you like a sherry, dear?"

"Who can say no to that?"

Joseph's compact three-room apartment (comprised of a sitting room, bedroom, and office as well as facilities) was as cozy and luxurious as an English manor. It was masculine in that the walls of the various rooms were high-gloss hunter green and chocolate brown, and plaids, stripes, and tweeds were the favored patterns of upholstery and throw pillows. Almost the entire sitting room and office walls were comprised of bookshelves that held dog-eared copies of paperbacks and hardcovers. Joseph, a voracious reader, had an appetite for books much in the way Antonia had, well, an appetite. As Joseph took most if not all of his meals downstairs in the restaurant, he did not have a kitchen but instead had a microwave and a hot plate for a kettle. He also had a well-equipped bar cart that was stocked not only with a medley of liquor but all of the garnishes and stemware that matched them.

He handed Antonia a small sherry glass.

"The young lady from the liquor store hunted me down on

Main Street and told me I had to come by and pick up this brand. Said it's selling out quickly. I'd like to hear what you think."

"Sure. Sounds like a sales pitch."

"I am an old man easily influenced by attractive salespeople. That said, she's a little young for my taste. But please, tell me what you think of it."

Antonia sipped it daintily.

"It's nice."

"I think so too."

She nestled back into the comfortable sofa and briefly closed her eyes.

"I just can't make sense of it. Did you hear anything, Joseph? Were there any strange sounds last night? They are bound to interview you."

Joseph shook his head. "Indeed I did not. I slept very well last night, actually. I had the window open and the fresh air knocked me out. I know it's only the beginning of September, but fall is already in the air. I can sense the subtle chill."

"I both dread and look forward to it."

"What's to dread? Fall is beautiful in East Hampton."

"I guess, but after fall comes winter and that can be miserable out here. Business is slow; it's cold and gray. Don't forget, I was born and raised in California. Once a California girl, always a California girl."

"Undoubtedly. However, you have to take the good with the bad. We have the most spectacular weather in the summer and fall. Spring can be hit or miss, but there is so much beauty for the majority of the year."

"And so much death, it turns out."

"Yes, that is a sad state of affairs these days," agreed Joseph.

He had a small cut-glass dish of dark chocolate, sea salt caramels that he slid toward Antonia. She took a small handful and popped them one by one into her mouth.

"These are delicious."

"I bought them at the Monogram Shop."

"Yum."

There was a knock at the door, and Joseph scootered over to open it. Jonathan stood on the threshold.

"I'm sorry to bother you. I just wanted to follow up on some things," he said.

"Do come in. Can I offer you a drink?"

"Thanks, no, I'm still working," said Jonathan. "Although I can assure you I will be having one after I get off work."

"What's up?" asked Antonia. "Come and sit down."

"I have to get back downstairs, but I wanted to give you an update. I had Jesse and Glen come into my office and look through Dawn's pictures on her social media accounts. They said she was not the woman who was with Mr. Boskin and Mr. DiAngelo at the bar last night."

"Really?" asked Antonia, sitting up. "Are they sure?"

"Yes. Dawn had been in the bar on Saturday night for dinner. She had spent the evening chatting with Jesse, and Glen had been the one to seat her. They both said they would have recognized her if she was the one with the victims."

"Interesting," said Antonia.

"What about the other young lady," asked Joseph. "Lauren?"

"Yes, I showed Jesse and Glen her profile as you instructed. They couldn't be certain, but they don't think she was the woman at the bar either."

"But they couldn't be certain?" echoed Antonia.

Jonathan nodded. "Jesse remembered the woman at the bar as quite plain, and he thought the Lauren Wayne that he saw online was quite attractive. He said he would have noticed."

"But maybe she dressed down?" asked Antonia, thinking out loud.

"It's possible. I can concur that I never saw her before. Not that I was at the bar last night, but I don't remember her being in the inn."

"Okay, thanks. Are the police still in with Dawn?"

"Yes, they're still talking to her. One more thing I wanted to mention..."

"What's that?"

"I asked Rosita if anyone in housekeeping serviced the room today. She said they had not because there was a DO NOT DISTURB sign on the door."

"That's strange," said Antonia. "There wasn't a DO NOT DISTURB sign on the door when we knocked."

"I know. There most certainly wasn't. That would have given me pause."

"So at some point she had it on, but then it wasn't there. Which means either Dawn didn't black out for the entire day, she woke up and took the sign off, or the person who allegedly tied her up put it on and later came back to take it off," mused Antonia.

"It would appear so," said Jonathan.

"Didn't you say you had surveillance cameras?" asked Joseph.

"There are no cameras on this floor," admitted Jonathan.

"Yes, I told a little fib to Dawn," admitted Antonia.

"A pity," said Joseph.

"There are cameras in the main floor and by the staircase," said Jonathan. "I did a quick run through, but I didn't see anyone suspicious or that I didn't recognize as a guest."

"Then the only way they would have gotten upstairs is the elevator. There is no camera there," said Joseph.

"Or they didn't get up here," said Antonia.

"What do you mean?" asked Jonathan.

"I mean maybe Dawn did this to herself. Maybe nothing really happened. She didn't seem very upset."

"What would be her motive?" asked Joseph.

"That is what we have to find out."

The police left without revealing anything of their investigation to Antonia. Unfortunately Sergeant Flanagan had departed while Antonia was still in Joseph's apartment, so she couldn't use all of her charm to coax some information out of him. The grim officer duo that remained was close-lipped. They did tell her that she did not need to treat the room as a crime scene and housekeeping could come in and service the room whenever need be. They slightly hesitated when asked if she needed to secure the inn and if her guests were in some sort of danger, but they said in an almost offhand way that they thought everything was okay.

Antonia returned to Room Eight to find a cheerful Dawn packing up her belongings. She was wearing one of those shorts-romper things that had come back in style and had her hair up in a messy knot.

"Checking out?"

"Yeah, gonna hit the road," she said, as she threw her makeup kit into her duffel bag.

"Where are you heading?"

Dawn paused a moment before shrugging. "Just gonna stay at a friend's for now."

"I'm very sorry this happened to you at the inn."

"Yeah, it's a bummer. But look, I'm not going to sue you. I figure you just comp my bill and we're even."

A giant ball of rage swept through Antonia's body along with an intense primal urge to fling herself on top of Dawn and start pummeling her. Lawsuit? Free room? This all felt like a scam. Antonia's palms were instinctively curling into fists, and she had to use all of her self-control and bite her tongue. An innkeeper who attacked rude guests would be bad for business. Sometimes it really sucked being in the service industry. Antonia regretted it, but she knew that until she had clarity from the police and talked to her lawyer, she couldn't really argue with the girl. She could always send her the bill at a later date if things proved to be suspect. She wanted to bitch-slap Dawn, but instead she responded in her most saccharine tone:

"Sure, of course."

"Thanks," Dawn said without a flicker of gratitude.

Antonia swallowed deeply and counted to three.

"So, who else was staying here with you?"

"What do you mean?" asked Dawn evenly.

Antonia motioned toward the bathroom. "I noticed two toothbrushes."

"Oh, that…"

"Yeah."

"I really like clean teeth, so I always have two brushes. One for the top and one for the bottom."

She stared at Antonia in a challenging way.

"I've never heard of that."

"Oral hygiene is really important. My mom is actually a dental hygienist."

"Interesting."

Antonia lingered in the room, trying to figure out her next move. She felt as if she were playing chess against a formidable opponent and had to be as strategic as possible.

"Do you think you'll obtain a restraining order against Lauren?"

"I'm not sure yet. The police said they'd talk to her. But probably I will."

"I got the impression that you were still friends."

Dawn stopped tossing her personal items into her bag long enough to give Antonia a sideways glance. "Where did you get that impression?"

"I actually met Lauren today."

"You did?"

Antonia studied Dawn's face for some sort of tell but gauged nothing. "Yes, I did. She was found wandering around the Northwest Woods in a daze. She said she'd been at your house in Napeague and then woke up to find herself in the woods."

Dawn shook her head. "See, she's clearly delusional. I was here. She's just trying to cover her tracks."

"But why would she do that?"

"Did you ever see the movie *Single White Female*? It's about these two women who are friends and then one becomes obsessed with the other and tries to steal her life. She dresses like her and goes after her boyfriend and is a total psycho. That's Lauren. She idolizes me. At first I thought it was cute, you know? I was flattered. But now it totally freaks me out. I just can't deal with her energy and want her out of my life."

"Of course you do if she tied you up! You must be terrified of her."

"Yeah, I am," said Dawn without fear in her voice.

"Did the police say they were going to arrest her?"

"They didn't say."

"So she could be out there still. Doesn't that scare you?"

Dawn turned to Antonia and gave her a fake smile. "Thanks so much for your concern, but I really have to go. Also, I don't want to talk about this anymore. I want to move on. I'm still in shock; it's really distressing."

"I'm so sorry to hear that."

"Thanks," she said as she heaved her bag over her shoulder. "No need to call the bellboy. I'll just carry this down and head out on my own."

"Okay," said Antonia. Her mind was racing to come up with more questions to ask Dawn, but before she could think of something, the girl was out the door. She soon heard footsteps clomping down the stairs. There was nothing more that she could do right now.

7

COOKING WAS THERAPY FOR ANTONIA. IT WAS A TOTAL AND complete brain cleanser. It demanded focus and swiftness, especially when the kitchen was busy and the orders were coming in at a rapid pace. Between chopping, dicing, stirring, ladling, whipping, and baking, there was no room for thoughts other than the task at hand. Tonight Antonia was relieved to bury herself in her work and push aside any contemplation of the day's events.

Soyla had spent the afternoon assembling tomato tartes tatin with the last of the summer's heirloom bounty, and Antonia was sprinkling ribbons of chopped basil and flakes of sea salt as she plated them with a small arugula salad. It was a recipe that Antonia had developed after several attempts at a perfect tomato tart. She had experimented with various cheeses: mozzarella, which was tasty, but the result was too similar to pizza; ricotta, which was nice, if a bit plain; Gruyère which was a strong, meaty flavor but felt somewhat more autumn than summer to Antonia. In the end, she had comprised a medley of local goat cheese, cream cheese, and mayonnaise as the base. The concoction enhanced the sweet baby orange Sungolds and allowed the tomatoes to show off. Arugula was perfect at this time of year: peppery and zesty—a nice accompaniment to the tart.

By early September the farm stands and gardens were bursting with vegetables and fruits at their peak. Antonia savored every moment. She loved tasting a peach that tasted like a peach and not some frozen rock that had limited hints of its glorious past. Her garden, overseen by Hector, Soyla's husband, had been an embarrassment of riches this season. Antonia was taking full advantage, and tonight's menu was particularly produce-focused. There had been a bumper crop of sweet mini peppers, which Antonia was grilling with olive oil and a pinch of sea salt and offering as a side dish, as well as zucchini blossoms that she stuffed with cheese and roasted. Tonight's menu also included Japanese eggplant brushed with a miso glaze, charred corn salad with cilantro and pickled jalapeño peppers, and spiced kale chips. The red baby potatoes that had arrived in abundance were boiled, roasted, and then smashed with Parmesan, and they were a total crowd pleaser.

Dinner service was winding down at about ten o'clock. Antonia wiped up her workstation where she prepped her food. She put away the squirt bottles that she used to garnish dishes and washed her cutting boards. Her knives would be sorted and cleaned and packed up for the evening. When Antonia had first started cooking—catering, actually—her boss had told her that a clean workstation separated a good chef from a bad chef. She had taken that note seriously.

Next to Antonia, Soyla blanketed key lime pie with a thick layer of whipped cream. She was finishing off the last of the dessert orders. Glen popped his head into the kitchen.

"Antonia, can I talk to you?"

"What's up?"

"Cindy Boskin just got here and ordered dinner. She was asking me some questions about her husband—you know he's the one who was here last night. Anyway, I thought maybe you'd want to, you know, maybe talk to her."

"I probably should."

Antonia turned toward the grill. "Marty, do you need me for any reason?"

Marty grunted from behind a pile of saucepans. "Do I ever need you for any reason?"

"Touché. I'm heading out."

Glen motioned in the direction of the last booth on the right, where a woman sat alone, her head bent down over a notepad in which she scribbled fiercely with an expensive-looking pen. There was a glass of chilled white wine in front of her that appeared untouched. Antonia wasn't sure what she had been expecting when she imagined Shane Boskin's wife, but it definitely wasn't the Cindy Boskin that appeared in front of her. Shane had been described as somewhat of an obnoxious, loudmouthed partier, and Antonia had conjured up an image of an overgrown frat boy hurling blond teenage cheerleaders over his shoulder, not unlike one of those idiot football players from the movie *Revenge of the Nerds*. With all respect to the dead, the words "meathead" and "jerk" swirled through Antonia's mind when she conjured up the deceased.

At first blush anyway, Cindy Boskin did not appear to be the perky trophy wife that Antonia thought would be joined with Shane in matrimony until (quite literally) death did them part. Despite her recent loss, Cindy exuded the impression of someone in control and not frivolous. She was petite—about five feet, two inches—Asian, and wore her hair in a well-tended bob with bangs leveled across her forehead so evenly that Antonia wondered if her stylist cut them with a ruler every day. The black suit she wore was tailored and probably expensive, and the crisp white blouse underneath had a collar so professionally starched that even if Antonia sat on it, it was unlikely to become smashed. When she heard Antonia approach, Cindy glanced up, and through her dark, black glasses, Antonia could detect wariness in her eyes.

"Mrs. Boskin? I'm Antonia Bingham, the innkeeper. I'm so sorry for your loss."

"Thank you," she said with a brisk nod. "And I appreciate you allowing me to stay the night. I was unsure if the police would need anything from me, so I wanted to secure a place to stay just in case. In the meantime, I'm making a list of the friends and family as well as business acquaintances that I will need to notify as well as other funeral arrangements."

"If you need help with anything, please let us know what we can do."

She nodded. "I appreciate that. Won't you sit down? My eyes are swimming from concentration, and I suppose I should take a break."

"I don't want to intrude…"

"I would like it. In fact, that's why I requested to meet you."

She motioned toward the seat opposite her, and Antonia slid into the booth.

"Why don't you join me in a glass of wine?" Cindy waved to the waiter and tapped on her wineglass before motioning to Antonia to indicate that he should bring her one. He nodded and went to the bar.

"I assume he knows what you like to drink," Cindy said more as a statement than a question.

"Yes, they are familiar with my preferences, that's for sure."

"As they should be."

People who were able to command a situation always amazed Antonia; Cindy Boskin appeared to be one of those types. Here Antonia was at her own inn, her home turf, and yet Cindy was the one calling the shots. *Impressive*, thought Antonia.

"You have a very nice inn," Cindy remarked. "Well taken care of, modern and yet traditional. I particularly appreciate that it's not frowzy and lace-curtained like so many bed-and-breakfasts out here."

"I tried to add a level of sophistication."

Cindy nodded. "You did a thorough job. Inns are usually dreary."

"Have you stayed in many inns?" Antonia asked, determined to make small talk.

Cindy was about to shake her head and then stopped and spoke. "We went to the Cotswolds on our honeymoon and stayed in a multitude of dumpy little B and Bs. I had thought in theory it would be a charming idea, but after about a week, Shane ordered a car and booked a room at the Mandarin Oriental in London. He said he didn't care if I stayed but he was going."

Antonia's eyebrows shot up in surprise though she thought it best not to editorialize. "He sounds like he knew what he liked."

Cindy emitted a small laugh—the sort that might be described as an evil chuckle in a children's cartoon. "He certainly did."

"How did you meet?"

"He was a client. I work in equity research for a bank and cover healthcare. He is—was—at a hedge fund. He read my coverage, and we used to chat on the phone. I was able to bill his company quite a lot for his time. An unapologetic flirt, he asked me out constantly. He was relentless and had fallen madly in love with me—and this is someone who doesn't take no for an answer. I think I presented a challenge to him because I demurred for so many months. I was not very impressed by him when we engaged in discourse, but when we finally met, there was definitely raw animal attraction. I have a weakness for blonds. I appreciated his masculinity and virility, which is fortunate because he was determined that he would have me. He doesn't—didn't—like it when people refused him. I ultimately succumbed. That was four years ago."

Antonia nodded. The portrait of Shane that his wife was painting was not exactly one of an altar boy. "Do you have kids?"

"No. Quite honestly, the marriage was in a precarious state, which I am sure comes as no surprise. Of course Shane adored me, but we had some hindrances. We had talked about children, but I was unwilling to commit until Shane settled down and eliminated his obstacles. I thought for certain by now I would have Ella and Julian—"

"Ella and Julian?"

"Yes. I had the names picked out. I wanted a girl and a boy. I did not, however, want to procreate with someone who was out partying every night. I had been naive in assuming Shane would become more domesticated after our union, but he was not a cat. More like a dog. In fact, it was not my idea, but this August we were on somewhat of a break. Not officially, in that he was supposed to run out and party like a rock star, but our therapist had suggested that we take some time apart for contemplation and to evaluate. It was important for Shane to understand that I was a precious gift and he could not take me for granted. Partying was a no-no. However, judging from last night, that was certainly what Shane was doing."

Antonia was unsure how to respond. "Maybe he was evaluating in his own particular way?"

Cindy sniffed. "We had a ten-point list of instructions as to how to determine if our marriage was sustainable. I can assure you that doing drugs in a hot tub was not one of them. But I was certain it was a phase and Shane would come to his senses. He loved me very much."

After only a very superficial knowledge of this couple, Antonia was amazed at how they ended up together at all. It must be the "animal attraction."

"And did you know Gary very well?"

"Ah, Gary," said Cindy, rolling her eyes up at the ceiling. "The quintessential sales guy—and I specifically say guy, not sales*man*. When you dress up a pig, it's still a pig. These individuals that work sales in finance are essentially cruise directors. They are there to wine and dine clients, play golf with them, order expensive bottles of brandy, head to strip clubs or massage establishments where the conclusions are happy. Gary could not have been better suited to a profession. He was Shane's best man, and Shane had been his best man when Gary was married, a union that lasted all of three months. Gary was blasé about the demise of his marriage and continued to refer to the wedding as 'an epic party.' I am certain the bride's father would prefer to have retained the four hundred thousand dollars he spent at Cipriani and Vera Wang. But Gary thought it was hilarious."

"Wow, sounds like a great guy."

"Indeed. My husband's best friend. Quite honestly, I believe it's Gary who made Shane behave badly. He led him astray."

"I'm sorry to hear all of this."

"Yes, well, it is what it is," said Cindy, hastily pushing her notebook away and finally taking a large swig of wine. "I went in with my eyes wide open and here is where I end up."

"And did Shane have family?"

"Oh yes, parents and stepparents and a brother. They all live down in Tampa. Shane wasn't very close to them, and we saw little of them, which was more than enough for me, but I suppose I have one last hump to deal with and then they can be out of my life forever."

She gave Antonia an almost defiant look, but Antonia remained silent. Who was she to judge? Hell, she herself had a tenuous relationship with her in-laws when she was married. Her ex-husband Philip's parents were blind and dumb to the pain that he inflicted on Antonia. She had attempted to enlist them in helping her, but they refused.

"I know how tough in-laws can be," conceded Antonia.

"You do? What are yours like?"

"*Were* like; I'm divorced."

"Oh yes. If you don't mind me asking, what was the cause?"

Normally Antonia avoided discussing her marriage, but she could discern that Cindy was trying to deflect from her current pain. She was probably one of those people who feels that suffering is a weakness, Antonia surmised, and perhaps it was cathartic for her to hear about other people's challenges. Antonia had meant to give her the Cliff's Notes version of her marriage to Philip, but Cindy was a talented interrogator, and Antonia ended up oversharing. She felt like she had a talk-show hangover by the time she got to the part of purchasing and refurbishing the inn, so she changed the subject.

"Cindy, by any chance do you know who the woman was who was with Shane and Gary when they were here at the bar?"

Cindy shook her head. "No."

"I wonder who she was…"

"Shane flirted with danger. The consequences are somewhat inevitable."

Antonia wasn't sure what that meant, but the snoop inside of her propelled her to probe. "I hate to ask, but do you have any idea who might have done this…committed this horrible crime?"

"The hypothetical list is long. My husband was a flawed man.

He cheated, so it could be a spurned lover. He gambled, so it could be a bookie. He mentioned recently that some 'chick was making trouble for him,' but he assured me of his innocence. I'm not sure what that meant, but I can surmise. Gary was no different. They were accomplices. I'm not sure who was the target— Shane or Gary or both—but they had been known to cause tremendous pain to the people in their lives and who they came into contact with."

Something shimmered in her eyes, a deep hurt. It was evident that she didn't want to acknowledge her pain, so she gave Antonia a stern look before turning away. Antonia had an unsettling sensation that she couldn't quite pinpoint.

"What do you mean that a 'chick' was making trouble for him?"

Cindy kept her eyes down before lifting her head and responding.

"I believe she accused Shane of sexual assault. And not just Shane, but Gary as well. Which is absurd. There is no way Shane would do that. Gary, maybe."

8

ANTONIA WAS DEEP IN SLUMBERLAND, ENCLOSED BY HER creamy sheets and marshmallow duvet, when her phone rang. She was disoriented as one is when awoken from a restful sleep and blinked several times before snatching her cell phone out of the charger and placing it next to her ear.

"Hello?" she said hoarsely.

"It's me."

It took a split second to register before all of the hair on the back of Antonia's neck shot up as if a canon had exploded behind her. With fear and adrenaline bursting inside every part of her body, she immediately sat erect.

"Who is this?" she asked lamely, her voice wavering.

"Oh, come on, don't play that game. *You* know who it is."

Unfortunately, she did.

"What do you want? Why are you calling me?"

"Where are your manners?"

Antonia didn't respond. She wasn't going to be lured into this sick game.

"Antonia? TonTon, you there?"

Once again, Antonia was quiet. She had to gather her thoughts before she responded.

"Don't ever call me again."

The man on the other end of the phone clucked his disapproval. "Now, now, sweetie. Is that the way to talk to your husband?"

"You are not my husband."

"I'll always be your husband."

Antonia ended the call and flung the phone down on her bed as if it were virulent. Her heart was pounding. How in the world did Philip find her number? Well, duh, she had been liberal about handing it out on her card to various guests. Why, just last week she was scattering it around a charity event like she was a card dealer in Vegas. But he wasn't supposed to call her. She had a restraining order. He was not allowed to have *any* contact with her whatsoever. Why was he trying to infiltrate her life again?

Only a few weeks prior, Antonia had learned that Philip was attempting to manipulate his way back into her world. He had uncovered a family member who was unknown to Antonia and tried to use her as some form of revenge against Antonia. Luckily the girl had figured out what sort of a monster he was before it was too late. But now here he was yet again, persistent and unshakable, insidiously imposing himself on her.

After Antonia left Philip, she had met with a therapist as well as a support group to try to decipher how she had been lulled in by a man as evil and twisted as he. It was reassuring to learn that she was not the first to fall for a psychopath but just as heartbreaking to realize that she would not be the last. What was gratifying was to see that there were many normal people who became prey for deranged people. That sounded wrong, but Antonia had blamed herself for so long and felt nothing but shame and fear. What was so amiss with her that she had married an abuser? But the members of Antonia's support group had been compassionate, thoughtful, and successful people for the most part. People whose best intentions and efforts to look for the good in individuals had been their downfall. They had tried to help her acknowledge that she wasn't the bad guy, Philip was. He was like Julia

Roberts's husband in *Sleeping with the Enemy*, one group counselor had remarked. Yes, indeed. She had slept with the enemy for too long.

Yet now sleep was completely off the table. Antonia remained in bed but had a fitful night of rest. She finally abandoned her attempts at slumber at five thirty and dressed for her walk on the beach. She set out at daybreak to clear her mind along the cool shores of the Atlantic and was privy to one of the most spectacular sunrises she had seen in a while. As the sun rose, the sky was alight with bursts of orange and red and purple with a teal backdrop, all accompanied by the song of the thrushes. Antonia decided to count it as a blessing that she had been awoken to experience such beauty. That was one of the things that she had learned in her support group: count your blessings. Life was too short to do otherwise. She had the expansive white sand beach exclusively to herself except for one lone walker a mile ahead that looked only like a dot in the distance. The glossy rays of the sun were reflected off the shimmering water and Antonia felt as if the sun had risen specifically for her. What could be better?

On her way home, the absence of bikers and joggers on Lily Pond Lane confounded Antonia until she realized with a thud that it was Tumbleweed Tuesday. That's what the locals called the day after Labor Day, when all the summer people fled the area for the season. Whereas the day before, the streets and beaches were clotted with libidinous and hedonistic seasonal folk, the light congestion today was exclusively comprised of local society, give or take a few stragglers. It was actually remarkable to experience the difference between Labor Day and Tumbleweed Tuesday, and some people compared it to living in a pre- and post-apocalyptic world. The swollen population evacuated with one thunderous clap and disappeared back to the city. Antonia thought about Shane Boskin and Gary DiAngelo. No doubt they would have left by today, and yet now they lay cold in the morgue, never to venture anywhere again.

Back at the inn, Connie informed Antonia that Sergeant Flanagan was in Jonathan's office and had asked that Antonia join them as soon as she returned. She found him seated comfortably in the chair across from Jonathan, but ever the gentleman, he stood when she entered the room.

"Two days in a row, what an honor," Antonia announced as she strolled into the room.

"I know. It's a habit."

"But you appear much more relaxed in Jonathan's office than my own," Antonia remarked.

"His is neater."

"Sad, but true," said Antonia, glancing around the office. The bookshelves behind Jonathan's desk were neatly arranged with files and binders, all dated and labeled in an orderly manner. There was no clutter, not a pile of books or knickknacks to be found anywhere. It was almost antiseptic except for the perky row of plants that were thriving on the windowsill, which was an affront to Antonia, who had little success with gardening. She'd never spotted a dead leaf on one of Jonathan's ferns, and yet hers were dead by the time she returned from the garden center.

Jonathan rose and pulled over a chair for Antonia.

"To what do I owe the honor, Sergeant?" Antonia inquired.

Sergeant Flanagan flipped through his brown notebook before sighing and placing it in his lap.

"I'm trying to fill in the blanks."

"Okay, what do you need from us?"

"I had asked Jonathan when Dawn Costa had booked her reservation. He said she booked it in April."

"Yes, I informed the sergeant that Labor Day was one of our most in-demand weekends of the year," confirmed Jonathan.

"That's true," concurred Antonia. "But I see why you have that look on your face, Sergeant."

His eyebrows shot up. "What look?"

"I may be presumptuous, but I think I have interacted with you regarding criminal matters enough to know when something doesn't add up for you."

Sergeant Flanagan appeared amused. "And what would that be?"

"I obviously wasn't there when the police interviewed Dawn Costa, but I did chat with her myself. She told me that she decided last minute to book the inn because Lauren Wayne was stalking her and she needed to hide. It sounded off to me at the time, but I was way more distracted by her crocodile tears and lack of fear than anything else. As you know, I personally have lived with a stalker. It's not something I take lightly. If I had been tied up by him in a room, the second I was untied, I would be out of there like a bat out of hell. Dawn was in no rush, and appeared unruffled."

"My thoughts exactly."

"Can I ask what Lauren said when she was told that Dawn said she stalked her?" Antonia queried.

"You can ask, but I can't tell. Ongoing investigation."

"Annoying."

Sergeant Flanagan returned his attention to Jonathan. "Can you tell me who was in the adjoining room?"

"Certainly. I know the door was locked, but I can look it up."

He clicked through his laptop.

"How do you know the door was locked?" asked the sergeant.

"When the rooms are not booked by the same guest, we lock them," answered Jonathan.

"Can the guests unlock them?"

Jonathan nodded. "Yes, if they both unlock their doors, they can access each other's rooms." He slid his computer screen around toward Sergeant Flanagan and Antonia. "This is the guest."

Sergeant Flanagan and Antonia squinted at the screen. There was a scanned driver's license with a picture of a thirty-year-old man with a mop of dark hair and wireless glasses. Like most official government-issued portraits, it was unflattering, and the subject appeared to be irritated.

"Tomas Stefanowski," said Sergeant Flanagan, scribbling the name in his notebooks. "Would you mind printing that out for me?"

"Done," said Jonathan, swiveling his chair to reach the printer behind him. Two sheets of paper came slithering out, which Jonathan retrieved and dispersed to Antonia and Sergeant Flanagan.

Antonia looked carefully at the picture. It said Tomas was six feet tall (which meant he was five ten or eleven because every man she knew gave himself a few inches). He had brown eyes and was born on January 23, 1988.

"He's really nondescript-looking," Antonia noted.

"Yes, quite generic," concurred Jonathan.

"Do you recognize him?" asked the sergeant.

Both Antonia and Jonathan shook their heads. "Not at all," Jonathan said and sighed. "And I'm usually pretty good about it."

"Me too," added Antonia.

"Anyone else who might be able to tell us about him?"

"I'll ask Connie to stop by and tell us. She would have been on reception at the time," said Jonathan, before pressing a button to buzz Connie.

"Also, can we get housekeeping down here? Maybe they know something?" asked the sergeant.

"Certainly," replied Jonathan.

Antonia was perplexed. She really did pride herself on meeting and greeting everyone who was staying at her inn and making sure that she had her finger on the pulse, so to speak. How did she totally miss Dawn and this Tomas? What had she been up to all Labor Day that she had not even laid eyes on either of these guests? The inn only boasted eight guest rooms. That wasn't a large number of people to keep track of, and yet Antonia had been remiss. Was it because it was the climax of a very long and eventful summer? Or was she too distracted to do her job well?

"In the meantime, can you please tell me when Tomas booked his room?" asked the sergeant.

Jonathan furrowed his brow as he looked at the computer. He pressed a few buttons and then clicked back and forth. He glanced up, a concerned look on his face.

"They both booked the same day, right?" asked the sergeant.

Jonathan nodded.

"So he was her accomplice," said Antonia. "He must have been the one who tied her up. But where is he now?"

There was a knock at the door, and Connie peered her head in. "You wanted to see me?"

She strode in the door, her manner cheerful as always. Although in her thirties, Connie dressed like a much older woman. Today she had on pleated khakis and a long orange tunic that was belted around her midsection so that the sides below the belt flared out like a tutu. She favored bright colors and sported a large turquoise necklace and bright yellow earrings.

"Yes, thank you, Connie. We want to know about Tomas Stefanowski, our guest in Room Seven."

"Oh, right. Yes, he was supposed to arrive on Friday, but his flight was canceled, so he arrived on Saturday. He left first thing yesterday morning."

"And what was he like?" asked Antonia.

Sergeant Flanagan gave Antonia a warning look. He wanted to control the line of questioning, but Antonia couldn't help herself.

"Well, you know, I never met him."

This got the attention of the trio in the room.

"What?" asked Antonia.

"Never met him?" repeated Jonathan.

Connie was instantly flustered. "Uh-oh, did I do something wrong?"

"No, no, just, how is that possible?" asked Antonia.

Sergeant Flanagan scribbled something in his notebook.

"Well, he called Friday and said his flight was canceled and he would be a late arrival on Saturday, maybe even after hours. I said that's fine, just email me a copy of his driver's license or a passport and I would leave the key to his room in an envelope in his name at the front desk. We've done this before. I didn't think there was anything wrong…"

"No, no, of course," said Jonathan.

"Then what happened?" asked Antonia.

"When I left Saturday he wasn't here, but when I arrived Sunday morning, I saw that the envelope was gone. I assumed he had checked in. I asked Soyla if he'd been down for breakfast, and she said she didn't think so. I wanted to confirm that he did indeed have the key, and so I asked Rosita and she told me he was here. She said he had a DO NOT DISTURB sign on his door, which made sense. After all, he'd had all those travel delays and no doubt he was tired. Honestly, I didn't think much of it. I was busy with other guests, and I just assumed I missed him going in and out."

"What about yesterday?" asked the sergeant.

"Well, he checked out before I arrived. We allow our guests the option of a room checkout, which makes it easier. Nobody really likes paperwork and the last thing anyone wants to do when they're leaving is to wait on a long line. We already have their credit card information anyway. Once people are ready to leave, we have found they are truly ready to leave. They become angry if that process is delayed. Well, Mr. Stefanowski took advantage of our speedy checkout and left yesterday on his own accord."

"How do you know when he left?" asked Jonathan.

"Rosita said his door was open and his things were gone."

"Just to clarify, you never actually saw Tomas Stefanowski?" asked the sergeant.

Connie pursed her lips. "Well, I suppose you are right. It's kind of strange, because normally I see people coming and going. I like to chat with our guests, and they always ask me for restaurant recommendations or what the best beaches are. I tell them if they want a snack bar, then they should go to Main Beach or Atlantic Beach. I personally prefer Indian Wells, although Georgica is a lot of fun also. I think people really appreciate the insider tips. They also want to know where all the celebrities live and I tell them. I actually put it on the map. I know I shouldn't do that, but people just love it. But, well, Mr. Stefanowski never came down to ask about anything. I mean, this is unusual. I never laid eyes on the man!"

"Thank you, Connie," said the sergeant.

Before the group could confer, Rosita appeared at the door. For someone so tiny, Rosita was a force to be reckoned with, although you would never know it from her small stature and timid demeanor. She had a beautiful face, thick, black hair swept back, and dark, soulful eyes that could light up a room when she smiled. She was in charge of housekeeping, working with her sisters. Soyla and Hector were her relatives also; it was truly a family affair at the inn.

"You wanted to see me, Miss?" asked Rosita uneasily. Her eyes instantly darted to the police officer in the room and Antonia detected fear.

"Yes, it's all okay, we had a few questions about our guest in Room Seven?" asked Antonia, attempting to assure Rosita with her comforting tone.

Rosita nodded. "Yes, Miss?"

"Did you meet this guest?" asked the sergeant.

Rosita shook her head. She kept her responses short and didn't look the officer in the eye. "No."

"No?" repeated Antonia.

Rosita looked alarmed. "Something wrong, Miss?"

"Antonia, can you please let me conduct this interview?" chided the sergeant.

"Yes, sure."

"Did you ever see him at all?" asked the sergeant.

"No. He had his sign on his door. I didn't want to disturb him."

"You never went into his room?"

"No. He came late I think Saturday and left Monday early. When I got to work Monday, the door was open and he had already left."

"What about the condition of his room?" asked the sergeant. "Did he leave much trash? Was he messy, was he neat?"

Rosita took a moment to contemplate the question. "He was neat. There was nothing. He didn't use the towels, I don't think. No garbage."

"What about the bed?"

"The bed…he had opened the bed, but the sheets were still tight at the bottom."

"Like he didn't sleep there!" conjectured Antonia.

The sergeant gave her a withering look. "Please don't lead the witness." He turned back to Rosita. "But, yes, I do want to ask. Did it look like he slept on the sheets?"

"I thought it was strange…but no, it didn't look like that. I don't know… The bed was very neat. I thought maybe he made the bed himself… I wasn't sure."

The sergeant nodded. "Anything else strike you as odd or important to note?"

Rosita shook her head, but something in her demeanor conveyed hesitation.

"You can tell us, Rosita," prompted Jonathan.

"Any little thing can help," added Antonia.

She addressed Antonia when she responded. "I found a picture… I wasn't sure what to do. It was on the desk…"

"What kind of picture?" asked the sergeant.

"It was…I have it here. I kept it. I wanted to ask Hector what he thought I should do but I didn't have a chance yet."

"Can we see it?" asked Antonia.

Reluctantly Rosita pulled a small photograph out of the pocket of her dress. Her face was awash with regret and apology. "Sorry, Miss…"

She handed the photograph to Sergeant Flanagan. He stared at it, his face betraying no sign of impression, before glancing up at the group.

"What is it?" asked Antonia.

He slowly turned it around in his fingertips for Antonia to see. She instantly felt like she had the wind knocked out of her. She moved forward and took the photograph from his hand and held it.

"This is my wedding…" she said in barely a whisper.

Jonathan leaned over to glance at the photo. It had been taken in California many years before, on her wedding day. Antonia in her ethereal white gown was standing next to Philip, who sported a tuxedo. Her expression was that of astonishment and his of wicked contempt. At least that's what Antonia saw now. At the time she would have said he wore a mischievous grin, but now that she knew his soul better, she knew that evil was broadcasting all over his face like a billboard. The image had captured the moment after they cut the cake when Philip was shoving it into her face. Actually, more like smashing it. She remembered the moment so vividly. They had plated the cake—an enchanting huckleberry confection with a buttermilk frosting, lovingly prepared by her catering staff and gifted to her as a present—and then *BOOM!* She turns to stare up at her new husband and he smears it all over her mug. She looked like a clown with the white smears and chunks of ripe berries hanging off her lower lip. She should have known then that only jerks actually smash you in the face with wedding cake. Some people find it cute, but it is truly an act of aggression. She remembered seeing the faces of her catering friends at the time. They were horrified.

The picture brought up so many bad memories for Antonia.

But now, the truly frightening part was not that remembrance of things past. What was more frightening was that Antonia's face had been scribbled out with a black Sharpie. And the word *BITCH* was written across her forehead.

"Who would do this?" asked Jonathan.

"I can think of one person," said Antonia with a shiver.

9

THE IRONY WAS NOT LOST ON ANTONIA THAT PHILIP HAD decided to insinuate himself back into her life on Tumbleweed Tuesday, the day that locals "reclaim" East Hampton for themselves. If there was ever a day that conjured up old-fashioned turf wars and feelings of freedom and redemption, it was the day the interlopers cleared out and locals regained their town. This was normally a relaxing day for Antonia, one where she was reminded how much space and peace there was to be found on the east end. Now Philip had interjected himself into the moment by calling her and quite literally waking her up from her dreams. The wedding picture was the cherry on top of the poison sundae. If it wasn't Philip who left the picture in Room Seven, then it was surely one of his agents, a thought almost more frightening.

With assurances from Sergeant Flanagan that he would be on high alert for Philip, as well as preparing a door-to-door casing of the entire inn and surrounding area by his fellow officers, Antonia had no choice but to proceed with her day. Unfortunately, she knew Philip well enough to know that he liked to prolong his torture. He was calculating and would contrive the most devious plans to torment her. In the past she had been crushed and immobilized by his twisted games, but now that she had personally faced down serial killers, she was not going to allow him to affect her. No matter how much willpower it required.

In an effort to retain control of her life and business, Antonia decided to supervise reception with Connie for the rest of the morning. Between chatting with guests, fielding phone calls, refilling the iced-water pitcher with flavored water, and wiping the bird poop off the Adirondack chairs on the porch, Antonia kept herself busy. At an inn, mornings are a bit easier, because after breakfast is cleared, guests either check out or set off for town. Afternoons are more difficult because of the elusive check-in time—anywhere between three and eight p.m. That was when an innkeeper and her staff had to be really "on." And that was when Antonia would head to the kitchen.

At about half past eleven, Larry Lipper came strolling through the front door, a serene expression on his face, an uncharacteristically breezy manner encompassing him. He wore a baseball cap, his scruffy hair peeking out of the sides, and a Bonac sweatshirt, in deference to the local school team. With his stature he could have passed for a peewee baseball player, if not for the twelve o'clock shadow on his chin.

"Why do you seem like the cat that swallowed the canary, Larry?" Antonia inquired, feeling quite proud of herself that she had included a rhyme.

"Got lucky last night," confessed Larry. "You should try it some time."

He leaned across the reception desk, completely disrupting the neat pile of maps that were available to guests. Several fluttered to the ground. Larry made no attempt to retrieve them until he acquiesced to Antonia's withering look, then he bent to pick them up.

"Thanks for the advice."

He popped back up and thrust the now-crushed maps at Antonia, making no effort to restore them to their previously folded condition.

"Listen, Bingham, I know you want every detail of my conquest, and I'm sure you're burning with jealousy, but I came here to talk business, not to have you hound me with questions over who I am sleeping with."

She would not deign to respond.

"Let's go talk somewhere," he suggested.

"I need to stay here to greet guests."

Larry rolled his eyes. "Whatever. Don't you pay her for this?"

Antonia was becoming very impatient. "What did you want to talk about, Larry?" she asked sternly.

"Okay, well, when I went over to Dawn Costa's house…"

"Let me guess, she wasn't there."

"You had a fifty-fifty chance, yes or no, so I'm not handing out a medal to you, Bingham."

"Well, I suppose you could say that I cheated because I knew she wasn't there. She was here, staying at the inn."

"What?" exclaimed Larry, his face turning shades of purple. "Tell me everything. *Now!*"

Antonia sighed and took a mint from the small dish she kept next to the register. She took her sweet time unwrapping it, while bubbles of frustration emanated from Larry. She knew she would cave and tell him everything, but it didn't hurt to make him wait for it. After popping the mint in her mouth as he tapped his fingers on the counter, she filled him in on the previous day's interaction, ending with the mysterious Tomas Stefanowski. She even told him about the wedding picture they found in his room. Bravery comes from acknowledgment and not surrendering to fear, Antonia reminded herself. She felt that she had control of the situation and could undermine Philip's power the more she talked about it.

"Do we think this Tomas is Dawn's accomplice or some friend of your crazy ex?" asked Larry when she had concluded her discourse.

"I don't know. The police are running down the leads."

"This whole Dawn and Lauren thing is weird. Let's nutshell it: Lauren says she and Dawn were watching TV together and the next thing she knows she's in the woods, at the scene of a crime, remembering nothing. Apparently drugged, scratched up, and claiming to be a victim of some sort. It's all cookies and milk, tragic and weird, you're rubbing her back and the librarian's irrigating her with tap water, sad face emoji—but then her face contorts when we mention Shane and Gary. That expression made it clear she knew the deceased. Maybe she's not Miss Victim after all. Then you find Dawn here, at the inn, tied up by her supposed stalker, Lauren. Another quote unquote victim. But you say she wasn't scared at all, the ropes were loosely tied, she was ordering up frothy Italian coffees, insisted she be comped, and took off into the wind. Adding to this was your mysterious guest Tomas Polish-Last-Name, who nobody laid eyes on, and he may or may not be an accomplice. We have no proof except he's the invisible man. But he may be somehow connected to your ex because of the memento he left you. It doesn't make sense."

"I know. Unless it's all fake."

"Fake except for the dead bodies in the hot tub."

"Maybe Dawn and Lauren did it together. One accuses the other and then they both get off because the jury can't decide which one did it."

"That's possible. After I went to Dawn's empty house, I headed over to the Shore Lodge, where Lauren works."

"How did you know she works there?"

"Sources, Bingham. Sources."

"What did they say?"

"They said that Lauren has waitressed there all summer. They said she's an okay waitress, what she lacks in serving skills she makes up for in looks, so that works for them. This is her second summer there. And guess what? Turns out Dawn worked there last summer. She abruptly quit last August, left them in the lurch, so they are not too thrilled with Miss Costa. Did one of those moves like calling in sick at five o'clock on a Friday, and they had no replacement set up in time. Said it was weird, though, because she was usually all about the money, and she didn't even come by to pick up her tips or check. Never laid eyes on her again."

"Did they offer up a theory?"

"Not really. They just thought maybe she shacked up with some rich dude and it was no longer about the dinero for her."

"What about Shane and Gary? Did they know them?"

"The manager said they looked like just about every dude that comes through the place. But that said, he did me a solid and ran their names through his credit card machine, and they were regulars. Not just this summer, but last summer. And this is where it gets interesting. They were there the night before Dawn did her disappearing act."

"Talk about burying the lead, Larry," Antonia exclaimed. "So maybe they hooked up with her last year? Did something bad to her and this is a revenge kill?"

"Exactly what I was thinking and then…well, Bingham, it seems too easy. I mean, I know I've solved a bunch of murders lately, with your help a little, but I mean, how could this be what happened?"

"There are no perfect murders and no brilliant murderers. Almost everyone gets caught. We're smarter than Dawn and Lauren. That's why we caught them."

"If we're so smart, where's our proof? All we have now is conjecture. I need some hard evidence."

Antonia and Larry drifted off into uncharacteristic silence. She knew he was right. They had a good theory that would be a nice movie plot—hell, it probably was! How could they link Dawn and Lauren directly to the murders? An irritating thought sprung into Antonia's head.

"Larry, here we are thinking we're all sleuth-y, but the fact is the police have probably already come to the same conclusion. And they had the additional benefit of interviewing both Lauren and Dawn at length. I'm sure they would have pressed on both of them to figure out what happened."

"Could be, Bingham, could be," confessed Larry.

Antonia was instantly surprised and realized her hunch must be correct if even Larry conceded it.

"You know, there's something wrong with us if we are disappointed that law enforcement solves a crime and we don't. Maybe we're in the wrong profession. We should be grateful that we don't live in a world…"

As Antonia droned on with her saccharine and debatably sincere pep talk, she realized that Larry's attention was being pulled in another direction. Cindy Boskin was walking down the stairs in a short black dress with black high heels. She held a monogrammed weekend bag in one hand and had a leather purse with a giant logo on her other arm. She paused when she saw Larry in his little boy hat staring up at her.

"What are you doing here?" he blurted out, before moving toward her.

Cindy hesitated then continued down the steps gingerly. She shot a glance in Antonia's direction before mumbling a morning salutation, taking Larry by the arm, and leading him into the parlor off the front hall.

"Come with me," she commanded Larry.

That was strange, mused Antonia. She wondered how those two knew each other. But the world was small and perhaps Larry knew Cindy from some other iteration of his life. As they were out of earshot, Antonia could only hear murmurs of their conversation, which sounded like white noise. She realized that she and Larry had been totally indiscreet chatting about Shane's murder with his widow just upstairs. She hoped she hadn't heard anything. That was a total party foul.

A few minutes passed before Cindy and Larry emerged from the parlor. Cindy was all business while Larry appeared amused.

"I'm checking out now. Thank you for accommodating me," said Cindy.

"No problem. Please let me know if there's anything I can do. Again, I want to say how sorry I am for your loss."

Cindy nodded brusquely before giving one more piercing gaze at Larry. She nodded her head and quickly left the inn.

"What was that all about?" asked Antonia.

Larry beamed. "She made me promise not to tell you."

"Tell me what?"

"Oh, come on, Bingham. You know I can't kiss and tell."

Antonia was confused. "Larry, you know that was Shane Boskin's widow, right?"

Larry's face went from enraptured to shocked in one second. It would have been comical had he not been so totally stunned. "Wait…what?"

"That was Cindy Boskin. She was here to meet with the police and identify the body."

Larry rubbed his eyes with his hands. "That's messed up! She didn't mention any of that. I'm not surprised she's married because she just begged me to keep our little tryst a secret, not to mention that she was a wildcat in bed. Clearly it's been a while as with most married women…"

"Spare me the details," Antonia chided. "When was your tryst?"

"Yesterday."

"Yesterday? But I was with her. She was here around ten."

"Oh no, it was much earlier than that. After I went to the Shore Lodge to ask about Lauren, I stopped by the Clam Bar on the way home. I hadn't had anything fried in six hours, and I was jonesing. I'm sitting there, she's next to me alone at the bar and instantly drawn to my rocking body, and the next thing I know I'm in her room at White Sands Motel across the street having lots of fun."

Antonia's brain was swimming. There was so much wrong with his statement that she didn't know where to start. "Wait, back up. What time was this?"

"I don't know…around three or something. And I get it; it's weird that she didn't mention Shane. Maybe they hadn't found her yet and told her about him being offed."

"I thought they told the family in the morning. That's why Sergeant Flanagan could be candid with me."

Larry considered this. "Look, I do want to say that she just couldn't resist me, but I agree with you, this was strange. If it was a revenge thing since her hubby was found dead after partying, I get it, but she didn't seem at all disturbed or upset. She was…totally relaxed. People process grief differently, but this would make her one cold broad."

"It's also strange that she called us and begged for a room at the inn when she already had a room at the White Sands Motel. She specifically told Jonathan that she was driving out from the city. And he said she was hysterical."

"She's a good actress."

"What else did she tell you?"

"There wasn't much conversation if you know what I mean," said Larry, winking. "But she said she was passing through town. I had no indication that she was here for anything other than a vacation."

Antonia had a thought. "What was she wearing?"

"You know, short shorts up to the thigh and a tank top. She's very fit and can pull that off."

"But did you notice right now that she had on a black dress and formal black shoes? It's like she was prepared to play the role of a grieving widow."

"The chick is whacked. I mean, I could tell she wasn't really into talking and just wanted a good roll in the hay. She didn't even tell me where she was from. Just said her name was Ella…"

"Ella? Her name is Cindy. She told me she wanted to name her daughter Ella."

Larry shrugged. "If she was married, she probably didn't want to be tracked down if she's cheating. I could ask the guys at the Clam Bar what the name was on her credit card, but I specifically remember her paying cash. I can return to the motel and ask them there."

"Let me see what credit card she used here."

Antonia clicked on the computer. She typed in Room Two, which is where they had put Cindy Boskin. It only listed her name and no other information. In terms of payment, there was a note: *Comped.*

"Nothing," said Antonia, her heart sinking. "I think I told Jonathan to not bother with payment because her husband just died."

"How do you even know she was his wife?" asked Larry.

"What do you mean?"

"She calls and says she needs a room and shows up. Gives you no identification, no credit card, then leaves."

He was right, how did she know? Not only that, but she also was able to cajole Antonia into telling her everything about Philip and all of her personal details, stuff that Antonia generally kept to herself. She had commiserated with "Cindy" on lousy husbands and irritating in-laws. She'd been quite loose with the grim facts of her marriage. *Well done, Antonia.*

"I'm scared of what you're implying."

"Google Shane Boskin and wife," commanded Larry.

Antonia did as she was told. The screen filled with a LinkedIn headshot of Shane, looking quite slick in that Wall Street way, as well as some pictures of him at conferences with assorted groups of other business types. When she scrolled down the screen, there were several party pictures at charity events. In most of them, Shane was quite cozy with a perky blond with big white teeth that would make a dentist proud, just the type of bride that Antonia had imagined he would have. She clicked on the picture and the couple was identified: Shane and Cindy Boskin.

"I'm going to be sick."

"She may still be out front. Let's see if we can catch her."

They both hastened outside, down the steps, and scanned the parking lot. "Cindy" was nowhere to be found.

10

When you are having a bad day, do what you can to help someone else have a good day. That was one of Antonia's mother's nuggets of advice. It was a sound philosophy, because it always made her feel better to make someone else feel better, and it is a clever idea to pull one's head out of a small world of problems and have perspective. In the scheme of things, nothing terrible was happening to Antonia. She had her health, her friends, and hell, even a dinner engagement! But she was feeling like a professional failure—her inn had allowed two questionable—okay, downright sketchy—guests to stay there for free, which was just sloppy. There had been zero background checks and just the naive assumption that people would be honest. That was definitely bad for business. Not to mention that her ex-husband was creeping his way back into her life. Those were enough to put her on edge and make the day careen downhill.

But this time, Antonia took her mother's advice. She called up her best friend, Genevieve, and allowed her to do what she had been begging Antonia to let her do for years: give Antonia a makeover. Genevieve and Antonia's friendship went back to California when they catered together, and Genevieve was actually the one who had coaxed Antonia into moving to East Hampton, where she had set up shop after spending childhood summers here. She was a manager at a Ralph Lauren store and used herself as a human billboard for his clothes. Whatever the current fashion trend, Genevieve dove into it wholeheartedly and with a feverish zeal. She was a person who took the mantra "no white pants after Labor Day" as gospel, and as soon as a glossy magazine declared animal print or suede out of style, Genevieve couldn't rush fast enough to the Ladies Village Improvement Society thrift shop to dump off outfits made of the offensive prints that she had donned as recently as the prior day. She lived as if the fashion police lurked around the corner.

"This is such a great idea. You made my day, literally!" squealed Genevieve.

Genevieve was an attractive woman in her early thirties, tall in stature and thin as a model. She had beautiful skin and arresting large green eyes that always seemed to convey an inquisitive expression and quite literally made one think of the phrase "wide-eyed." In true fashionista form, she had on a tight camel dress with layers of beaded and feathered necklaces and wore the highest and thinnest strappy heels, the kind usually reserved for the runway. She had only been at Antonia's house for half an hour, but she had managed to fling almost everything out of Antonia's closet onto the bed and had a teetering pile of "reject" clothes that she was planning to drop off at the thrift store, whether Antonia liked it or not.

"I'm glad to be of service," sighed Antonia, who was holding up a lavender paisley print long-sleeved shirt in front of the mirror.

Genevieve was wading through the back of Antonia's closet, throwing shoes out one by one, and glanced up at Antonia. "I can tell you right now that that is a definite no. You are not the symbol formerly known as Prince, God rest his soul. That shirt should have been buried in the nineties."

"I like this shirt," said Antonia defensively.

"And I like you too much to have you commit a crime by wearing it."

"Fine," Antonia conceded, before throwing it on the reject pile. She knew that Genevieve was right, but she had a hard time relinquishing clothes that were once so beloved. She clearly remembered purchasing that shirt in a small shop she had wandered into in Carmel, California. There had been no question in her mind that it would be hers once she laid eyes on it. True, that might have been about twelve years ago, so perhaps Genevieve was right.

"These are great shoes," said Genevieve, holding up a pair of leopard mules.

"You gave them to me."

"I did? Huh, I have good taste."

"I don't think I ever wore them. Sorry, but they are so uncomfortable."

Genevieve sighed. "Antonia, fashion is not supposed to be comfortable. Anything beautiful comes with pain. You have to suffer through it to look good."

"No thank you."

"Okay, well, maybe not every day, but now and then! Tonight for example, for your hot date."

A flash of anticipation shot through Antonia's veins. It was so odd that she had a "hot date." She was never the gal with the "hot date." Before and after her marriage, she had been the *friend* of the gal who had the "hot date." Her courtship with Philip had been brief and secretive, preventing any opportunity to relish the wooing process. In retrospect, that probably should have been a red flag.

"I honestly can't believe that I'm having dinner with Nick tonight."

"Not just dinner, honey, hopefully there will be a little hokey-pokey afterward."

"I'm not prepared for that."

"You should be!" exclaimed Genevieve. "And because I knew

you wouldn't be prepared for that, I purposely stopped by Bonne Nuit and bought you some sexy undergarments."

Genevieve threw a small bag over to Antonia. "How did you know my size?"

"Duh, I'm in retail. I can size a person up the second I see them."

Antonia waded through the tissue paper and pulled out a lacy white bra with matching panties. "I don't know if I can wear this…"

"You can."

"This is crazy."

"Yes, but so is life. And so is your closet. Antonia, you need to come into the store and I can outfit you for future romantic interludes. If you're dating a celeb, you need to dress the part. For now, we have very few things to work with. You know you look good in jewel tones, you need to show cleavage, and wrap dresses suit you very well. I like you in long, dangling earrings because of your long hair; it's a good combo. Tonight you're wearing kitten heels whether you like it or not. I think going forward you have to remember not to be afraid of accessories: they are your friend. And if you've got it, flaunt it, which is what you need to do with your chest."

Antonia wanted to groan, but she kept herself in check. Genevieve was a professional, and fashion was her expertise, and despite all of Antonia's reluctance, she did need a complete closet renovation. Hell, a complete fashion renovation. She decided to let her friend run with it.

"I think you should wear this."

Genevieve held up a ruby-colored dress.

"I wore that last time I went out with him. You also gave me that."

"I have great taste. Don't worry. I'll keep looking. And I'll keep in mind that if I like it, I probably gave it to you."

"True."

An hour later Antonia's closet was as bare as a baby's bottom. Lonely hangers dangled in the wind. The dusty back shelf that housed footwear had been stripped of practically everything. Not even handbags were spared; the offensive passé contents were cleared out by Genevieve and packed in garbage bags to cart to the LVIS. Antonia was strapped into a clingy, jade dress, with the aforementioned kitten heels on her feet and dangling earrings in her lobes. Genevieve was gratified to discover that Antonia was not remiss in the makeup and skincare department—they were actually a favorite indulgence of hers. With a plethora of goodies to select from, Genevieve was now putting the finishing touches on Antonia's visage. She had spritzed and styled Antonia's hair and managed to make her look her best.

"Almost done with the smoky eye," said Genevieve, poking at Antonia's lids with a brush. The rims she had outlined with charcoal liner, and she put a thick layer of mascara on the lashes. Antonia worried that if she blinked, her eyelashes would crack off.

"Don't overdo it."

"Shhhh…hush, child. I know what I'm doing."

"Okay."

"Honestly, it really is surreal that you are dating Nick Darrow. Here I am, scouring the globe for a man, dating loser after loser, and you're like, I don't ever need a man, I'm all good, and yet you land the biggest catch on the planet!"

"I'm not sure that's exactly how it went down."

"What's your secret?"

"No secret. I think the fact that I never thought we would have a romantic future helped a lot. We started as friends, walking on the beach."

"I suppose I always skip that part. I just get overexcited! But maybe I should try it."

"You should. I also think romance comes when you are not searching for it. That sounds so cliché, but honestly, I've been super busy with the inn and with all these murders. The last thing I was thinking of was dating."

"I don't know how that's possible. I always think of dating. I always think of men. I love that they come in all shapes and sizes and colors and ages. There are so many to choose from, it's hard to settle on one."

"Perhaps that is where we differ."

"Ta-da!" said Genevieve, doing one last fluff of Antonia's hair. "You are ready to go, my lady."

Antonia appraised herself in the mirror. Genevieve had done an excellent job concealing, shading, contouring, manipulating, teasing, and padding—all the stuff Antonia generally eschewed and had little patience for. Maintenance was too high maintenance for her. But today it was worth it, not to mention more palatable if someone else did it for you. Antonia was excited; she did look good.

"Nick Darrow, I'm ready," said Antonia.

Genevieve responded with sounds that could only be associated with wild animals in the cat family. She even pantomimed a lion scratching the air.

After a brief stop in the kitchen to put in her two cents, which were received by Marty and Kendra with only moderate enthusiasm, Antonia headed toward the parking lot. It was an easy walk to the 1770 House, but not in the shoes she had on. Besides, it was okay to show up looking put together with nary a hair out of place, and not all disheveled. Genevieve had told her that tonight should be all about seduction, and although she rarely took Genevieve's advice, she planned on heeding it this evening.

It was not yet seven, but the sky was already unveiling its darkness. The sun was slowly descending, and it was that gauzy hour that made visibility a challenge. That the days grew shorter was perhaps her least favorite part of impending fall and winter. She was a creature of light; it was the California in her.

As she opened the door of her beloved but abused blue Saab, which probably should have been put out to pasture several years prior, something caught Antonia's eye by the hedge that abutted the adjacent property. It was just a flicker of movement, but there was a furtiveness to it that captured her attention. She squinted. The privet was at its most robust this time of year, proving it to be a beneficial barrier between the inn and the neighbor's house. It was too thick for a person to abscond into. But it did seem like it had been a human form that darted deep into its breast. She shook off her worry. If it was anyone, it was a guest who was probably on a walk. No crime in that.

She sat down in her bucket seat and flipped on the CD player. The Saab was not iPod or iPhone compatible, which was just as well considering Antonia's tech skills. She was still congratulating herself that she'd been able to figure out the CD player ten years ago. Simon & Garfunkel's mellow voices came floating through the speakers, singing about a bridge over troubled waters. She'd heard the song a million times, but the lyrics always escaped her. I will lay you down? Or was it, I will lay me down? She wasn't sure. Remembering the lyrics to songs was also, sadly, not her skill set.

After steering the car out of its spot, she drove carefully to the end of the driveway. Making a left on Route 27 was always tricky; there was a relentless stream of cars proceeding from one direction or another. She glanced right and then left. She waited for a few cars to pass, her eyes bobbing back and forth like windshield wipers on the highest setting. She was about to pull out when she thought she caught movement by the hedge. She squinted, but there was nothing there. Finally there was a lapse in traffic, and she steadily turned the wheel and made a left. It was the one quick last glance to the right that chilled her to the bone, as Philip stepped out of the shadows on the corner. Even from a distance, she could read the expression on his face. It was the smirk that she knew only too well. The one he loved to mock her with. Her entire body surged with fear, but as she was in the process of turning and oncoming cars were heading straight at her, it made it impossible to stop. She was so rattled that her hands were shaking, and it took all of her strength to make sure she didn't keep proceeding forward and drive directly into the town pond. What was Philip doing here?

She looked into her rearview mirror. He wasn't there; he'd vanished. Had she imagined him? No, it couldn't be. She had seen him. He was standing by the edge of the driveway. Waiting for her. All of her senses exploded with the tension that he exuded. Antonia didn't consider herself mystical or influenced by astrology or crystals or anything of the sort, but she did believe in energy. Sometimes she could feel her late mother or father's presence around her. That made her happy. But she could also feel Philip's presence—his nefarious energy that strangled her to the core. And she was certain that right now it was near her.

She was at the 1770 House in less than two minutes and decided to sit in her car for a moment to pull herself together. What should she do? Should she call Sergeant Flanagan? How could he help? She ran the playbook in her mind. She'd have to cancel her date, return to the inn, and wait for the police to come. That could be minutes or hours. She was certain by then that Philip would be long gone; he was too crafty to stand around violating the order of protection that she had against him. No, it was no use to call the sergeant now. She didn't want to bother him at night; she would tell him in the morning. It was so perfect that Philip would show up to rattle her on the one day when she had a date. How could he have sensed that? Or maybe he didn't sense that, maybe he *knew* that. Antonia shivered. Had he been coming to her inn undetected? Sure, they had considered that the wedding photo might have been left by Philip, but Antonia had dismissed that idea. She had been too hasty. Hadn't she learned never to underestimate her ex-husband? Never to assume that he would cease his mission to ruin her life? Maybe he had been coming and going at the inn for weeks or even months and she had no idea.

Antonia wanted to cry. Ugh, but she couldn't; her makeup would smear and she'd look awful. Should she call off the date? That would be exactly what Philip wanted. No, she couldn't let him win. But she also couldn't go into the restaurant as rattled and emotional as she was. She needed a distraction. She picked up her phone to call Genevieve and then remembered that Gen was heading to a dinner party where her ex-boyfriend and his new wife would be in attendance. Gen was very excited to wear her sexiest outfit and show the guy what he was missing. Antonia had thought it a feeble plan, especially since it had failed several times before. Who could Antonia call to cheer her up?

"Bingham, miss me already?" Larry squeaked on the other end of the phone.

"No, I—" Antonia cleared her throat. She didn't realize how hoarse her voice would sound after suppressing the avalanche of tears that clogged her throat. "Any update on the case?"

Antonia could hear the sounds of munching on the other end of the line. Larry spoke with his mouth full.

"The motel said Ella, or Cindy Boskin, paid cash. The credit card that held the reservation was registered to a business—Force Partners. It's an LLC registered out of Delaware. That doesn't say much, most LLCs come out of Delaware even if the owners have never stepped foot in Delaware. It's better for taxes."

"Did they say when she made the reservation?"

"A couple of months ago."

"Anything else?"

"My police source says they found very big shoe prints by the hot tub."

"Really?"

"Yeah. I think they are going to chase down the guy who was at your bar the same night as them. The one who got upset."

"Huh. I should go back and look into that. Maybe Glen or Jesse remembers more."

"Yeah, you should do it." Antonia could tell Larry had taken another bite of food.

"What are you eating?"

"Me? Dinner."

"Yeah, but what?"

"Kraft Mac and Cheese with chopped up hot dogs."

"Cute."

"Cute? I'm waiting for the lecture."

"No lecture."

"Come on, you always ride me about how I eat like a kid and I eat junk, blah blah, like you're the food police."

"Not going to ride you tonight."

Larry's tone became serious. "You okay, Bingham?"

The lump in Antonia's throat became bigger. It was endearing that Larry actually sounded like he cared. It made her want to burst into tears. That would be a bummer after he had done so well in distracting her.

"I'm fine, Larry."

"You'd tell me if you weren't, right?"

"Of course. Don't be silly."

"Okay."

"I should go, Larry."

"What, you got a hot date?"

She smiled through the phone. "Something like that."

11

THEY WERE SEATED AT A CORNER TABLE IN THE TAVERN, THE dimly lit and intimate dining room that was cozier and less formal than its upstairs sister restaurant. Antonia had deftly maneuvered the miniature, winding staircase in her kitten heels, making every effort not to sound like a horse clanking down a steel plank, and was now ensconced in one of the plush cushioned banquettes that wrapped around the low-ceilinged room. The atmosphere was redolent of a British pub, and indeed the adjacent room was replete with a fireplace and a bar with a smattering of regulars having a tipple.

Nick had arrived cleanly shaven, his hair damp, and a fresh-scrubbed air enveloping him. Antonia's thoughts about Philip and her past life quickly dissipated once she laid eyes on her handsome dinner date. There are people in this world who have that shiny aura—they seem brighter and more luminescent than others—and Nick Darrow was certainly one of those. It was no fluke that he was a famous actor. He had a luster to him that could not be artificially cultivated.

They chatted about nothing of consequence before Nick began to regale her with a story about his dog's latest visit to the vet. It seemed as if Jack, his golden retriever, had developed a romantic attachment to the vet's pug. It wasn't so much the story that entranced Antonia, it was listening to Nick narrate it with his rich, baritone voice. His tone was so enchanting to Antonia that she believed she could listen no matter the topic. Antonia suddenly had a small recovered memory that Nick had at one time been hawking some insurance company on the radio years prior and she had not turned the station despite her deep aversion to commercials.

The waiter came to bring them menus and Nick ordered a bottle of Burgundy wine. The atmosphere was quiet, not many tables were full, but there was the muted hum of conversation and the occasional sound of corks being popped or the clatter of silverware placed on china plates. The air smelled of sautéed onions, ketchup, and chowder. The conversation flowed freely, stopping only when the waiter returned to present the wine, uncorking and decanting it for a tasting. Nick nodded his acceptance of the wine, and then they gave their orders. Antonia had debated a prissy entrée like a Caesar salad but instead decided to show her true self and went with the house meatloaf that promised potato purée, spinach, and roasted garlic sauce on the side. Nick ordered the Tavern Burger cooked medium-rare, extra pickles but hold the lettuce, specifications that Antonia filed away in her mental recipe Rolodex in case she ever cooked a burger for him.

Once the waiter had left and they had tasted their drinks, a moment of silence crept across their table. Suddenly Antonia found herself smiling dumbly but sitting mutely, and Nick staring across from her. She hadn't felt at all self-conscious until this point, and now it smacked her in the head with a thud.

"You look great, Toni."

"Thank you." She was about to embark on a long-winded and self-effacing diatribe that she had enlisted her friend Genevieve to help her primp and they had spent the entire afternoon readying her for this dinner, but she bit her tongue. One of Genevieve's parting statements to her was to watch the TMI, and Antonia thought it best to adhere to that.

"Tell me something about yourself that I don't know."

He gave her a look, and she found herself blushing. "Me?" she sputtered. "Oh, wow. I don't love talking about myself."

"I know that. That's why I'm asking. I have little interest in hearing myself talk all night."

"Okay. Hmmm. Let me think."

"Why don't you tell me how you became a chef? Was cooking a big deal in your family?"

"Yes, actually. We were a house of foodies."

"Who taught you to cook?"

"I learned by watching my mother. Her parents were from Italy and she had in turn learned from them. I was an only child—the blessing that my parents had waited for after almost sixteen years of trying—and was treated as such. They literally thought I could walk on water, for better or worse. When I returned home from school, I never wanted to go outside and play or head over to friends' houses; I always preferred to assist my mother in the kitchen. She insisted on preparing big family-style meals every night, and my uncle and aunt would join us most evenings. The kitchen was her sanctuary and laboratory. My mother would joke that other women ask for jewelry for their birthday, but she always would ask for things like new brass pots or a mandoline or lemon squeezer. There was no kitchen gadget that did not mesmerize her. Williams-Sonoma was founded out in Northern California and we used to make the pilgrimage to their mothership store several times a year. I was as excited as some kids are to go to Disneyland.

"There was so much I loved about the kitchen with my mother. The smells of garlic simmering on the stove; the fresh-cut herbs like tarragon, basil, and sage. I used to watch her simmer sauces, make beef and chicken broths from scratch, braise beans and sear the veal for osso buco. She would let me ladle the chicken broth into the risotto and stir it—a true Italian knows that it can take up to an hour to make the rice the perfect consistency. It was California in the eighties and nineties and many of my friends ate pretty well at home, thanks to Alice Waters and Chez Panisse. But they ate differently than we did, it was all very healthy and fat-free—they had salads that were green and lettuce-y, and skinless chicken breasts or filleted fish. We had salads also, but they were comprised of shaved fennel, pepperoncini, oregano, capers, olives, artichokes, and tomatoes. Always tomatoes. And my mother used a lot of butter and cheese. No chicken breast would land on our plates unless it was draped in mozzarella, blanketed in tomato sauce, and stuffed with several cloves of garlic. There was a different olive oil for everything—cooking, salads, bread dipping, or garnishing soups. Same with vinegar—red wine, sherry, champagne, rice, and balsamic were all on the lazy Susan.

"It's funny. I remember it all like it was yesterday. I can still smell the kitchen; I can smell my mother's perfume and the flowers on the windowsill. I can see her face smiling at me, and I can feel how happy I was then. It's like I'm looking at my past through a window when I think of this, or watching a movie. And the title is *Happy Family* because that's really how I felt at the time."

Antonia stopped talking. She was unused to exposing this much of herself, but she didn't care. It had been nice to revisit her past. "I'm not sure you wanted the long answer, but there you have it."

Nick smiled at her. "I wanted the long answer."

"Phew."

The waiter came with their food and placed it in front of them. A busboy came rushing over proffering pepper and a tray of condiments for the burger. Nick spoke when they had left.

"You're lucky you had such a wonderful childhood."

"I know."

"Not everyone can say that."

"I'm aware. I'm grateful every day."

They left the restaurant at about nine o'clock, which was still early, but they had been finished with their food and drinks for a while. Even after lingering over coffee and a shared bowl of ice cream, the dinner was condensed into two hours. They walked out to the parking lot without a discussion as to what would transpire next, and Antonia felt a nervous tension coursing through her veins. Would this be the night that she went home with Nick? Was he ready? More importantly, was *she* ready?

"Did you walk or drive?"

"I was lazy," she said, pulling her shawl tightly around her shoulders. The air had cooled significantly, and the slinky dress gave little help in the way of warmth.

"I'll walk you to your car."

There was the answer she was waiting for. She would not be heading home with Nick. Had she done something wrong? Suddenly her face felt flushed with embarrassment.

As if he were reading her mind, he continued. "It's not that I want this night to end. Actually, that's not what I want at all, especially after seeing you in that very sexy dress. I think, though, right now we should take things slow and not complicate anything. Is that okay with you?"

She nodded. Was it? She wasn't sure. "Sure," she said.

"Good."

They walked across the brick path toward her Saab, which was tucked into a shadowy corner. The sky was now an inky black with stars scattered about and a slice of fuzzy moon that was dim due to thin clouds passing. She retrieved her key from her clutch and unlocked and opened the car door. With feigned casualness, she turned to face him once more.

"Thank you for dinner."

"Thank you."

She was about to settle in the car when he pulled her toward him and gave her a long, deep kiss that would melt icebergs. After what seemed like a very lengthy and enjoyable time, they broke apart.

"You didn't think I'd let you go without a good-night kiss, did you?"

"I wasn't sure."

He cocked his head to the side. "Antonia, I like you. A lot. I just don't want to mess this up. I respect you too much to do that."

"Maybe I would rather that you don't respect me."

He gave her a crooked grin. "I plan on doing that very soon. It is something I'm looking forward to very much."

Antonia replayed the kiss over and over in her head on the short drive home. Maybe her expectations had been too large. She had hoped for more, and then Genevieve had sort of fueled her fire by bringing her lingerie and insisting that something would happen. Antonia had been swept away by the fairy tale. But was it a rebuff? Maybe he really did want to take things slowly. After all, he was only just disentangled from a marriage, which was ripe with innumerable complications. She should allow him some time to extricate himself from his relationship of over a decade before he hopped in the sack with her.

As Antonia made the turn into the parking lot of her inn, her eyes darted around the bushes and the hedges. All of her fear returned with a rush. Was Philip lurking there? Had she really seen him, or was she going crazy? She cautiously exited her car, furtively scanning the area before dashing into the back door. She shivered when she closed the door behind her and switched the lock. Feeling antsy and uneasy, she decided to head up to Joseph's apartment and see if he wanted to have a nightcap. She had noted that his light was on when she pulled into the drive, which wasn't really unusual as he was something of a night owl.

Joseph's face was friendly but hesitant, and Antonia felt at once that she was interrupting him.

"Oh, hello, my dear, I was just chatting about you."

"Sorry, I didn't mean to intrude..."

She spotted a striking woman in her late fifties sitting daintily on the armchair, sipping a glass of wine, her legs crossed seductively and her foot idly swirling figure eights in the air. Antonia was initially confused; this was perhaps the first time she had ever encountered someone in Joseph's apartment, except when his grown sons and their families were visiting. She was momentarily disconcerted. Suddenly everything clicked into place at once. Joseph was on a date. Just the mere fact that he had approached the door to open it on his crutches and not his scooter should have told her that something was up. Not to mention that there were votive candles flickering shadows off the walls and Adele's voice softly crooning in the background. (Adele? She was pretty sure Joseph hated Adele. He preferred classical music.)

If he was perturbed by the interruption, he showed no signs of it and quite elegantly responded, "Would you like to come in? I'm just having a glass of wine with my friend Cheryl. This is Antonia, Cheryl Cooke."

"Nice to meet you!" Cheryl boomed in a southern accent. "I've heard a lot about you. I love your inn!"

"Nice to meet you also," said Antonia.

Cheryl was slim, slight, and meticulously groomed: her blond, buttery highlights and extensively layered coif smacked of an upscale salon. Even from a distance, Antonia could decipher that her makeup was applied with expertise, her nails recently filed and painted, and the large diamonds in her ears were real. The scent of her perfume—Chanel or some other designer brand— permeated the room. In one eyeball, Antonia pegged her as a high-maintenance broad who had mastered basic feminine grooming skills that Antonia had never been able to achieve. If Cheryl felt any self-consciousness at being caught out on a date, she certainly didn't show it. In fact, she appeared totally at ease. Antonia slowly backed away.

"I can't stay, just wanted to make sure that, well, that everyone enjoyed Tumbleweed Tuesday. I'm off to check on other guests now, bye-bye!"

She quickly moved away from the door. It was hard to read Joseph's expression, but if she had to guess, it was one of perplexity. Indeed, Antonia couldn't blame him. What was she thinking when she said she wanted to make sure everyone enjoyed Tumbleweed Tuesday? How lame was that? She needed to think on her feet better; even a toddler could have contrived a better excuse.

"Thanks, Antonia, good night!" said Joseph, before shutting his door.

How in the world could Joseph have a date and Antonia not know about it? She poured her guts out to him every day and yet he had held his cards close to his chest, that was for sure. She was excited for him, but there was the tiny bristle of hurt that he hadn't confided in her in advance. Who was this Cheryl? Why had Antonia never even heard of her? Was she a gold digger? Antonia wasn't sure how much gold there was to be dug from Joseph, but Cheryl should know to watch her back. Antonia was protective and, let's face it, possessive of Joseph, and any lady that came into his life had to be prepared for scrutiny.

She was about to head downstairs when she paused. A little sparkle of revelation tingled in her memory and pulled her toward the door of Room Eight. She walked down the dark, carpeted hall and stopped in front of it, but instead of facing the doorway, she turned and faced the console across from it. Once again, the bouillotte lamp was unplugged, just as it had been yesterday. Had Rosita or one of her sisters unplugged it for the vacuum and then forgotten to replace it? That seemed unusual. They were pretty thorough. She bent down by the shadowy corner and waded under the console's skirt to plug it back in. However, nothing happened. She stood up and reached under the shade to touch the bulb. It was loose and cool to the touch. When she twisted it, the light came on, illuminating the hallway. Antonia glanced around with unease. Something was bothering her. She couldn't quite pinpoint it.

Antonia bent her head and ran her hand all around the interior of the lampshade. Her fingers glided along the seam before stumbling across a bump. At first she thought it was just where the fabric gathered, but a few more presses with her fingertips and a little jiggling led her to believe it was something more. She wiggled the bump, working it out of the seam, finally pulling out a small metal object the size of a postage stamp that had been tucked into the fabric. It took a split second for her to comprehend that she was staring at a microsize pinhole camera. She knew exactly what it was because she had seen one before: in the kitchen of the house that she shared with Philip in California.

She remembered that day all too well. Antonia had been fiddling with the old-fashioned electric can opener that was mounted on her wall, attempting to open coconut milk, when the same metallic rectangle fell out. She had thought it was a part of the can opener, which was already giving her trouble, so she dismounted it, pocketed the piece, and brought them both to her local hardware store to ascertain how it could be fixed. The store owner gave her a strange look before he told her what the little piece was: a pinhole camera. She was confused, until finally the store owner said, "Is someone spying on you?" That's when Antonia went into frantic mode, returned home, and made a very thorough sweep of every room of her split-level house. She was traumatized to find various cameras scattered around every room. She had first hastily removed them one by one, and then, realizing with fear that she would only incur Philip's wrath, she put them back until she plotted her escape. That had been the tipping point, but she had been frightened and young and needed to muster courage to make a move. She didn't feel that way this time. She threw the camera on the floor and stomped on it with rage.

12

ANTONIA SPENT THE NEXT HOUR RUMMAGING THROUGH ALL of the public rooms and hallways for surveillance devices. Her hunt garnered six more mini-cameras, lodged in lamps and concealed in painting frames and even stuffed in a potted plant in the parlor. She was certain there were more. The guest rooms were currently occupied, so she didn't have the opportunity to canvas those areas at all. It probably wouldn't be wise to have the innkeeper skulking around for recording devices while visitors slept. She would have to hold off until the morning, and she planned on calling in the professionals as well. There would be nothing more pleasurable than siccing Sergeant Flanagan on Philip.

With increasing dread, Antonia saved the search in her apartment for last. It would be beyond infuriating to her to find Philip's cameras in her own private domain. It was bad enough to discover them in the inn; she was enraged that either Philip or one of his henchmen (or henchwomen) had been there planting surveillance equipment. But if they had achieved access to her apartment, she would feel totally violated. Very few people had even been in her personal quarters; she kept the doors locked and limited guests to only a very small group of select friends. If Philip had gained access under her nose, she wasn't sure how she would react.

While Antonia had painstakingly renovated and supplied the Windmill Inn with polished antiques and expensive fabrics and curtains, her own garden apartment was more modest, to say the least. It wasn't that she had simply given up by the time she got around to furnishing her small dwelling (although she was certainly overwhelmed by decorating at that point), it was that she wanted supreme comfort above style and all else. Her mantra for her home—which consisted of a bedroom, living room, kitchenette, and, of course, facilities—was that everything had to be soft and squishy—from the deep upholstered sofa and armchairs to her king-size sleigh bed—and ultrafeminine (which meant an explosion of pink on the walls). The sensualist in her craved a hedonistic palace full of throw pillows, wall-to-wall carpeting, magazines within reach of every couch and chair, a giant television, and framed posters of impressionist masterpieces that hung in the best museums in the world. There would be no features in shelter magazines for her personal decor, but she was cozier than anyone else she knew when she was at home.

Antonia walked down the back hallway toward her private rooms and hesitated before she unlocked the door. What if someone was inside? What if it was Philip? Should she go and wake up Hector and Soyla? One of the reasons she had installed them in the inn was to assist her in times of danger (which seemed to be more frequent these days). Should she interrupt Joseph on his date with Cheryl? Probably not. It wasn't that late; there were still guests lingering in the bar. Her lungs were robust; she could probably scream loudly if need be. Fear was irrational for her right now. She had to pull up her big girl pants and do this on her own. After unlocking the door with her key, she banged it open dramatically, hoping to startle any potential interlopers. She was met with silence.

There was no one in the living room. She remained where she was and did a visual survey, but fortunately, it appeared to be exactly as she had left it, down to the mug of half-drunk tea that she had left on the side table before departing for her date. She would give her housekeeping skills these days a giant red F.

"I'm here with a gun, so you better come out now!" said Antonia with more confidence than she felt. She wondered if Philip would believe her. She had made it quite clear back when they were married that she loathed firearms. She would never even touch his government-issued piece and regarded it as toxic. Sometimes just to be cruel, Philip dangled it at her in a taunting manner, and she would recoil with revulsion. Now she wished she had learned how to shoot and did indeed have a gun. Maybe it was something she should look into.

Antonia slowly moved across her carpet, peering up and down to make sure no one was lurking behind any furniture. The living room folded into the kitchenette, the only divider was a counter with a stool, which held appliances on one side. There was a possibility that someone could conceal himself or herself behind it, so wasting no time to allow them any advantage, Antonia jumped into the kitchenette like a ninja.

"Hi-YA!" she screamed, throwing in a few karate chops in the air.

There was no one there, just cold linoleum. Her eyes scanned the lone cereal bowl and glass that were drying in the dish rack and the dish towel hanging neatly on the oven door handle. Nothing was amiss. It did provide her with the opportunity to grab one of her fancy knives. She ran her fingers along the blade with pride. That is one advantage a chef has—her knives are always sharp.

After she had reconnoitered the public rooms, only her bedroom and bathroom remained. Antonia moved swiftly toward her boudoir, adrenaline coursing through her body. She could hear the murmurs of people walking by outside in the parking lot on their way to their cars, but she still had an irrational fear that she was cornered. Philip could do that to her; he was a master of manipulating her and making her feel isolated and trapped. Antonia closed her eyes hard and said a silent prayer to her mother for help. Emboldened, she entered her bedroom. It was empty, her fluffy duvet cover immaculately in place. In what can only be described as acrobatic moves, she kicked open her closet, did a quick scan before falling to the ground to scope under her bed, and then banged her way into the bathroom to survey the scene. No Philip. Honestly, she didn't truly expect to find him there in the flesh, although she had learned never to underestimate him. But now that she was certain he wasn't there, she had to do a sweep for bugs. A glance at the clock revealed that it was almost eleven, and Antonia was tired. She locked her apartment door, went back into the kitchen, and pulled out a bottle of cabernet sauvignon from her wine rack. After popping the cork and pouring herself a steep glass, she continued her search. The extra glass of wine would be regretted in the morning, but right now her nerves were shot and her mood dampened and she felt tired and pissed, so she deserved that extra glass of wine, dammit!

Antonia practically tore her apartment apart in her quest for the cameras. Her mission proved futile; she found nothing. She should have been happy and relieved, and she *was* on a certain level, but she also couldn't relax. If Philip had taken the effort to bug her inn, why had he stopped at her apartment? Was it access? Perhaps. She did have a deadbolt and the only other person who held a key was Joseph, who had concealed it carefully in a hollowed-out copy of *Crime and Punishment* on the bottom of his bookshelf. Maybe Philip had planned something else? Why bug her inn? Then there was also the question of whether it was actually Philip who had done it. If not him, then who? Had she really seen him tonight? Was she making this all up? She collapsed into her puffy bed and fell into a restless sleep.

Antonia called Sergeant Flanagan first thing in the morning but was told he was unavailable until noon. She decided to proceed with her day, which included her monthly visit to the Salon in Amagansett. The older she became, the more she realized the necessity of physical maintenance, as much as she perceived it to be a giant time suck. It wasn't so much that she didn't enjoy it, only that when she was in the salon, her mind was racing with a million other tasks she should be doing. But with each new wrinkle or chipped nail, the concept of taking preventive measures to sustain attractiveness won out; she now took time to have her hair cut and get manicures and pedicures regularly. She would also indulge in the occasional facial and a bimonthly massage, which she would do with much less reluctance. Having other people primp and work on her body was better than having to exercise or style herself. And at the end of the day, it was amazing what a good blowout could do for one's self-esteem.

After Richard and the gang at the salon performed their magic, Antonia strolled through Amagansett Square. Tucked away off Main Street, the Square was a series of white clapboard buildings surrounding a grassy yard that was intersected by small brick paths. (Square was somewhat of a misnomer; it was more like a misshapen pentagon, as if a child had drawn the site plan.) In the summer they held weekly movies outdoors, and families would picnic and bring dogs and kids to scamper about. It had a nice community feel. Among the several businesses that were huddled, there was French Presse, which sold the creamiest sheets and bathrobes; Cavaniola's Gourmet Cheese, where Antonia could find lush soft cheeses; Mandala Yoga, which Antonia was certain was popular for people who worked out; Pink Chicken for kids' clothes; and Hampton Chutney, where Antonia was currently heading to pick up a dosa for lunch.

It took time for Antonia to select which crispy sourdough lentil rice crepe she wanted for lunch. She was torn between the Masala Deluxe—which included spicy Indian potatoes, roasted tomatoes, spinach, and jack cheese—or the Grilled Chicken—which included roasted peppers, roasted onions, and arugula. As the girl behind the counter patiently waited, she ultimately chose the former, before then being confounded with the choice of chutney to accompany it. Curry and mango won out in the end, and she was satisfied with her selection. As it was a bright day with only a small sampling of clouds sliding across the sun and temperatures in the low seventies, Antonia took her tray with her dosa and iced chai to sit outside at one of the outdoor tables. This was a luxury that would have been unavailable to her even a week ago. The mobs of summer folk that flocked to the square had disappeared and there were mostly locals in abundance. The only other interlopers were the herds of European tourists weaving their way in and out of the various storefronts, clutching Jack's coffees. Antonia had noted that the majority of tourists this time of year were European, a disproportionate number Scandinavian. It was true with the guests at the inn as well. When she had questioned a few, they remarked that they enjoyed the off-season and that the chance of a cold front didn't scare them.

After a leisurely lunch, during which time she people-watched, Antonia dabbed her mouth with her thin recycled paper napkin, dumped out the remainder of her lunch (which was really only the wrapping that the dosa came in), and returned her tray to its proper place. On her way to retrieve her car, the sound of two women laughing caught her attention. She wasn't sure what compelled her to turn and look, but she stopped dead in her tracks when she did. At a picnic table in the shade of the trees, Lauren Wayne and Dawn Costa were sitting eating lunch. They had their heads together like two children nonchalantly telling secrets during naptime at school, and appeared footloose and fancy-free, as Antonia's mom would have said. What was that about? Wasn't it only five minutes ago that Dawn was weeping at her inn, saying she feared for her life from her "stalker," Lauren? It had been a majestic performance, brimming with crocodile tears and histrionics.

It took a heck of a lot of self-control for Antonia to restrain herself from bursting over to them and demanding an explanation; she knew she had to be strategic. Experience had taught her that if you confront someone, nine times out of ten, they immediately deny whatever it is you are accusing them of. Then they are backed into a corner and that primal urge to survive clicks in and you are just given a whole lot of baloney and lies in order for them to save face. No, that couldn't happen. If Antonia had remembered to bring her ancient cell phone from her desk, she could have snapped a photo of the two conspirators together.

Antonia decided to allow them to recognize her so she might catch them off guard. She moseyed over to the table next to theirs and sat down casually. The previous occupants had not been as fastidious as Antonia and had left their used tray and half-eaten sandwich for someone else to clean up. She slid it to the side with disdain; more disgusted that someone wouldn't finish a delicious dosa than the fact that they had left evidence of it. She eyed her prey. Dawn was facing her and Lauren's back was to her. They were both clad in sundresses with visible bikinis underneath and were sipping iced coffees through straws. There was no sign of tension or of friends confronting each other: they were "hanging out." Antonia could overhear snippets of their conversation: Dawn was telling Lauren about a "hot" guy she had met the previous week. She was so engrossed in her anecdote that she didn't even bother to glance at Antonia's table.

"He's like, almost thirty-five, but he still looks good. He's a total gym rat," Dawn regaled.

"What does he do?" asked Lauren.

"Wall Street."

"Aren't you over that? I thought you said Wall Street guys were super boring or full of themselves."

"They are, but *duh*! He's got a place downtown in the city. I just want him to wine and dine me. Besides, I'm obviously not going to marry him."

"Yeah, that could be a problem considering he's already married."

"Those are the best kind! They're so grateful."

"Well, not always..." said Lauren.

Dawn raised her hand to shush her friend. "Let's not talk about that. It's over, payback city."

"Yeah, I guess."

Just when Antonia's interest was piqued, the conversation digressed into a discussion about celebrity fashion. But now Antonia was left with more questions than answers. Had Lauren and Dawn been alluding to the murder of Shane and Gary? Had the women killed them in retaliation for something the men had done to them? What was "payback city"?

She listened for another few minutes as they continued their superficial banter, amazed on several levels. First off, she was astounded that grown women could be so interested in discussing the minutiae of celebrities' lives. Did people discuss Nick Darrow this way? What he wore to an awards ceremony and what type of food allergies he had? She wondered. It was so boring to her. Well, not with Nick, because she knew him. And probably not with his soon-to-be ex-wife Melanie, because, well, for obvious reasons. But Antonia had never cared what, say, Nicole Kidman had for lunch or wore to the gym. Why did these girls? She was also struck by how self-involved they were, as they had not once looked around to notice anything or anyone other than themselves. And Antonia was becoming restless. She decided it was time for them to notice her. She stretched her arms to the sky. Nothing. Dawn continued her chatter. Antonia yawned loudly. Nothing. She sneezed. Neither of them even said "God bless you," they were so engrossed in analyzing Goop's list of recommended diet regimes.

Finally, Antonia bobbed her head back and forth as if she were dancing so that the movement would catch Dawn's eye. When it did, Antonia looked away as if oblivious.

"Oh my God!" Dawn hissed to Lauren.

"What?"

"Shhhh."

They bent their heads together.

"Don't turn around," Dawn commanded.

But it was too late. Lauren turned around and Antonia met her eye. Why is it when people say "don't look," people immediately look?

"Oh, why, hello," said Antonia with faux innocence.

"Hi," Lauren replied. She quickly whipped her head back toward Dawn so that Antonia could not see her face. Her body language, however, was another story, and Antonia could see her flail and gesticulate wildly.

Dawn bent her head down, trying to obstruct herself from Antonia's view by using Lauren as a human shield. It was almost comical.

"How are you feeling?" Antonia trilled across the tables.

Lauren turned back around. "Oh, me. I'm better, thank you."

"That's great. You looked really shook up."

"Yeah, um, thanks for your help."

"Not a problem." Antonia stood up and walked over to their table. There was no hiding now for Dawn, whose face conveyed her irritation. "Fancy meeting you here as well."

"Yeah, um, Lauren and I are just working things out."

"You do seem awfully chummy," said Antonia, peering down at the young women. She was using the fact that she was looming over them to her advantage.

Dawn sighed with impatience before responding tersely. "Yes, she apologized for everything and we're all good now."

"That's wonderful. She said she was sorry for tying you up?"

Out of the corner of her eye, Antonia saw Lauren turn to Dawn and give her an incredulous look. But Dawn held Antonia's gaze and didn't blink. "Yes."

There was a petulance to Dawn that drove Antonia crazy. It was smug entitlement, the kind of stuff that gave millennials a bad rap. Right now Antonia wanted to take a cart of artisanal craft beers and smash it over Dawn's know-it-all, "I can do it better and you are irrelevant" head. A vague fantasy of doing just that appeared in Antonia's mind before she snapped out of it.

Antonia turned toward Lauren. "I'd love to know how it all went down. How you entered my inn, pulled your friend out of bed, tied her up for hours. She was quite distraught."

Lauren squirmed slightly, obviously not as adept at lying as

Dawn was. She bit down on her bottom lip, contorting it to the side, and glanced anxiously at Dawn, who answered for her.

"It's all good now, thanks for asking. We actually have to go."

Dawn abruptly stood up, and Lauren followed.

"Are you able to pay for your bill at my inn now?" asked Antonia. "I mean, now that it's all good?"

Dawn temporarily froze before shrugging her shoulders. "You'd have to talk to my lawyer about that. He actually wanted me to press charges against the inn."

"Really?" Now Antonia was pissed. "And what did he say about falsifying a statement to the police?"

"I didn't falsify anything. I don't think we should talk anymore about this without my lawyer present." She crossed her arms and made a defiant stance.

"What's his name?"

"I'll have him get in touch with you."

"Please do so." Antonia turned to Lauren. "And what about you? The police are probably investigating you as we speak."

Lauren quickly glanced at Dawn before answering. "She dropped the charges."

"Of course she did," said Antonia. "But now the police probably think you killed Shane Boskin and Gary DiAngelo. Your friend says you stalked her and tied her up, and then you're found wandering around the woods near a crime scene. They think you're crazy."

"That's ridiculous," said Dawn. "Let's go, Lauren."

Lauren momentarily wavered as if she wanted to say something before shrugging and following her friend. "Bye," she mumbled on her way. Dawn didn't bother with any closing statement.

13

ANTONIA CAUGHT SERGEANT FLANAGAN IN THE MIDDLE OF lunch. He was seated behind his desk in a swivel leather chair, and spread out neatly in front of him on wax paper was a half-eaten roast beef and cheddar sandwich, accompanied by a pickle on the side and a small pile of salt and pepper potato chips that he had sprinkled out of the bag. There was a Diet Dr Pepper next to his computer. The rest of the paraphernalia on the desk included a stapler, tape dispenser, and a well-maintained inbox. All in all the office emitted the general appearance of tidiness.

"Sorry to interrupt."

"It's okay," he said, sliding his wax paper "place mat" over to the side. "You said it was urgent."

"It is, but you can keep eating."

"It's okay."

Antonia looked at his sandwich. She hated to bother people when they were in the middle of a good meal. "That looks tasty. Do you take it with mustard or mayo?"

"Both."

"Nice."

"I'm sure you didn't come here to talk to me about my lunch. What's going on?"

"I just saw Lauren Wayne and Dawn Costa looking thick as thieves. Literally, they may as well have been wearing matching necklaces that said 'Best Friends Forever.' This whole stalker thing is a pile of you-know-what. I heard them discussing payback, but then Dawn says she's forgiven Lauren, and she has a lawyer, so she won't pay me. I smell a rat."

Sergeant Flanagan nodded. He brushed invisible crumbs off the front of his neatly pressed uniform. "I'm aware that they are not estranged."

"Not estranged? They were practically braiding each other's hair."

"Don't worry, Antonia, we're looking into it."

"I want to know what's going on. I feel like I'm living in Surreal Land. Did they kill those guys? Why were they in my inn? Oh, and here's the latest, the initial reason I called you this morning: there are recording devices planted all over the Windmill Inn! I removed about seven of them last night and haven't even entered the guest rooms!"

Sergeant Flanagan's eyes grew wider. "Okay, let's start from the beginning."

Antonia recounted her discovery of the pinhole lens cameras. Sergeant Flanagan already knew that Antonia had a restraining order against Philip, but he hadn't previously heard the details of Philip playing Big Brother and sprinkling her house in California with recording devices. Sergeant Flanagan scribbled notes as she talked. She also relayed the middle of the night phone call that she had with Philip and her suspicion that she had seen him lurking in the bushes by her place. Lastly, she reported her interaction with "Cindy Boskin," who played the role of grieving widow but didn't hold back from having a one-night stand (more like, one-afternoon stand) with Larry Lipper, of all people.

"What I can't figure out is who this 'Cindy Boskin' is," sighed Antonia. "On the one hand, she is obviously connected somehow with Shane, because she knew he had been at the inn. Yet I can't help but think she has some connection to Philip as well. Maybe I'm wrong, but it's very coincidental that she stays in my inn and sneakily pumps me for information about Philip around the same time he reappears in my life."

Sergeant Flanagan nodded. "Could be."

He took a sip of his soda.

"Could be? That doesn't help me, Sergeant Flanagan."

He placed the can back on the desk. "Listen, I don't want to jump to conclusions. You know that's not my style. Did Larry Lipper indicate that he had any way of getting in touch with this alleged Cindy Boskin?"

"No. He was thrilled to have a one-night stand."

"I'll call over to the motel and see if they can give me any information they didn't give him. In the meantime, someone from the Boskin and DiAngelo families has come to identify the bodies. They're at the coroner's now. I will head over there and see if I can make sense of all this."

"Can I please come?"

"No."

Antonia folded her arms and pouted like a small child. "I need to know what I'm up against."

"I will keep you abreast of anything pertinent to your situation. In the meantime, I will distribute a picture of Philip to all of my officers to make sure they are on the lookout for him. I will also send someone over to sweep for bugs or other surveillance equipment." Sergeant Flanagan stood.

"That's great, but I don't want to scare off the guests. What will they do if they see cops crawling all over the place?"

"Good point. I'll send him in plain clothes."

"And how do I explain what he's doing?"

"You'll think of something. You're a mistress of deception." He smiled and left the room.

Was he mocking her? With a sigh, Antonia departed.

Antonia was still bristling from Sergeant Flanagan's comment on her ride home. How could he suggest that she was a bad liar? The nerve of him! What, did she not have a poker face? Was she not great at bluffing her way into situations where she wasn't supposed to be? Well, okay. Maybe not, come to think of it. The dawn of enlightenment burst in Antonia's head. Fine. So perhaps a better strategy was to consider his statement a compliment rather than an insult. Who'd want to be a *good* liar, anyway?

Antonia realized she needed to make a phone call. She pulled over on Main Street (now that it was officially "off-season," one could find street parking in the village) and placed a call to the coroner's office. After relaying her request and obtaining the information she needed, she ended the call, quite pleased with herself. The window of BookHampton caught her eye, and Antonia simply had to pop in for a browse.

She browsed through the glossy new interior design books, bought an armload of motivational books, and drove home in a better mood. She allowed her mind to wander to Nick Darrow. When they parted, Antonia felt certain that he would get in touch swiftly with a plan. Then he had emailed her that morning and said he had to head to the city for meetings, wasn't sure when he would be back, but had a great time at dinner and couldn't wait to get together again. So, when was *again*? He hadn't suggested an actual time or place yet. Should she? Would that make her a hussy? She took a deep breath.

She had to take it easy. It hadn't even been twenty-four hours since she'd last seen him. What did she expect? Antonia was no good at this courtship stuff.

Jonathan had left word with Connie to have Antonia find him when she returned. When she stopped by his office she found it empty, and a quick walk through the public rooms revealed only guests lounging in various seating arrangements. She popped by the kitchen, certain she wouldn't find him there, but her stomach was rumbling and in dire need of sating. Her mouth had been watering since she spied Sergeant Flanagan's sandwich, and she rifled through the refrigerator for something as tasty. She emerged with a honey-glazed barbequed chicken drumstick, which would have to do for now. She devoured it in a quick three minutes, popped a few cherry tomatoes in her mouth, then retraced her steps to reception and queried Connie.

"Maybe he's upstairs?" Connie offered from her perch. She was busy stapling the list of town events that they presented to the guests each Thursday.

"I'll check."

Antonia trudged up the stairs, along the way adjusting the framed antique maps of Long Island that were askew. Though she had used a special putty to secure the frames to the wall, somehow they always managed to be banged around by guests as they marched up and down the stairs. Perhaps it was the luggage knocking into them, but she really wished people would be more careful. It had taken a lot of legwork to find those maps on eBay, and they were anything but free. A quick perusal of the second floor revealed no activity. Antonia's eyes flickered from door to door of the guest rooms, which were sealed shut. She heard Jonathan's voice on the floor above and continued further upstairs, until she found him with Rosita in Room Seven.

"Oh, Antonia, I'm glad you're back," Jonathan said with a sigh of relief. "We've found something most upsetting."

He was standing by the window, peering at something behind the shade. Rosita was next to him, holding the curtains as far back as possible to enhance his view.

"What's up?"

"It appears to be some sort of telescope perched here on the windowsill. It's very small and was concealed behind the curtain. A person might not notice it, but thankfully Rosita and her staff are extremely diligent in servicing the bedrooms, and she noticed it when she went to dust the ledge."

Antonia felt a sense of dread swishing around her stomach. Philip—or whoever had planted the cameras around the halls and public rooms—had clearly also planted surveillance inside the guest bedrooms.

"Let me see," she said, moving toward the window. Jonathan stepped aside and Antonia peered down at the telescope. It had been attached to the wooden frame, and was painted the same white as the window in an effort to camouflage itself.

"As you'll notice, it is not facing in the room, it's facing out. I suppose there is some consolation in that, meaning that whoever planted it was not trying to spy on our guests in their various states of undress," offered Jonathan.

"But you see where it looks," Rosita interjected, her large eyes worried.

Antonia crouched down and pressed her eyeball against the telescope. Her heart began thumping wildly when she realized what she was looking at. From this angle, the telescope peered straight into the living room window of her small garden apartment. Although she frequently kept her curtains drawn, as she was usually only there at night, this angle afforded an excellent view of any movements she would make when her curtains were open. She could make out her couch and her fireplace and the framed posters on her pink walls. There was enough in that view to give someone an impression of Antonia's existence. In addition, the telescope had a clear shot of the door to her apartment, so whoever was in this room could trace her comings and goings. Adrenaline coursed through her veins as she comprehended the level of violation. Thank God she hadn't taken a man to her apartment!

Antonia stood up straight. "Rosita, when was the last time you tidied up this windowsill?"

"I do it every time, Miss Antonia," said Rosita.

"Do you think it's possible that you could have missed this telescope? Now I'm not accusing you of anything, I know you do a wonderful job and you are not in trouble at all. I just want to figure out how long this might have been here without drawing attention."

Rosita's lip trembled slightly as she spoke. "I always clean top to bottom. But Miss Antonia, last week my sister Angela was sick and I had my niece Natalia helping me. She is good, but maybe she didn't notice that."

"Or perhaps she noticed it, but didn't realize that it should not be there," offered Jonathan.

Antonia nodded. "Good point."

"I'm so sorry, Miss Antonia," said Rosita.

"It's not your fault. In fact, I want to tell you both, and please be discreet. I found a number of cameras scattered all over the inn last night."

Jonathan audibly gasped. "What do you mean?"

"I know. It's horrible. They were small lenses, barely noticeable, stuffed in lamps and frames all over the inn. I think I removed all of them, but be extra cautious and on the lookout. I informed the police, and they are sending someone today to sweep the inn and make sure I have removed all of them. We will have to be vigilant from now on to make sure they are not replaced once we remove them."

"Absolutely."

"And it goes without saying that it's crucial we keep this to ourselves and not worry our guests. Can you imagine how bad this would be for business?" mused Antonia.

"I think we'd be out of business, actually," said Jonathan.

"I know," said Antonia, with a shudder.

"I've seen *Dateline* episodes about this. It's straight out of *Psycho*, with Anthony Perkins staring through the wall. It's reprehensible. Who do we think would do this?" Jonathan asked.

"Fortunately, or rather unfortunately, I think I know the culprit," Antonia admitted.

"Is it that Tomas Stefanowski?" asked Jonathan. "This is the very room where he stayed, supposedly. Of course we never saw him and can only conjecture that it was he who stayed here. But could it be him?"

"Yes. But I don't think that's his real name. I think it's Philip, my ex-husband."

"Oh dear," said Jonathan.

That's an understatement, thought Antonia.

14

"I WAS DELIGHTED TO RECEIVE THE CALL FROM CONNIE," SAID Ruth Thompson, as she nestled into the plush sofa in the marine blue parlor. She picked up the linen napkin at her place setting and with one thrust and flap, unfolded it and positioned it on her lap. "Will you now be offering tea every afternoon and not just Thursday? If yes, I will have to do a bit of rearranging of my schedule. I currently have my hair done on Wednesdays, but today Annie was out of town, so I postponed. But if tea will be offered on Wednesdays as well as Thursdays, as is usual, I might have to move my hair to Friday. I have bridge on Tuesday afternoons, so that is not an option."

"I can't commit to it being a standing event, but I thought that it would be nice this week to offer an additional tea service to celebrate the new season. Of course we all love the summer folk, but it is special to have our village back to ourselves, and what better way to celebrate than with raisin scones and clotted cream?" Antonia replied, as she poured ice water from a pitcher into Ruth's glass.

"Traffic is definitely better today, although I dare say it is still buzzing out there! How about the inn? Are you full?"

"We are, actually. Lots of Europeans this week."

"Well, it is the nicest time of year. It's so glorious to see all of those westbound cars heading back to the city on Labor Day. Their departing headlights curling around Route 27 look like a string of pearls to me! I certainly feel like the joke is on them: September is the prettiest month out here."

"I'd agree," concurred Antonia. "Now, will Penny be joining you today?"

"Yes. I managed to catch her on her way out the door when she was heading to an aquatic fitness class for seniors at the Y. Can you believe that? Aquatic fitness? Does she have no dignity? I suppose I should applaud her efforts to stay in shape. I myself play tennis at the club or East Hampton Indoor Tennis, but I would never flail myself around in a public pool. Kicking and treading water in a petri dish whilst moving my arms about like Janet Jackson? No thank you. Oh, here she is now."

Although the two best friends were both in their seventies, they couldn't differ more physically. Whereas Ruth Thompson was tall and svelte and exuded patrician elegance and efficiency, and possessed the grit and determination that enabled her ancestors to endure their rough journey to America on the *Mayflower*, her best friend Penny Halsey was round and plump and reminded one of a friendly grandmother who would distribute homemade cookies from a designated jar in her cozy kitchen.

"I know what you're talking about, and I think you're being unfair," Penny trilled as she slid into the sofa next to her friend. Her words may have been strident, but her expression was warm and friendly. Antonia noted that there was something about Penny's rosy cheeks and twinkling blue eyes that would make it impossible for her to seem harsh. She looked not unlike Mrs. Claus.

"Of course you know what I'm talking about. I wouldn't have said it if it was a secret," said Ruth haughtily. "I think the pool games are undignified."

Penny chuckled as she loosened the knotted silk scarf around her neck. "I do not participate in pool games. I exercise in the pool. My doctor said I needed to keep my heart vibrant and shed some pounds. I thought this would be fun, and you know what, Antonia? It is."

She winked at the innkeeper, while Ruth shook her head. "I don't know..."

Penny ignored her. "But on to more pressing issues. Antonia, did you hear, there was a double murder this week?"

"I did," replied Antonia, hesitating about how much to divulge.

"Apparently it was like a scene out of a slasher movie!" boomed Ruth. "The men were cut up as if a samurai had gone to town on them!"

"Yes, I heard," replied Antonia in a low tone, as she glanced around the room to make sure no one was eavesdropping.

Ruth and Penny immediately read her body language. "What, is someone here that knows something?" asked Ruth.

"Perhaps a suspect!" Penny exclaimed with giddy pleasure. "Is that why you had us all here today? I remember you did this before—invited all of the suspects to the inn and then captured the murderer!"

"What are you talking about? Of course that's not why I offered tea today," lied Antonia.

Ruth and Penny exchanged skeptical glances with each other. Antonia could not believe that her plan was so transparent! Within two minutes, Ruth and Penny had nailed it. She had indeed decided to offer tea today in an effort to lure the real Boskin and DiAngelo family members to her inn. She had extended an invitation through the coroner's office to those who were identifying the body and suggested they come in for a respite and a cup of tea before they head back to the city. She wasn't sure they would accept, and it might all be for naught, but there was a chance they might come, and therefore it was important to keep a lid on her covert agenda. She had to do damage control fast.

Antonia bent down and whispered to Ruth and Penny. "Okay, listen. Maybe you are right. I can't divulge the details but I did ask some of the key players here today. And I would love your help."

Penny's face lit up like a child's on Christmas morning. "What do you need us to do?" she responded in her worst stage whisper.

"There will be people coming today; at least I think they will. I need you two ladies to be the eyes and ears of the inn. I'll seat them near you so you can try and overhear their conversation. Keep in mind something that may seem unimportant could be useful."

"I love it!" boomed Ruth.

"Shh," both Antonia and Penny chided in unison.

"Who are they?" asked Penny.

Once again Antonia hesitated. Should she tell them? Did it matter? She glanced down at Ruth and Penny's eager faces. Enlisting them in this endeavor was low-hanging fruit. It wouldn't hurt to have them know what was going on, would it? Antonia sighed and bent down to her companions and told them what to expect.

Forty-five minutes later Antonia had abandoned hope that the Boskin and DiAngelo relatives would stop by for a cup of tea. She should have known that it was a dumb plan. They were probably in a rush to return to the city and finalize the funeral plans. Why in the world would they come to a country inn and sit down for an afternoon snack? She felt a bit guilty about raising Ruth and Penny's hopes up. Every time she glanced in their direction, they either winked or nodded knowingly. When she was escorting the

Norwegian couple who were staying in Room Three to a table by the window, Penny and Ruth stopped her.

"Shouldn't they be sitting here!" announced Ruth, sotto voce.

Penny wiggled her eyebrows suggestively. "Yes, there is a bad breeze by the window."

The Norwegian couple capitulated and started to sit down at the table next to Penny and Ruth before Antonia halted them. "No, no, the table by the window is better," she said trying to guide them away.

"So hard to *hear* from over there," said Ruth with a wink.

"Yes, they should sit near us," Penny concurred.

The Norwegian couple was confused. "This is fine," said the man. He began to place his book on the table and remove his shoulder bag.

"No, no, this table is reserved," said Antonia sternly. "You must come this way."

She directed to the window, but not before whispering to Penny and Ruth over her shoulder, "It's not *them*."

"Our mistake!" Ruth warbled as Antonia moved away.

That was the problem with amateur sleuths, thought Antonia. They are always a little too eager and not very tactful. Oh well, what did it matter? It didn't appear that anyone relevant to the crime was coming. But just when Antonia had accepted that fact, the real Cindy Boskin and a man appeared at the threshold of the parlor, where Antonia was standing as hostess.

"Table for two?" Antonia blurted out.

"Yes, thank you," said the man. "We actually got a call…not sure that it matters, but, well, we're here on sad business."

"I'm Antonia Bingham, the innkeeper and owner. You must be relatives of…" She was at a loss for words. Gary and Shane? Mr. Boskin and Mr. DiAngelo? She let her voice fade.

"I'm Paul DiAngelo...Gary's brother. And this is Cindy Boskin, Shane's wife. Thanks for inviting us to tea. It's been a really rough day for us. Few days, I should say. Like a nightmare."

Antonia clasped his hands and looked into his sorrowful eyes. "I'm so sorry for your losses. If there is anything I can do to help..."

"We're just exhausted right now. I think we could use some sandwiches before we hit the road."

"Of course, right this way."

Antonia extended her arm and motioned toward the seating arrangement next to Penny and Ruth. Cindy and Paul set off in the direction of the table with Antonia following. As she passed Ruth and Penny, they gave her wide-eyed looks and nodded vigorously. Antonia tried not to meet their eyes and fervently wished they wouldn't be so obvious. Fortunately, Paul and Cindy appeared oblivious to them.

Antonia waited as her new guests settled into their armchairs, which gave her a moment to study them. Paul was late thirties, clean-cut with blondish-gray hair styled in the manner of a news-caster. He was attractive, with a straight row of pearly white teeth that looked like caps and neat eyebrows that were perfectly shaped. He exuded an aura of competence and ease, the type of guy you would want on your side during a tough situation, although today the heavy, dark bags under his eyes, and two days' worth of patchy stubble on his face gave him a tired and sad appearance, which was to be expected. Unlike her companion, Cindy Boskin (the real Cindy Boskin!) had not let her grief get in the way of her groom-ing. She wore a thick layer of makeup: base, concealer, blush, heavy eyeliner, and bronzer. She was young enough that she didn't need all that makeup, Antonia noted, although perhaps it was a shield with her or she suffered from bad skin. That could be why she wore her expensively highlighted hair framed around her face and not swept back. Cindy's eyes were a pretty blue and Antonia could swear she had on those fake eyelashes that all the society girls wore these days—they were just a little too long and a little too pointy. Her tight black dress was conservatively cut but somehow came off as sexy as it enhanced all of her curves and showcased a body that a model would envy: chiseled, muscled, and nary an extra pound to spare. She was as pretty as her pictures, but there was a certain hardness to her in person that was not visible in the images on the internet, and Antonia didn't think that it had anything to do with her husband's death. Antonia didn't like to make unfavorable opinions about people, but this Cindy Boskin had clearly suffered some hard knocks before her husband's murder and it had made her tough as nails.

"Would you like some tea? Or maybe something stronger?" Antonia offered.

"I'll have an iced tea," said Cindy.

"I'd love a vodka tonic. I know, it's early and I'm driving, but I need something to take the edge off," Paul explained as if they had questioned him.

"No problem. And I'll send over a tiered tray of tea goodies unless you would like something else?"

"I'm pretty starving. We left early this morning and had stale Dunkin' Donuts when we stopped for gas. I'd appreciate it if there were sandwiches," said Paul.

"Oh yes, there are. Today we have pimento cheese, cucumber, and smoked salmon."

"Great. As many as you can pile on, thanks."

Antonia was about to leave and place the order when Cindy spoke. "Excuse me, do you mind if I ask you a question?"

She gazed up at Antonia evenly.

"Sure."

"Why did you invite us to the inn?"

"Why did I invite you?" repeated Antonia. "I, well, I wanted to extend my hospitality. I was so sorry to hear of your loss."

Cindy took in the information without changing the expression on her face. "Did you know my husband?"

"Did I know him?" Antonia realized that she was repeating everything Cindy said in an effort to stall. "No, I didn't know him. But he had been here, to the inn."

"Yes, the detective told us," Paul chimed in. "He gave us a rundown on Gary and Paul's...well, their last night. Did you talk to my brother and Shane? Did you get any sense of what was going on?"

The look on his face was one of quiet desperation. Antonia was overwhelmed with pity for him. She shook her head gently. "I'm sorry, but I wasn't at the bar that night. I wish so much I had been."

Paul sighed. "There was nothing you could do."

Cindy continued to hold her gaze on Antonia and watch her carefully. "I feel like there is something else that you are not telling us."

"Something else?" Antonia repeated and once again kicked herself for doing that. As Soyla was passing by refilling water glasses, Antonia jumped on the opportunity to relay Cindy and Paul's order. When Antonia returned her attention to Cindy, she was still staring at her.

"Yes, well, I do have something else to say. Do you mind if I join you for a bit?"

"Of course."

Antonia retrieved a side chair from another table and pulled it up to their table. They looked at her expectantly.

"This is awkward, and I am not sure if it's relevant, but a woman called my hotel and claimed to be Cindy Boskin."

Antonia paused and waited for theatrical gasps, but when her audience didn't even flinch she continued. "She said she was coming out here to make funeral arrangements and could she stay at the inn. We, of course, wanted to be accommodating, so we said sure. She arrived late and when she was having dinner, she asked me to join her, and I did. I was completely fooled into believing that she was you. Of course now having met you, I know the truth. But I can't understand why this woman would come to the inn and do this."

She had expected astonishment, but Paul appeared confused and Cindy remained stoic. She merely arched an eyebrow and looked down at the table.

"I'm not sure I understand," Paul responded. "Cindy, did you call?"

"No, it wasn't me."

"It was someone pretending to be you? Wait, this is weird, can we back up? Do you know what's going on, Cindy?"

"It doesn't surprise me," she said finally. "This woman has been out there pretending to be me."

"What?" gasped Paul.

Antonia bit her tongue. She wanted to hear Cindy talk.

"Look, there's no other way to say it: Shane was a cheater. I turned a blind eye for years and then it became impossible because he was so flagrant. It was like I couldn't avoid it even if I wanted to. He left hotel receipts all over the place, and he came home reeking of perfume. When I first understood what was going on, I was devastated. Shocked, really. I shouldn't have been. When I started dating him, he had a long-term girlfriend. But I thought he cheated on her because she wasn't the one. But once a cheater, always a cheater. You can't teach an old dog new tricks, as they say, and it's damn true. So I learned to live with it. I had no choice. For my kids' sakes..."

"You have children?" Antonia asked softly.

"Two. Ella and Julian."

Antonia wanted to throw up. The fake Cindy Boskin had said she wanted to name *her* kids Ella and Julian!

"And you said you knew this woman was out there pretending to be you?" asked Paul.

"Yes, I mean, a parent in Julian's class was confused when I met her because she said she had met my husband with another woman who was introduced as me."

"That's sick," said Paul.

"I know. I think they liked to play house."

"Do you think this is the woman who came to the inn?"

"Probably. Lately Shane had become increasingly distraught. I could tell. We don't—or at least, didn't—talk much anymore. Although we lived together, we went our separate ways. I didn't even come out here this summer. Not once. I vacationed in the Vineyard with friends. We needed a break from each other. I don't really know what happened. What I gleaned from some of the telephone conversations I overheard was that someone was not taking no for an answer, and that was making Shane frantic. It was like despite the fact that he cheated and didn't take his marital vows at all seriously, he was still determined to continue the charade that we were happily married, and he didn't want this woman to wreck that. It's a joke. Look, I may sound like a monster, but I was secretly glad he was sweating it out. Let him suffer a little. Of course, I never wanted it to end like this. Not at all. I hate that my children won't have a father."

She stopped abruptly, choking back emotions in an effort to keep them in check. She took a sip of her water and wiggled her shoulders as if shaking off her sorrow. Antonia felt sorry for her. She understood the hardness now. When someone has been cheated on, lied to, and embarrassed, it was pretty hard to keep it together.

"Cindy, I'm so sorry I didn't know this," said Paul, gently placing a hand on top of hers. "I had absolutely no idea."

She grimaced and gave him her best effort at a smile. "It's okay."

"Tell us more about this woman," Paul commanded. "What did she say exactly?"

Antonia filled them in on the conversation, including the fact that the fake Cindy had said that she wanted kids named Ella and Julian and about their trip to the Cotswolds.

"She must have known him pretty well," conceded Cindy. "He hated country inns. No offense."

"None taken," said Antonia.

"Shane liked the flashy life. Glitz and glamour. Quiet nights in were revolting to him."

"Do you know if this woman threatened him in any way?" Antonia asked.

"She was clearly a stalker," Paul added. "To come here and pretend to be Shane's wife? That's just sick. I hope you told the police."

"I did," Antonia replied. "Don't worry, they are on it."

"I don't know if she made threats, but Shane was agitated. Lots of phone calls where he would leave the room and whisper loudly. I heard him tell someone to stay away from him. I heard him say it was all a lie. Someone was giving him a hard time, and I can't say I didn't enjoy it. I didn't have it in me."

"Did anyone ever approach you directly?" asked Antonia.

"There have been a number of phone calls over the years."

"Really?"

"Yes. The first ten times, I was really upset, but Shane always denied it or lied about it, said women hit on him constantly and were angry when he refused them. And by the way, I do know that there were women out there hitting on him. He was a hotshot Wall Street guy. There were some he may have refused, but he was a dog. I figured it was all discarded lovers calling him. It was scary and annoying at first. But then I realized that he was never going to leave me. We could live together but live separate lives. I would ride it out until my kids were older. Why get divorced and only get half his money when I have to deal with the pain and suffering of infidelity? I'd rather spend it and make him feel guilty."

"I can understand that," Paul said gently. "He really hurt you."

"Did anyone call recently?" asked Antonia.

Cindy glanced up at the ceiling while she pondered the question. Suddenly she snapped back to attention.

"You know, there was a call a few weeks ago. I was at the beach on the Vineyard with my kids and a bunch of other families, and very distracted. A woman called to tell me she was a neighbor and did I know that my husband was bringing women home with him every night and cheating on me? I was pissed because I couldn't believe that Shane would bring people back to my apartment. That's where I drew the line. I have custom Egyptian sheets with like a ten thousand thread count; I do not want some hussy getting off in them. I confronted him on this one, but he denied it. He said he would never bring someone to our apartment. I believed him."

"Why did you believe him?"

"I could just tell," she said. "This time, I knew he was telling the truth. I could hear the stress in his voice, and it wasn't stress with me, it was stress with her."

Soyla arrived with the tea tray and set it up on the table. It was probably time for Antonia to leave them alone, she knew, but she had an arsenal of questions that she wanted to ask them. She cataloged her queries in her mind and decided to select the most pressing one, which hopefully would lead to further illumination. She posed the question when Soyla had finished arranging the tea plates.

"If it was this woman, this fake Cindy Boskin, why do you think she would kill Gary? What did he do to her?" asked Antonia, trying to be sensitive to Paul's feelings.

He chimed in: "I was thinking the same thing."

Cindy shook her head. "I have no idea."

Both of the bereaved then tucked into their sandwiches and Antonia knew it was time for the interrogation to come to a conclusion.

15

Antonia made a big deal of letting Marty and Kendra know that she would be in the kitchen for the entire dinner prep and service. She thanked them for always picking up the slack and informed them that there was nothing she wanted to do more than to cook for her restaurant guests that evening. They gave her expressionless nods and said very little, which resulted in Antonia practically delivering a soliloquy on how important cooking was to her, what it meant to her to provide food to the masses, and how all of her creative enjoyment came out of these efforts. There was nothing better than to fortify people and no greater joy than feeding the hungry.

She felt like a fool an hour into prep when Larry Lipper arrived to pick her up and have her accompany him on a mission she couldn't refuse. All of her apologies to the staff were futile. Marty waved her away and told her he cooked better without her there, and Kendra just gave her an arched eyebrow as if to imply that she knew all along that Antonia would be heading out the door on some hackneyed adventure. In these sorts of moments, Antonia took solace in the fact that she had such a competent staff.

"Where are we headed?" asked Antonia, after she had strapped herself into the passenger seat of Larry's car.

"The Gig Shack," he replied. "She said she was working tonight."

"How did you find her?"

"Bingham, you know I can't reveal my sources."

Antonia rolled her eyes. "Come on."

"All right, 'cause it's you. Just this once. And I actually have to pat myself on the back for this one," said Larry, who literally took his hand off the steering wheel and patted himself on the back. "I figured we know this type of guy, or these types of guys, right? They come out here to party and they go to all the places. We know they went to the Shore Lodge, and we know they were hanging out with waitresses and picking up easy lays. We're still not sure who the Asian Cindy Boskin is…"

"Hey, be careful," cautioned Antonia.

"What, I can't call her Asian? That's not politically correct? What am I supposed to say? She is Asian."

"Well, you wouldn't say we still don't know who the white Cindy Boskin is."

"Then how do you want to discern between the two?"

"Call the first one the fake one and the other the real one."

"Whatever, Bingham. I would hate to live in your world of political correctness. But I will humor you. So the *fake* Cindy Boskin was an easy lay."

"I hate that phrase also."

"Listen, what do you want me to say? She was a 'loose woman'? I picked her up at the Clam Bar and I'm in her bed in fifteen minutes. There is no way to sugarcoat this. And do you want to hear the story or not?"

"Okay, yes. Watch out for the crosswalk, please. The light is blinking and there are people waiting to cross."

The village had recently installed flashing lights along the crosswalks for pedestrian safety. It was a wise move. Because East Hampton's Main Street was part of Route 27, often drivers would gun it through town on their way further east to Amagansett, Springs, or Montauk. It was a necessary precaution that had enhanced village life. Larry waited for a man and a woman to cross before continuing.

"My thought was that I should call around to some of these restaurants and club-type places to see if anyone knew these guys. I myself make the rounds and know a lot of people who work at these places. And I got a hit when I called the Gig Shack. My friend Tara waitresses there. She said she knew the guys and she had a story so come on over and she'd meet up with us and let us know."

"I'm flattered that you thought to include me."

"Oh, it wasn't my choice," confessed Larry. "She at first was like, you are just using this as a pretext to hit on me. But I swore up and down that it wasn't the case and told her I had a girlfriend who wouldn't let me out of her sight, so that's where you come in."

"Gross, I have to pretend to be your girlfriend?" asked Antonia.

"You should be so lucky, Bingham."

They secured a spot on the street a few doors down from the Gig Shack, properly known as 668 The Gig Shack. It was located in the heart of Montauk on the main drag. The restaurant had primarily outdoor seating, the front tables covered by a striped yellow and white awning and the side section protected from the elements by a thin roof. The restaurant had a strong beachy vibe with an open front and potted palms sprinkled among a row of flower boxes. As it was still relatively early, six p.m., the restaurant was not very crowded, just a few people scattered about in the bistro chairs, mostly sipping cocktails.

Larry and Antonia were seated at a table by a young, pretty brunette hostess. When Larry informed her that he wanted to talk to

Tara, she said she would send her over, but in the meantime took their drink orders. The atmosphere called for something fruity so Antonia eschewed her normal red wine and ordered a grapefruit margarita on the rocks with salt. Larry asked for a light beer.

"I'm surprised you don't get a daiquiri or something that comes with a little umbrella," teased Antonia.

"Why's that?"

"I don't know. You seem to be the type who would go for those sorts of things."

"That's a weird statement."

As they waited for Tara, Antonia glanced around the town. Montauk had always been somewhat scruffy and laid-back, full of family-run restaurants, pancake houses, great surfing beaches, and shabby charm. Instead of designer label stores and posh chains, the storefronts were mostly shops touting various "Montauk: The End" paraphernalia like sweatshirts and baseball caps. The no-frills fishing village was always a cheaper and more mellow alternative to its fancier sister villages, East Hampton and Amagansett. However, within the past decade, the town had been "discovered" and enthusiastically embraced by hipsters, partiers, young professionals, and even high rollers. This meant that marquee restaurants had started to replace some of its more humble lobster shack predecessors, and live music venues had popped up all over the place. The local population who lived there year-round, numbering approximately three thousand, was becoming increasingly annoyed that their quaint hamlet was turning into an amped-up summer version of Fort Lauderdale on spring break. Recently efforts had been made to control the zoning and ensure that the noise was contained. Needless to say it was a very controversial standoff between those who thought it was a good thing for the town to have crowds and those who thought it compromised the unique character of Montauk.

"Hey there, handsome, you drove all this way to see me?" asked a tall woman with wavy dark hair in her midthirties.

Antonia glanced up, and was face to face with the woman's ample breasts that were secured into a black tight-fitting shirt.

"Don't you know it," said Larry, flirting back.

The woman, presumably Tara, placed her hand on Larry's shoulder and squeezed. She rubbed his shoulder back and forth then slid her hand down his back before finally placing it by her side. Antonia wondered if perhaps it was an aphrodisiac for her that Larry had said he had a girlfriend? Because her body language was not at all suggesting that she was tired of his hitting on her.

Larry made introductions and asked her if she could sit, so she motioned to the hostess that she was taking a break and the hostess nodded in accordance.

"How come you never come to see me?" asked Tara.

"Work has been nuts, but I missed you like crazy."

"I missed you too, baby. But you don't come visit anymore."

"I feel old here! This town is owned by twentysomethings now."

"You look great for your age," purred Tara.

Tara had barely given Antonia a glance after offering her a limp hand to shake and kept her eyes glued to Larry as if he were the most interesting man in the world. Antonia took a sip of her cocktail, brushing away the pebbles of sea salt that dotted the rim of her glass and planted themselves on her lips, and studied their interaction. Larry's eyes appeared gleeful, and he was clearly enjoying Tara's attention.

"But let's get serious. You said you knew Shane Boskin and Gary DiAngelo."

Tara leaned back in her chair and twisted her dark hair into a knot. Antonia noticed she had a pronounced clavicle and around her neck, she wore a long dangly gold necklace with an arrow pointing directly into her cleavage. Also, her skirt was so short that it was possible to see her panties by the way she sat.

"Okay, well *knew* is a strong word."

"It is?" asked Antonia skeptically.

Tara gave her a derisive sidelong glance, as if to convey the message that she was offended that Antonia had interjected. She continued addressing Larry. "I mean, I knew them, but not very well."

"Okay, talk to me. How did you meet them?"

"I was working here last month, and they were at one of my tables. They were with a bunch of people—there were maybe two or three women and a couple of guys. They were drinking hard, eating, you know, having fun."

"Right."

"Then, some of them got up to dance. We had a great band going that night. And this group was pretty blitzed. So they all got up, except one guy. And I said, 'What, you don't dance?' And then he said he wasn't very good and didn't like to do it. So he asked me to come sit down, and as my shift was over, I said 'Sure.'"

"Which guy was this? Shane or Gary?" asked Larry.

"It was Gary. Shane was out there on the dance floor dirty dancing some chick."

"Sorry to interrupt, but do you happen to remember what the chick looked like?" asked Antonia.

Tara gave her an irritated look. "Not really. I mean, she was Asian."

Antonia's eyebrows flew up, and she gave Larry a knowing look. He nodded and then returned his attention to Tara.

"Okay, so what happened then?"

"I talked to Gary for a while. He was a nice guy. He was pretty drunk, so he wasn't making much sense. But he said he lived in the city and he worked on Wall Street. He was out here to have a good time. He asked me if I wanted to have a good time with him, and I said sure."

"I'm sure you did." Larry giggled. "You went back to his place?"

"No, he came to mine."

"Wait a minute," interrupted Antonia. "I thought you said you didn't *know* him."

"I didn't," Tara said firmly. "We just had a fun night. Not much conversation. Then he left."

"Was there anything he said that might suggest why he was killed? Anything he did here? Was he aggressive?" asked Larry.

"You know, since we planned to meet up today, I thought about that a lot. I asked him if he was single, and he said he was, thank God, but that Shane wasn't and was having a lot of problems. I said something like, oh, his wife must be pissed he's running around on her, and he said it wasn't his wife. That it was Shane's girlfriend who was super possessive and wouldn't let him out of her sight."

"Did you catch her name?" asked Larry.

"Hmmm…no. It was something plain. Like Jane or Francesca."

"Francesca's a plain name?" mused Antonia.

"I didn't really pay attention. It wasn't Shane I was interested in."

She took a sip of her water and retrieved an ice cube with her tongue, which she then proceeded to crunch on loudly.

"Interesting," said Larry.

"Yeah," agreed Tara through the chewed ice.

Antonia was impatient and wanted to pose more questions, but it was obvious that Tara resented her, so she had to bite her tongue. She kept trying to prompt Larry with her eyeballs into asking follow-ups, but he was busy ogling Tara. The waitress came over and took their orders (spicy tuna tartare taquitos for Antonia and braised Hawaiian-style baby back ribs with cornbread and cole-slaw for Larry). Tara refused the offer of food, citing that she was on the clock. Antonia finally had to speak or she would explode.

"Okay, so can you tell me anything more about the interaction between Shane and this Jane or Francesca, whatever her name was?"

"No."

Antonia gave Larry an exasperated look. He leaned toward Tara and put his hand on her knee. "Nothing you can think of, sweetie? You are so perceptive, I can't imagine that you didn't notice anything."

"Well, he didn't look happy."

"He didn't?" Antonia echoed too eagerly.

"No," replied Tara, almost offended that Antonia had spoken. "She kind of dragged him up to the dance floor and then kept putting her head on his shoulder wanting to slow dance. And he kept trying to, you know, dance around, not romantic dance, but she was having none of it. Oh, and also, now I remember this. She wasn't there initially. They were all sitting together and then she walked up and asked the hostess to add her to their table. We were kind of pissed because they had said that it was only a table for like six and then she squeezes in. I don't think they were that psyched. Although maybe I'm projecting because other people around them complained that it was too tight."

"Wow, so she really was making his life miserable," said Antonia to Larry.

"I guess," replied Tara.

"If she was so into him, why would she go for you, Larry?" asked Antonia.

"Wait, what?" asked Tara. She swiveled her head in Larry's direction. "You hooked up with her?"

Larry laughed. "No, Antonia's just being crazy. She thinks every woman is after me. She's a possessive girlfriend, just like that woman."

Tara looked back and forth between Larry and Antonia. "You know, I don't see you two together at all."

"Thank you," Antonia began to say before Larry shot her a look.

"She just wouldn't take no for an answer," said Larry.

"Not sure why that worked with her and not me," said Tara with a pout on her face.

"Honey, you are marriage material. When I'm ready to settle down, you are my number one call. Right now I'm just sowing my wild oats."

"Geez, Larry, thanks," said Antonia.

She was glad the waitress was setting their food on the table. She couldn't take any more of the baloney she was hearing.

"You know, now that you say that, it reminds me of one thing," said Tara. "Sowing wild oats. Gary said that to me. Before we hooked up, he said he wanted to make sure that I was okay with it, and he even asked me to sign something on his phone. I thought it was weird, but he said he was a guy who liked to sow his wild oats, all innocent. But there had been a girl last summer who accused him and Shane of taking advantage, even though she had been the one who initiated things."

"Didn't that alarm you?" asked Antonia.

"Naw. He was a good-looking guy. And girls make things up. I mean, I'm a feminist, but I see these women in town flinging themselves at guys. They get drunk, and they're all over them. Gary and

Shane could have their pick of them. No way they took advantage of any woman."

"You sound so sure," said Antonia.

"I just know that a lot of women are liars."

16

As soon as they pulled out of their parking space, Antonia spoke.

"Well, she's a piece of work."

"Yes, she is."

"What I don't understand, Larry, is why you needed me to go with you. It was evident that she has a crush on you and was irritated by my presence. Why the heck was it so urgent I come? You made it seem like she wouldn't divulge anything without me."

"Yeah, I know I gave you that impression. The fact is, I just like to make her jealous."

"What? That's sick."

"I guess, but Tara and I have a twisted relationship. She's always been a Larry Lover and after me. I needed you there to protect me. Fend off her advances."

Antonia couldn't believe what she was hearing. She turned and stared at her diminutive companion. "Um, Larry, when did you become so discriminating? I've never heard you turn anyone down. In fact, you're what I would consider desperate."

"Bingham you are too funny. Naw, Tara's not my type. She's a beautiful woman, but a little too promiscuous for me."

"Promiscuous? What about the fake Cindy Boskin? This Francesca or Jane or whatever her name is? She sounds pretty forward, and that didn't stop you."

"That's different. I knew the rules. I knew I would never see her again."

"Okay, I didn't realize that you had some sort of playbook."

"Of course I do. What do you think I am, an amateur?"

Antonia settled back into her seat. "So where to now?"

"The Shore Lodge. Time to get more dirt on Lauren Wayne and Dawn Costa."

They made a right onto Edgemere Street, then drove into the parking lot of the Shore Lodge, which was located on the banks of Fort Pond. The white clapboard structure was a restaurant, motel, and nightclub all rolled into one. It had become the scourge of the locals who insisted that the relentless noise and party crowds that were generated by this hipster hangout made life in town unbearable. It was a trigger point for those who preferred old Montauk to new Montauk. Antonia could sympathize with both sides. It was hard when your quality of life was impinged upon by transient weekenders, but on the other hand, there were not many places for people who just wanted to go out and have a good time. Would she like to be living across the street from there? The answer was a resounding no. But would she have liked to have spent an evening there when she was single and fancy-free in her twenties? The answer was yes. It was hard to have your cake and eat it too.

The crowds had definitely dissipated now that it was the off-season, but there were still a robust number of people dining in the restaurant. The decor was a stylish and peppy mix of turquoise—the floor, the barstools, and the accents on the table linens—and white. The tables had that sustainable wood look, and there was a giant wall collage of candid photos of beachgoers and surfers. Antonia had heard that the food was quite good and made sure to elongate her neck into giraffe status to check out the fare that passing servers were bringing to outdoor guests. Looked pretty tasty, Antonia decided, and noted that her food intelligence had been correct.

A fortyish man with spiked salt-and-pepper hair, a carefully curated beard on his cleft chin, and thick black Warby Parker glasses waved to Larry from the edge of the bar, and they made their way over in his direction. He was lean and thin enough that he had to cinch his belt tightly around his black jeans to keep them from pooling at his ankles. He wore a snug black T-shirt that had a little pin on the shoulder that said "Love."

"Ezekiel," said Larry, clasping his hand in greeting. "How goes it?"

"Doing well, buddy, how are you?"

They engaged in a brief catch up about some woman they knew in common before Larry bothered to introduce Antonia.

Ezekiel gave a perfunctory smile, but his eyes quickly slid past Antonia to check out a bevy of tall, blond twentysomethings in tiny rompers that had entered the bar chattering loudly. He made no bones about gliding his eyes up and down over every inch of their bodies, and he did so with a smirk on his face. Larry took a moment to check them out as well, before returning his gaze to Ezekiel and snapping him back in to attention. Literally snapping, like putting his fingers in Ezekiel's face.

"Listen, Zeke, I'm on deadline, and, of course, you know I can't say anything, it's highly sensitive information that could make or break the investigation, but I know you hang out here a lot. Do you know either Lauren Wayne or Dawn Costa? They were waitresses here. Well, Lauren still is."

"Yeah, sure, I know those girls," Ezekiel responded with a nod. "Haven't seen much of Dawn this summer, but Lauren is around."

"She's here now?" asked Antonia.

"I think it's her night off," he said. "Actually, she may have taken the whole week off. I haven't seen her."

"What can you tell me about them?"

He ran his hair through his spiky hair (which Antonia marveled did not flatten under the pressure; each spike remained buoyant) and shrugged. "Lauren's a nice girl. I never noticed her doing anything crazy."

"Well, what could she possibly do that was crazy at work?" asked Antonia.

"Oh, you'd be surprised," said Ezekiel.

"Is she a big flirt? Going after the tips the good old-fashioned way?" asked Larry with a wink.

"I never saw her do that. She's kind of shy, I'd say, more of a low-key type. Not to be a jerk, but I wouldn't say she was the brightest girl I ever met. Not that you get into deep conversations here, but I'm a regular and I talk a lot with the waitresses, and some of them are smart cookies."

"What about Dawn?" asked Larry.

"Now she's a force to be reckoned with."

"How do you mean?" asked Larry eagerly.

"You know, she is one savvy chick. That's a girl who knows what she wants and will go after it."

"You mean she never gave you the time of day?" Larry said with a laugh.

"Well, I wouldn't even try. She's not my type at all. Zeroes in on anyone she thinks is a big ticket. You can tell she's ambitious a mile away, and she's got attitude. But I can say she is very smart. Gets her way."

"Do you know if she hooked up with any guys?" asked Larry.

Ezekiel nodded. "I'm sure. I mean, yes, I saw her leave with some guys late at night. But it was always, you know, the Wall Street types. Hedgies. She has her eyes on the prize. I figured that's why she wasn't working here this summer, probably caught herself a sugar daddy. Although I hear she wanted to focus on her blog."

"What kind of blog?" asked Antonia.

"Dawn believes herself to be an 'influencer.' She thinks people want her recommendations about where to stay and eat and drink in the Hamptons. The blog is pretty crappy. I checked it out once; it's like, how to spend a day in the Hamptons without paying a dime, and where the best beaches are. Her so-called tips with lame visuals. If I were Tripadvisor, I would not be panicking."

Antonia made a mental note to check it out before asking, "And did you ever see her pal around with Lauren? Or them leave together with guys?"

"Yeah, they were close. Still are, even though they have all those catfights."

"Was Dawn friends with any other waitresses?" asked Larry.

"I think all the waitresses hung out together. And Dawn ran the show. She's bossy. Gabriela and Irina were friends of theirs. They didn't return this summer. Actually, I do remember one thing. Okay, yes, now it's coming back to me. There was some sort of catfight toward the end of last summer. Irina told me about it. She's Russian, and she said American women are so…what was the word she used? Something like righteous, but her English wasn't that good so I don't think it was that. Angry? Or maybe it was naive? God, I wish I could remember. The gist was that she was implying Dawn was a tease, that she was leading on some guy and when he made the move, she got all offended. Irina thought she was overreacting. Maybe the word was touchy?"

"Do you know who the guy was?" Larry asked.

"No, but you know, like I said, she had a type."

"Did she tell you anything else? Details?" Antonia asked.

"I don't know what I remember or what I assumed. But my take-away is they met the guys here, they all went out, the guy hit on Dawn, Dawn didn't like it, she got mad at him, then she got mad at them for not agreeing with her that he was a jerk. Something like that."

"And that included Lauren?" asked Antonia.

"Yeah, I think they were all pissed off at each other. Then Dawn quit not long after that. And you know, someone keyed Irina's car, and she thought it was Dawn. I told her to report it to the police, but she was worried about her visa, so she didn't do it. She did say if she ever came across Dawn again, Dawn would pay."

"Where can we find Irina?" asked Larry.

"She's back in Russia. She was on one of those summer work visas."

"Bummer," Antonia lamented.

"But Gabriela's around. I ran into her a few weeks ago; she was working at a restaurant in Sag Harbor. She said she was looking for a job in decorating, so I gave her my card."

"You're in decorating?" asked Antonia.

"No, but I know people."

"Were you able to get her a job?"

"She emailed me her résumé. I wanted to make sure I got it to the right people, so I've been sitting on it. I can forward it to you."

"That would be great," said Larry.

"Why are you interested in talking with them? Are they wit-nesses or suspects?"

"Not sure what they are right now. Trying to find out the whole story," admitted Larry.

"Hopefully Gabriela can help you."

When they were back in the car, Larry's cell phone buzzed.

"It's Gabriela's résumé," he said, handing Antonia his phone.

"Gabriela Nesbo. Oh my gosh, Larry…"

"What?"

Antonia gave Larry a wide-eyed look. "She lives on Bull Path."

The entire ride home, Antonia felt uneasy. She wasn't quite sure why, but her sixth sense was blowing up. She kept looking around outside, scanning the trees and houses they passed, certain she would find something unpleasant. She flipped down the mirror on the visor to look at the cars behind her.

"Checking yourself out in the mirror, huh?" Larry asked with a smirk.

"Checking on the cars behind us, Einstein. Do you think we are being tailed?"

"What? No." Larry lurched upwards and stared in his rearview mirror. "Why would we be followed?"

Antonia didn't want to tell him about Philip. She just didn't have the energy. But she knew that it was Philip who was making her anxious, and sadly, whenever she felt his presence, he was usually around. She shuddered.

"I don't know, just thought maybe someone was following us."

"Ha! Maybe one of my girlfriends."

"Let's hope so."

Antonia stopped by her office when she returned to the inn. This was usually the time she accomplished the most at her desk, when

Connie was away and there was less foot traffic in the front hall and reception area. No distractions meant no excuses, her father used to say. It was true. She checked her email on her computer, and there was a message from Jonathan. He informed her that the police had swept the inn for cameras and had found nothing in the guest rooms, and only two others that Antonia had missed. One was located outside her apartment door and one in the garden shed out back. They had also scanned her apartment and found nothing. It was a relief that there was nothing inside her apartment, but dang, she was irritated that she had missed the others! Of course there would be a camera aimed at her door, Philip had always controlled her comings and goings. She felt sick to know that he had been that close to her. When would his obsession end?

Fortunately, most of Antonia's other emails were mundane except for three missives from Genevieve demanding to know all the details about her date with Nick. They were bursting with emojis and all sorts of exclamation points and question marks and demanding an immediate response. What could she say? Now that it had been twenty-four hours, she was able to examine it objectively. Okay, that was a lie, she knew, but with time comes clarity. She was confused by Nick's comings and goings to New York and everywhere else. They always seemed to pop up, and it wasn't that she didn't believe that he had to go to the city, but she wanted a stronger sense of what their timeline would be. Were they going to casually date every now and then? Was she going to be his "East Hampton" girlfriend and there would be other gals sprinkled around the world? She didn't know what to make of the courtship, or even if it was a courtship at all. Gosh, if she only had a rule book. It would be helpful.

She was about to click off her computer when she remembered

Dawn's blog. She wished she had asked what it was called. She typed in Dawn's name along with "Hamptons" and her search revealed a website called "Hamptons Influencers." Antonia opened the page.

Ezekiel was not wrong; the blog was pretty crappy. It did, however, have a nice header photo of Dawn in a seductive pose, scantily dressed (like in her social media pages) and staring suggestively at the camera. There were snapshots of beaches and drinks and small paragraphs with an abundance of hashtags delineating their favorite meals at restaurants and local bars to stop by. (The focus was more on drinks than food.) Dawn also included a rating of local inns and hotels and had given some five stars and others one star with brief commentary. Antonia scrolled down to look for the Windmill Inn and wasn't surprised to find they had given her only one star. It said underneath:

"The owner is a bitch and the place is stuffy as all hell. Paging all grandmothers, this is the waiting room to hell for you to spend your last hours. Death will come quickly, you'll be so bored."

Antonia bristled. Dawn did not have to be so nasty! She did a quick scan and saw that there were several comments below, one that said LOL and another that said "Why would you even go there?" Irritated, Antonia clicked off the page without reading any further. How dare she? Dawn was a conniving little brat. Antonia felt used and abused.

When she left her office to walk through the public rooms, she found Joseph in the parlor having an after-dinner drink. He sat at a quiet corner table flanked by bookshelves and steps away from the fireplace. He waved to Antonia.

"How are you, my dear? I have barely seen you this week."

Antonia shrugged. "I know, it's been a busy week."

She eyeballed the empty seat next to him, unsure if his friend Cheryl had joined him this evening and was merely powdering her nose at the moment. There was no trace of another presence. As if sensing her thought process, Joseph motioned for her to sit down.

"Is someone sitting here?" she asked tentatively.

"Just me. Please join me for a nightcap."

Antonia and Joseph shared a very close relationship, and she was possessive of him, having grown used to his being permanently available for pep talks and advice. But this new woman on the scene had made Antonia feel distant from him, and it annoyed her. She sat down and glanced around the room. Various guests were plopped around in the chairs and sofas, laughing and having drinks. Joseph eyed her carefully.

"Cheryl works at my publishing house," he said finally.

"Oh!" replied Antonia, relaxing somewhat. *That explains it*, she thought.

"I've never heard you mention her."

"She's new. She only recently contacted me and said she had joined the firm and she had enjoyed my books and was excited to be working with me."

"Is she an editor?"

"No, she's in the financial department."

"Oh, so then you won't *really* be working with her." Antonia sniffed. She wondered why this Cheryl had been so presumptuous.

"She'll be cutting my checks," replied Joseph with a mirthful laugh. "Thus the most important job."

"I see. And she lives in East Hampton?"

"She was out here for the long weekend with friends. We had been corresponding by email, and she asked if we could meet in person."

"Charming."

Joseph gave her a quizzical look. "Did you have a bad impression of her?"

"No, of course not. I barely met her. She just…"

"Just what?"

"Nothing."

"No, come on, dear, don't leave me in suspense."

"Well, she appeared to have made herself comfortable quite quickly."

Joseph burst into laughter. Antonia's face reddened.

"Why are you laughing?"

"No reason."

"No, seriously."

Joseph's face was merry. "I think you are right, my dear. She was very comfortable. I'm not quite used to that. I would say I'm a little old-fashioned and more formal. But I found it entertaining."

"Okay, but is this a romance thing, if I can ask?"

"Oh, I doubt she was interested in that," he said with a scoff.

"I don't think so at all, Joseph," said Antonia. "I can read body language and this woman was definitely interested."

Antonia could swear that Joseph blushed. He took a quick sip of his sherry. "I'm too old for all that nonsense."

"Now that's nonsense. You are in your prime. What, you're only in your midsixties, right? That's when you have to start dating up a storm. You will be the belle of the ball, so to speak."

"Then you approved of Cheryl?"

Every inch of Antonia wanted to say no, that she thought Cheryl was a hussy and too forward. But not only did she have no basis for that, and not only would it be mean, but the way Joseph was looking at her, an eager expression on his face, meant that it mattered to him what she thought.

"I barely met her, but I thought she was fabulous!" Antonia lied with a grin.

"I'm so glad. I liked her as well. The wonderful news is her friends have given her use of their guest cottage at their house on Huntting Lane, so she will be back every weekend!"

"How great!"

After Joseph retired, Antonia wandered through the dining room and finally into the bar to check on the state of affairs. It was pretty quiet, with only two giggly young women sitting on the stools and chatting with Jesse. He was flirting with them as he packed away the garnishes (olives, lemon, limes) in the fridge for the evening. He smiled when he saw Antonia.

"I was looking for you," he said.

"I'm here," she responded.

He motioned her to the other side of the bar, away from his admirers. Antonia sat down on a stool, and he leaned toward her.

"Listen, guess who I saw last night at the Talkhouse?"

"Who?"

"That big guy who was here on Sunday night. The one that was kind of weird and got really angry when a woman bumped into him? I know Glen told you and the police about him."

"Right!" said Antonia, smacking her head with the palm of her hand. "The one who was alone and paid cash."

"Yeah, he was kind of sketchy. I mean, I wouldn't have necessarily brought it up, but when the cops asked me and Glen if there was anything suspicious that night, he was the first person who came to mind."

"Okay, wait a minute," said Antonia. "I have so many questions.

First of all, I know that Glen thought he was weird because he got quote unquote triggered and really angry when a woman knocked his chair. Why was he sketchy?"

"He was kind of muttering while he drank. Like he was really pissed off about something. And at one point his phone rang, and I overheard a little, obviously not trying to eavesdrop, but he was sitting right in front of me and not trying to be discreet. He was saying things like 'It's your fault,' and he was cursing and saying how angry he was. And there was one point where I had to lean down and get some glasses from beneath where he was sitting, and I heard him say, 'You will live to regret this. I will make him pay. I know where he lives.' And then get this, I heard him say 'bull.'"

"Bull?"

"Yeah, didn't think anything of it, but when I heard those guys were murdered on Bull Path, I thought, Wow! He must be some disgruntled boyfriend or something."

"Wow, that is insane! Did you tell the police?"

"Yeah."

Antonia was momentarily deflated. She thought perhaps she had a lead in the case, something to break it open, but clearly the police already knew about it.

"But you saw him last night at the Talkhouse? Was he alone?"

"Yeah, he was alone. I did see him talking to a chick—girl—at one point, but I don't know if he knew her or he was hitting on her."

"Did you talk to him at all?"

"I was going to, but then right as I'm heading over to him, he leaves."

"Bummer, well, maybe you can ask the bartender if he remembers?"

"I can do better than that, Antonia. I followed him outside to the parking lot and watched him get into his car. It's a silver Audi, and I have the license plate number!"

Jesse held up his phone, where there was a picture of the back of a car. The New York license plate was prominently displayed.

"Good work! Did you send it to the police?"

"I'm going to, I know I have to do that. I just got busy, overslept this morning, and then raced here for work. I should do that now."

"Hang on a second," said Antonia, putting her hand out to stop him. She couldn't believe what she was going to do. This was interfering with a case. Wasn't it obstruction of justice? Could she go to jail?

"I know that the detectives will be in bed right now. Maybe you should wait until tomorrow morning to mail it?"

"I could," said Jesse. "But I'm not usually awake early in the morning. The guy might slip away."

He had a point, Antonia mused. "You're right. You should send it. But do you mind cc'ing me? Oh, and I have Sergeant Flanagan's email if you want to mail it to him directly."

"Sure."

Okay, Antonia did not have the advantage of time, which was probably for the best. But the cops were overwhelmed with leads and might not get to this part of the investigation right away. What she could do was put Larry Lipper on it pronto. He had contacts over at the police department and could pull up the owner of the license plate in no time. If she tipped him off tonight, there was no doubt he would find out some stuff by morning. Not to mention that he would owe her forever.

17

AT SIX THIRTY THE NEXT MORNING, ANTONIA ROLLED OUT OF bed, pulled on her stretchy pants, and drove to the beach for her morning walk. Already the sky was a gorgeous blue with an absence of clouds, and the air warm. Antonia parked her car next to a green Volvo and then walked to the entrance. There were dog walkers clustered by the poop bag dispenser, and Antonia smiled and greeted them with a hello. There was a daily crowd that she generally recognized and exchanged pleasantries with. She was so focused on making her way down the path that she didn't notice the person sitting on the fence to her right.

"What, you're not going to say hello?"

It was Nick. He was perched on the edge, a bag of Dreesen's donuts in his hand and two coffees in a cardboard carrying tray. His Lab and golden retriever were slobbering and bouncing around next to him, eager to hit the beach and chase after elusive birds and the moist tennis ball that they dragged in and out of the surf.

"I thought you were in New York!" she said, with genuine surprise.

"I was. But then I wanted to see you, so I drove back late last night. I almost stopped by the inn, but I figured you were sleeping."

"I probably wasn't, you should have! But I'm glad to see you today."

He extricated a coffee from the tray and handed it to her. "For you."

"That's so nice, thank you."

They headed down toward the water with the dogs leading the way. The two hounds were frantic with excitement, jumping, running, bobbing, and generally acting as if they had just secured release after years at a maximum-security penitentiary. The coffee had a watery deli flavor, but the fact that Nick had brought it especially for her made Antonia sip it with pleasure. There was a shininess to the day—the light on the water was sparkly, and the sand appeared to glint with brightness—that made Antonia feel exhilarated.

"What did I miss while I was gone?" asked Nick.

"Where do I start?"

She filled him in on everything she had learned about the murder investigation and all of her suspicions. Nick liked to hear about her "cases," and she had to admit that his interest fueled her own motivation in solving crimes (if she could call her snooping around solving crimes). After she gave him the rundown (although she neglected to confide in him anything about Philip—right now she did not want to inject her ex-husband into her burgeoning relationship), she paused to see what he made of it all.

"You know, you're a fabulous chef, and you run a great inn, but maybe you're in the wrong business. You seem to really like detective work. Have you ever thought of becoming a private investigator?"

"What? No. I can't imagine."

"No, seriously. Maybe at least get your license, then you can pursue these cases in an official manner."

Antonia shook her head. "I'll stick to the kitchen."

"Ah, but you don't stick to the kitchen. From what I'm hearing, you've spent a lot of time out of the kitchen."

She couldn't deny it. Her prioritizing had been completely out of whack of late. "You're right."

"What is it about this work that you find so exhilarating?"

"That's a good question. I guess I'm just nosy."

"It's not just that. Most people are nosy. But you are also relentless—and I mean that in a good way—and you're brave.

Not a lot of people would continue to investigate when there was danger. I think it's more than a hobby to you."

"I suppose I like the puzzle aspect of it all. Putting all the pieces together and discovering the who, what, where, when, and why. I always enjoyed that part of it; it reminds me of the game of Clue, which I played a lot with my parents as a kid. Although, actually, my favorite board game growing up was 221B Baker Street, based on, duh, Sherlock Holmes. It used bits from his cases and you had to solve the murder. That was the best."

"Right, but this is different than games. This is the real thing. You are pursuing bad people who have done the worst possible acts."

"Gosh, you make it so scary when you put it that way!"

"It is! What you're doing is hazardous."

"Huh. I think I just appreciate the concept of vengeance. I don't like it when people get away with doing bad things. I want accountability. And justice."

Nick gave her a look to suggest that he knew she was alluding to more than the crimes she had helped solve. And he was not wrong. It was deeper for her; she felt in control of her past if she could capture other bad guys. She had a major vigilante side to her. Philip may be elusive, but she couldn't allow his fellow evildoers to roam free.

They walked all the way from Georgica Beach to Main Beach, chatting, eating cinnamon donuts, and drinking coffee. Then they turned around and strolled back to their cars. Antonia did not want the morning to end. She felt so natural in these moments with Nick, so comfortable. They were without expectations, none of that "what's going to happen next" that added pressure to their other encounters. A beach walk was just a beach walk, and no need for anything else.

"Dinner tonight?" he asked, when they had reached the parking lot.

Antonia hesitated. "I want to, but Thursday is so busy and I really should be in the kitchen, which you very correctly pointed out I have been neglecting."

"I get it. Okay, how about this? I come to dinner there tonight?"

"That would be great. I'd love it!"

Before she had even finished, Nick leaned over and gave her a long kiss. Antonia felt as if someone were pulling her up from her toes and lifting her to the sky. Before she completely broke away, Nick gave her a firm hug.

"Do you want me to make you something special tonight? What's your favorite food?" she asked when they finally disentangled.

"I'm easy."

"No, come on, I want to. Remember, cooking is my thing."

"Okay then, make me some risotto. The kind you used to make with your mother."

"Will do."

Antonia was juiced up on endorphins after she left the beach. She turned up the stereo and blasted Billy Joel's "My Life" all the way down Lily Pond Lane. She sang along to the tune—more like shrieked along—and waved to passing joggers and bikers who looked at her askance. Instead of heading back to the inn, she decided to hit Riverhead Building Supply and see if they had more of that tape that held pictures in place on the wall.

The store was buzzing with contractors and painters picking up their supplies for the day or week. Although it was a vast warehouse space with aisles offering everything you would need to renovate a home, it was manageable. A sales associate directed her toward the section where she would find a selection of hanging necessities, and Antonia took a moment to peruse them. It was always overwhelming when there were so many options and she could second-guess herself.

"Well, hello there," said Iris Maple, sauntering up to Antonia. She had a red wicker basket hooked on her arm and Antonia instantly conjured up the image of Little Red Riding Hood.

"Hi, Iris. How are you holding up?"

"I was going to ask you the same thing. I was worried about you after you came over the other day. I dare say you suffered quite a shock. Are you recovered?"

"Yes, thanks for asking. How about you? Has it been crazy around here?"

"The police are still canvassing the area, but there are not as many of them. It's a little gloomy, but soon it will be over, I hope. I saw the owner of the house of horrors—that contractor— yesterday. He was all upset that now no one will want to rent the house because there was a murder there. And do you know what? I hope he's right. They should just raze the entire house and put up a little memorial sign. Let the woods grow back in and absorb the entire crime scene." Iris's eyes blazed with indignation.

"I hate to say it, but I can't see a contractor doing that."

"Of course not, they're only concerned with the almighty dollar. But one can fantasize."

"Iris, I was actually planning on swinging by your neighbor- hood. Do you happen to know someone named Gabriela Nesbo? She lives on Bull Path."

"Yes, of course. She's a few doors down. It was her aunt's house, and she inherited it."

Antonia's heart beat with excitement, and she responded a little too eagerly. "What can you tell me about her?"

"Her aunt Linda was a very nice woman. It was her second home; she lived in the city and came out on weekends or in the summer. She was fairly quiet and kept to herself and did not entertain often. She died a couple of years ago, and Gabriela moved in. I didn't even know Linda had died—I assumed she had business that kept her in the city, but then one day Gabriela shows up and I see a large dumpster and just about all the contents of the house were disposed of there and carted away. It's sad, really, when you see how one person's entire life can be erased in a minute like that. I know that Linda prided herself on her needlepoint, and what do I see on top of that dumpster but all of Linda's beautiful pillows. She liked to do ones with funny little sayings or messages on them, like 'Who's the boss?' with a picture of a cat. Very amusing."

"Yes, that is funny," lied Antonia, not thinking it was funny at all.

"Oh, and there was one that said 'Never trouble trouble until trouble troubles you.' That one was a hoot. I have to be honest, I thought of rescuing some of them out of the dumpster, but by then they were already dirty and it was unsanitary."

"Yes, you wouldn't want that in your house."

"No."

"Interesting about Linda's needlepoint. Anything more you can tell me about Gabriela?"

"She had a boyfriend for a while. I used to see a BMW parked there quite a bit. I don't see it anymore."

"Did you ever see the guy?"

"Yes, but he wasn't memorable."

"Young? Old?"

"Her age. She's probably somewhere in her twenties."

"Do you know why they broke up?"

"No, I haven't talked to her very often. She's not very neighborly."

"What do you mean?"

Iris shrugged. "We have a block party at Fourth of July, and I made sure I invited her in ample time to put it on her calendar. But she declined our invitation. She also had a few very loud parties this summer with an abundance of cars parked all over the street, including outside my house. The tire marks made a huge gash in the lawn, and I was forced to put up stakes until the grass recovered. It was thoughtless. I had my nephew go over and ask her what she planned to do about it, but she didn't give him an answer. He said it was as if she didn't care."

"Do you know if she ever partied with Shane and Gary?"

"I don't know for a fact, but I believe I saw them chatting at the end of the driveway one day when I was pulling out."

"Did they look happy or sad?"

"It was very fleeting. But I'm sure they were happy. Gabriela would be their type."

"What do you mean by that?"

"She's attractive. Brown hair, dark eyebrows, fit."

"I think I may have to talk with her. Do you think she would be home now?"

"I don't really know her habits, but I can tell you that her car is in her driveway until about noon. I believe she works at night," said Iris disdainfully.

"Thanks, Iris. I think I'll scoot up there now."

"Take care. And I hope to see you at the Author's Night meeting next week. We are doing a roundup on how it went."

"I'll be there."

When she sat down in her Saab, Antonia dialed Larry, but it went straight to voicemail. There were no emails from him, and she wondered what he had done with the license plate number she had sent him the previous night. His response had been a cryptic "got it," and she was disappointed because she thought she would at least elicit mild enthusiasm. Although, on the other hand, he also liked to play things down—especially her participation in his investigations—and then run with it. But she wanted to know if he had figured out who the big man was and why he had been so agitated the night of the murders.

On her drive to the Northwest Woods, Antonia mulled over all of the fragmented clues and information that she had gathered. Lauren, Dawn, and Gabriela all worked together. The previous summer Dawn had been angry at her colleagues slash friends and there had been some sort of "catfight" according to their fellow waitress Irina, who confided in Ezekiel. The implication was that a man had gone too far and Dawn was furious her friends didn't back her up on this, but Irina thought she was just a tease who was overreacting. Fast forward a summer and Lauren appeared on Bull Path the night after the murder of Shane and Gary, two frequent customers at the Shore Lodge where all the ladies had worked. Lauren was disoriented and unsure how she ended up in the woods when the last thing she remembered was sitting watching a movie at Dawn's house in Napeague. Her expression when the murder of Shane and Gary was mentioned was definitely one of shock, but that could be rehearsed. Not so her clear recognition as to who they were.

And then there was Dawn, who was a guest at the inn the night of the murders and claims that she booked there to avoid her stalker, Lauren. She claimed she booked last minute, although records showed she booked months in advance. She said that Lauren tied her up and she was scared of her, but the next day she was having a giggly lunch with Lauren and it was all water under the bridge. By all accounts, Dawn is smart and manipulative, and Lauren is nuts and a bit of a follower, although only Dawn has claimed Lauren is psychotic.

Then Gabriela enters the picture. She's their coworker who lives on Bull Path. That is too coincidental to dismiss. Did these three women conspire to kill Shane and Gary? Were they righting a wrong? Didn't fake Cindy Boskin (whoever she was) say that a woman had accused Shane and Gary of sexual assault? It all seemed so obvious to Antonia, and that's what worried her. She knew that murderers were not that clever, that some very high statistic like ninety-five percent of them were actually bungling idiots. But if this was a plan that Dawn had set into motion months ago, wouldn't she be more careful? Would it really be so easy for an overeager innkeeper to catch her? There had to be more to the story.

Gabriela's house was a modest one-story affair with tangled, overgrown bushes and a front lawn dotted with deer droppings. Although it was technically two doors down from the murder scene, it was closer than it would seem because the house in between them was situated on a flag lot. The three mailboxes sat together in a tight row, and Gabriela's house shared a pebbly drive-way with the flag lot house. Gabriela's driveway veered off to the right, and the neighbor's continued down a long, narrow stretch. There was a blue Subaru parked in front, and Antonia slid her car in behind it, hoping that she wasn't blocking access to anyone who needed to make a speedy departure. She opened a squeaky wrought-iron gate and followed a small, stone path to the front door and pressed the doorbell.

Nothing happened. Antonia was actually unsure if the bell even worked as she had heard nothing when she pressed it. Was it one of those super-high tones that only dogs and people with exceptional hearing could detect? She had no idea. She peered through the bay window adjacent to the door and saw no movement, only an empty staircase with a half-moon console table at the base, atop of which sat a decorative vase. The overhead light was not illuminated, although it was daytime, so that didn't mean much. It was possible that Gabriela was caught in some state of undress and was donning clothes before she opened her door, so Antonia thought she would give her some time until she pressed again. Meanwhile, she took the opportunity to scan the area.

Most of the houses in the Northwest Woods were situated behind dense woods or brush, concealing them from inquisitive eyes like Antonia's. Even in the winter, the foliage—especially on the pine trees—still hung on for dear life, making it difficult to have a proper visual of the houses tucked behind. Although sadly there had been a horrible outbreak of beetles in the woods this past year, and the town had been forced to knock down several thousand trees to prevent further infestations. The cherry on top of the pie in that situation was that once the town knocked the trees down, the owners of the houses were responsible for not only disposing of the trees but also paying for said disposal, which was not cheap. Many of Antonia's friends had been lamenting the unexpected landscaping costs. Not to mention that they now had gaping holes in their yard all over the place and were discovering neighbors they never knew they had.

When Gabriela didn't answer the door after a couple of minutes, Antonia lifted up the giant bronze door knocker and clanked it loudly several times. She waited a full minute before clanking it even louder. Finally she heard a voice trilling from somewhere inside telling her to hang on a minute.

Gabriela Nesbo opened the door bleary-eyed and with pillow-crease lines running all over her face. She wore gray sweatpants and a Lululemon black tank top. Her feet were bare, except for a gold toe ring that twinkled on her pinky. Her unbrushed hair was a tangled shoulder-length mass of thick brown with chunky streaks of lighter brown that had been applied with an unsubtle hand. Her features were pretty but generic, with her eyes slightly too far apart. It was clear that she was still in that caffeine-deprived, half-lucid sleep state, and Antonia felt guilty for having roused her.

"I'm so sorry to bother you," said Antonia.

"Can I help you?" asked Gabriela, wiping sleep from her eyes.

Antonia realized that she had not rehearsed a good reason for her presence on this young woman's doorstep. She hadn't been commissioned to solve this crime, she was not working with the police, and she was not really anyone but a nosy innkeeper who had a bad habit of looking into stuff that she had no business looking into. Maybe Nick Darrow was right and she should obtain a private investigator's license? Perhaps it was a good idea to be legitimate. It would certainly help in awkward situations such as this one.

"Hi, I'm Antonia Bingham, and I wanted to ask you a few questions about your neighbors."

Gabriela rolled her eyes. "Ugh, I'm so sick of it! Was it really so dastardly?"

"In my opinion, yes. I mean, they were killed."

Gabriela looked confused, and then realization dawned. "Oh. Shane and Gary."

"Yes, Shane Boskin and Gary DiAngelo. I want to talk about their murders. Would you mind if I came in?"

Antonia decided she would take advantage of Gabriela's drowsy state and talk with full confidence, as if she had a right to be there. Without waiting, Antonia made a step forward prompting Gabriela to open the front door wider and allow her passage.

"Sure, okay, are you the police?" asked Gabriela.

Antonia faux chuckled. "Oh, no, I'm not police, but I am doing an investigation. My, what a lovely home you have. Are you a decorator?"

Antonia remembered that Ezekiel had mentioned that Gabriela wanted to get into interior design. Without giving Gabriela a chance to hesitate, Antonia had moved past the front hall and made a right turn into the sunken living room, which was two steps below. The decor was not fancy—probably all out of a catalog like West Elm or Crate and Barrel, but it was nicely pulled together with a low-slung sofa, midcentury chairs, two strategically placed fig trees, and a few contemporary abstract paintings on the walls. It was what one would call minimalist and modern. There was also a giant orange beanbag chair in front of the fireplace with a stack of celebrity magazines situated next to it. From the memory foam dent the size of a human body, Antonia conjectured that this was where Gabriela spent much of her time.

"I'm not a decorator, but thanks for asking. I actually would like to be. I'm really passionate about home design, and I'm saving up to go to decorating school," Gabriela responded as she trailed behind Antonia.

"I think that's a smart move. You really have a flair."

"Thanks so much!"

Gabriela's enthusiastic response was a clue as to how Antonia could ingratiate herself.

"I love the modern lamp on the antique table."

"You do? Thanks!"

"Yes, very clever."

"I read in *Elle Decor* that it's great to juxtapose modern with antique."

"Very wise," Antonia replied with a nod, still surveying the room. "Do you mind if I take a picture? I just love it."

"Sure!"

"Hey, do you want to get in it? I have a friend who works at *House Beautiful*. Maybe I can send it to her? She'd really love this place and, hey, you never know..."

"Oh my god, that would be insane! I'm really trying to get press coverage. I just did a feature in my friends' blog about how to decorate on a budget, but I definitely need more."

Antonia took out her phone and snapped a picture of Gabriela beaming in front of her living room. "Great."

"Hey, you know, can I offer you something to drink? I can make some coffee?"

"If it's not too much trouble."

"No problem!" Gabriela said eagerly. "How do you take it?"

"Milk and sugar?"

"Be right back!"

Antonia knew from every single detective novel and crime show that she had watched that you always want a witness slash potential suspect to make you coffee or tea. That way, you were locked in and they had to answer your questions until you finished your coffee. It was often a scandal in some mystery novels if the inquisitor was not offered a second cup. It was basically the first rule of an interrogation. The second was to excuse yourself, head to the bathroom, and snoop around the medicine cabinet and any other adjacent rooms, without raising too much suspicion.

While she waited for Gabriela, Antonia situated herself on the sofa and picked up one of the many design books that were on the coffee table. It was by David Netto, a famous designer and East Hampton resident.

"Don't you love that book?" asked Gabriela, as she returned with two mugs of coffee. "So chic."

"Yes, totally."

Gabriela handed her the steaming mug then plopped herself in a chair, curling her feet underneath her.

"I'm taking notes on everything. It's amazing how you can study a room over and over and notice new details every single time."

Antonia saw an opening. "Interesting. Do you do that, say, when you're out and about town?"

Gabriela nodded. "Oh yeah. Every house I go into, every restaurant…"

"Restaurant?" asked Antonia, cutting her off. "Like, which ones would you say out here have the best style or decor?"

"There are so many. I love 1770 House, the American Hotel, the Windmill Inn…"

"The Windmill Inn? You've been?"

"Oh yeah. I really like the bar area there. It's lacquered this vibrant blue and the stools have nailhead trim, which I think is so cool."

"Have you been there a lot?"

"No, not really. I was actually just there…"

Gabriela stopped abruptly. She gave Antonia a quizzical look. "I'm sorry, can you remind me what this is about?"

"Oh, yes. I've just met with members of the Boskin and DiAngelo families. They had a lot of questions, as did I, and we were discussing that. That's why I'm here."

Antonia had not lied, but she had definitely made it seem like she was there in some sort of official capacity. She hoped Gabriela wouldn't know the difference.

"Why are you asking me?" Her tone was neutral, but Antonia could decipher anxiety in her voice.

"Because you're their neighbor. I was wondering if you knew them."

Gabriela paused. "I mean, a little."

"How did you know them?"

She took a deep breath. "I kind of recognized them when they moved in next door. I, um, waitressed at the Shore Lodge, and they used to go there sometimes. Then they rented that house."

She motioned toward the window.

"Oh, you must know Lauren and Dawn!"

Gabriela hesitated. "Yeah. I worked with them."

"I know them too. Was that whose blog you did the decorating stuff for?"

"Yes," admitted Gabriela. She quickly added, "We're not really good friends; we just worked together. It's like a business arrangement."

"We're not friends either. In fact, I think Dawn is a bit manipulative."

Gabriela didn't respond, instead taking a sip of her coffee.

"Don't you?" asked Antonia.

"Well, she likes to get her way."

"Yes, I agree. She may even bully people into things."

"To say the least," muttered Gabriela.

"Yeah, she can be a bully." Antonia hoped with these prompts that Gabriela would elaborate, but instead she changed the subject.

"What did you want to know about Shane and Gary?"

"Were they nice guys?"

Gabriela shrugged. "I mean, well, they were guys. But honestly, okay, no. They were not very nice. I mean, I can handle guys like that, but they can be too much sometimes."

"What do you mean by that?"

"You know, they were jerks, totally conceited. Like they had all these women throwing themselves at them and they loved it. Guys like that, who have money and are hot, they can do what they want, and they *do* do what they want. Doesn't matter if other people don't want it. They think they're so great."

"Did they ever do something that you didn't want?"

"I can handle myself," she responded, staring evenly at Antonia. "And besides, I'd never go for a guy like them. I have their number. They're not my type. Besides, I think Shane was married."

"He was. Do you know anyone who dated him?"

"I mean, no. I don't want to speak ill of the dead."

"What does that mean?"

"Just, like, they're dead. Nothing more to say. I told the police already that I didn't hear anything."

"Do you know who killed them?"

She shook her head. "Of course not."

"Was Lauren at your house that night?"

"I already told the police she wasn't."

"Then why do you think she was found just a few yards away, wandering in the woods? Isn't that a coincidence?"

"Lauren has a drug problem."

"She does? What kind?"

"I don't know...that's what Dawn told me. Lauren takes something and goes all crazy and then doesn't remember it. And she gets really violent, apparently. Dawn is her friend, but, like, she's scared of her. Terrified actually. She, like, pretends that it's all okay, but she is living in fear."

"Why doesn't she tell the police that?"

"Well, she did, but then Lauren threatened her. She said she would kill all of her family members."

"How would she do that?"

"Dawn says Lauren's family is in the mafia in New Jersey. Big time."

"That sounds...not true. I mean, come on."

"That's what I thought, but then I was at Dawn's house one day and she showed me all these articles on Lauren's family. She said she had told Lauren she didn't want to be her friend anymore, and then when I was at her house, Lauren shows up and asks to speak to Dawn outside. When Dawn came back, her shirt was ripped and her hair all messed up and she had scratch marks all over her and she was bleeding. She said Lauren attacked her."

"Really? Does Lauren strike you as violent?"

"Yes. I saw with my own eyes what she did to Dawn."

"But you didn't actually see her do it to Dawn."

"Look, maybe I had some doubt, but then look at Shane and Gary."

"So you do have an opinion of who killed them? You think it was Lauren?"

"I didn't say that...I don't know. But it could be."

"But Lauren wasn't at the bar with them. Do you know who was at the bar at the Windmill Inn with them before they were murdered?"

A strange expression came over Gabriela's face, but she quickly recovered. "Just because they were with some girl there doesn't mean that she was the one who killed them. I mean, why would that person go to a bar with them and then kill them? Maybe that person just went because, like, she wanted a drink or something. It doesn't mean anything."

Antonia was about to ask if she was the person with them at the bar, when Gabriela's cell phone rang. She jumped up and ran to the table where it was charging and answered it.

"You know what, I'm sorry, but I need to take this," she said.

"Can I ask you one more question?"

Gabriela shook her head and continued talking to the person on the other end. She was talking in a low tone, and all Antonia could hear was "uh-huh" and "there's someone here now."

Antonia knew she had lost her window, so she let herself out. At least she had a picture of Gabriela.

18

THE MINUTE ANTONIA LEFT GABRIELA'S HOUSE, SHE FELT A strong, almost magnetic pull that was yanking her in the direction of Dawn Costa's house in Napeague. She knew she had no business going there, and she wasn't even sure if she should bother because there was no guarantee that Dawn would even let her in, but she felt like she had to strike while the iron was hot, as they say. Her discussion with Gabriela had opened more questions rather than answered them, and she needed to gather as much information as possible before everyone got their story straight.

Antonia found it hard to reconcile the fact that Lauren was a crazed violent person. Now, granted, Antonia had met Lauren when she was disoriented and confused, stumbling out of the woods appearing all meek and vulnerable. Cue the violins. Could she have been faking it? Possibly. But it wasn't based on that interaction that Antonia was judging her; it was the time she saw her at Hampton Chutney with Dawn. By all accounts, Dawn was something of a leader, and that rang true when Antonia overheard her talking to Lauren. Dawn was bossy. It just didn't make sense that Lauren was scaring Dawn. It made more sense if it was the other way around. Antonia thought for sure Dawn was setting Lauren up in some way, and she needed to prove it.

The cinnamon donut that Nick had given her that morning had been a temporary fix, and Antonia found her stomach rumbling. She stopped at Mary's Marvelous to pick up a chicken sandwich with chipotle sauce on a baguette and a lime seltzer before continuing on her journey. It took her about two minutes to devour the sandwich, and she was glad that she had also grabbed a bag of Mary O's, which was Mary's Marvelous's answer to Oreo cookies, albeit with a chewier chocolate cookie dotted with chips. It didn't take much time for her to work her way through half the bag. When Antonia hit the stoplight by the post office where a long line of trade vehicles were streaming through on their way to lunch, she quickly tried Larry, but again the call went to voice-mail. She wondered why it was taking him so long to get back to her about the license plate and was irked to imagine that he was off investigating without her. If he was currently firing questions at that mysteriously aggressive man who was at the bar the same night as Shane and Gary, she would be pissed. Although she hated to, she had to admit that was the pot calling the kettle black. Here she was, setting off on her own line of inquiry and had left Larry oblivious. After she hung up with no answer, Genevieve called through, and although it was not convenient to talk on speaker, and the sound quality was less than cogent, Antonia felt that she owed Genevieve an update on her date with Nick.

"I'm sorry, I know I owe you a call..."

"Yes, I want to hear everything about Nick! All the gory deets! But first I have to tell you something kind of bad. Actually, very bad."

"What is it?"

"Are you driving?"

"Yes."

"Pull over," Genevieve commanded.

Antonia's hands became clammy and she did as she was told, slipping into the closest parking lot, which happened to be for the Yardley & Pino Funeral Home. *How ironic*, she thought, as she stared at a two-story brick building with white trim that thousands of dead bodies had passed in and out of for two decades. Her heart was thudding. She picked up the phone and switched it off speaker.

"What happened?"

"I saw Philip."

Antonia caught her breath. So he *was* in town. She had not been hallucinating. Of course she knew it, but it was one case where she hated to be proven right. "Where?"

"He came to the store this morning. He strolled in with that stupid smile on his face and then acts all casual and says, like, 'Hey, Genevieve, how's it going?'"

"What did you do?"

"I said, 'Philip, it's *not* nice to see you. What the hell are you doing here and you have to leave town.' He says, like, all smarmy, 'Oh, Genevieve, you shouldn't talk to me that way.' And I said, 'Antonia has a restraining order against you, and you have to leave. You have no business trying to get back into her life. She doesn't want anything to do with you. Get a life and get out.'"

"What did he say?"

"He laughed like a demon and told me it was a free country. I swear, I hate this guy. So you know what I did? I called the police. They came and are questioning him now."

"They are? Really?"

"Yes."

"But what will that do? I'm not optimistic. Unfortunately, the restraining order doesn't say that he can't be in the same town as me."

"Okay, maybe he can be, but we can make his life miserable while he's here. I've got all my friends on it, and we're calling every hotel and inn and telling them to turn him away."

Antonia loved Genevieve. "That's great, but not sure it can

help. He could stay at an Airbnb or something. Who knows? He's determined. And crafty."

"I'm going vigilante on his ass, Antonia. I don't want this guy to hassle you anymore. Don't worry, Antonia. I'll take care of him. I'm on it now, gotta go."

Antonia sat in the parking lot for a minute trying to compose herself. Her heart was racing as if she had just run ten miles at high speed. What could she do? Would Philip ever be out of her life for good, or was this something she would have to deal with forever? It didn't seem fair. She wasn't sure how to proceed and felt somewhat paralyzed. Now it seemed stupid to rush out to Napeague and try and interrogate Dawn; a total waste of time. She should head back to the inn and start cooking up a nice meal for Nick. He had requested risotto and he would get the best damn risotto he had ever tasted. It would melt in his mouth. She would swirl in mascarpone cheese and ensure that it was creamy as hell. They'd just received a nice shipment of chunky portobellos and fresh shiitake mushrooms, which would sauté up nicely and hold their own against the arborio rice. She put her car in drive and was about to pull out when she saw the door of the funeral home open and fake Cindy Boskin exit.

Now this was getting interesting, Antonia mused. What was she doing here? Was she here to claim Shane's body? Fake Cindy Boskin pulled sunglasses out of her purse and pushed them on her head to cover her eyes. She then checked her phone, sliding her fingertip up and down as if she was reviewing her emails, before throwing it back in her bag and moving across the lot toward a white car with Pennsylvania plates. Antonia quickly jumped out of her car.

"Cindy! Cindy!"

Fake Cindy Boskin did not even flinch, yet another reveal that her name was not Cindy.

"Hey, *you*!" yelled Antonia. "Fake Cindy Boskin!"

Fake Cindy Boskin froze. Antonia could see her body stiffen. She turned around. Her face did a complete one-eighty from friendly to angry. There was no flicker of hesitation, shame, or guilt in between.

"What do you want?" she sneered.

"It's me, Antonia Bingham from the Windmill Inn."

"I know." Fake Cindy Boskin folded her arms.

"I'm confused, did we end on bad terms?"

"I said, what do you want?"

"What I want is to know who are you? Because I know you're not Cindy Boskin. What's your real name and why did you lie to me?"

"It's really none of your business."

"Of course it's my business because it's legitimately my business. You pretended to be someone else and took advantage of my charity and stayed at my inn under false pretenses. For free, I might add. And then there was all that weird psychotic talk about children you don't have and honeymoons in charming little inns that you didn't visit."

A look of defiance appeared on Fake Cindy's face, and she dug in.

"I'm a grieving widow. I had to make arrangements."

"You're not the widow."

"Listen, Antonia, Shane was my husband for all intents and purposes. Of course we had our challenges, but we were ready to move forward."

"If you were so in love with him, why did you sleep with Larry on the morning of Shane's murder?"

She shrugged. "That was nothing. Sex isn't love. It was a mistake."

"I don't understand what's going on. Can you enlighten me?"

"I am going through a terrible time. I am suffering. People should be telling me how sorry they are for me and sending *me* condolences. She wants it all to be over, because she didn't care one bit about him."

"You mean Cindy Boskin?"

"Yes. I was the love of Shane's life and she knew it. I was his entire world. Of course we had challenges to overcome, but he was trying despite her. She hated Shane."

"How do you know?"

"Because Shane and I were inseparable. That bitch would call him and scream at him and make his life hell. He'd put it on speaker and let me hear her rant. She despised him. And I'm sure that she was the one who killed him."

"How can you be sure?"

"She had already tried to. Stabbed him once before. That's why he'd left her and was spending the summer out here. They were getting divorced, and we were to be united forever in matrimony. And now she's acting as if *she's* the legitimate widow. She won't tell me where his body is; she won't let me say goodbye. As a result I have to skulk around local funeral parlors to find him. I should be the one arranging everything. Not her."

"But that's no reason why you lied to me and stayed at my inn for free."

Her face became contorted. "Is this what it's all about for you? Money? You don't have a humane bone in your body to under-stand that I am suffering? You are a greedy person. If money means so much to you, then fine, here you go."

She pulled an envelope from Chase bank out of her purse and ripped it open. It was full of one-hundred-dollar bills, which she

promptly threw at Antonia. They cascaded in the air, mostly landing on the pavement. Antonia was glad it wasn't a windy day, and
she scurried to the ground to collect them.

"What are you doing?" Antonia asked. She shoved them back
at fake Cindy Boskin.

"Giving you your precious money. Now you can leave me alone."

"That's not the point. Here, take your money."

Fake Cindy recoiled as if Antonia were handing her a tarantula
on a platter. "I would rather die."

"Okay, that's so weird. Listen, I do want to help. What's your
real name?"

Fake Cindy Boskin gave her a look that indicated she was considering Antonia's question. Finally she answered. "Gloria. But I
won't tell you my last name for security reasons."

"Okay, Gloria. Listen, if you really think Cindy Boskin killed
Shane, why don't you tell the police?"

"They won't believe me."

"How do you know? If you have evidence that Cindy had
stabbed Shane, that would be useful to their investigation."

Antonia noted the look of hesitation on Gloria's face. There
was something she was not telling her.

"I can't do that."

"Why not? Gloria, is there something that you're not telling me?"

"Shane was stupid. He didn't want to get Cindy in trouble—he
said, mother of his children, blah, blah—so he told the hospital it
had been an accident, that he fell on his knife."

"Okay, well, maybe you can tell them it wasn't."

Gloria shook her head. "When it happened, I demanded he
leave her. I appeared at his office and..."

"And?"

"Well, he told his colleagues that I had stabbed him! That *I* was a crazy lunatic who wouldn't take no for an answer. Can you imagine?"

Yes, Antonia wanted to say. But instead she replied, "That's terrible. Is there any way you can prove otherwise? That Cindy did it?"

"I believe the only other person who knew the truth was Gary. And now he's dead also."

The visit to Dawn Costa's house was still an itch that Antonia needed to scratch, so she continued eastbound on her merry way. After Amagansett the landscape completely opened up and there were fewer commercial and residential buildings and a whole lot more sky and space. Antonia could feel her head clearing the instant she made the slight right toward Napeague, leaving gas stations and bait and tackle shops behind her. Like the rest of the Hamptons, this area had become incredibly trendy in recent years, attracting some celebrated designers and actresses. In addition, it was where the famous Lobster Roll (aka Lunch) restaurant was located, which had of late been featured in a famous television show that was a mating call for all of those who were starstruck and determined to seek out the "hippest" places.

Dawn's address, which Antonia had cribbed off Larry's notes earlier in the week, was on a street south of the highway, an area increasing in value daily. Antonia wondered how Dawn could afford such a location and thought of Ezekiel's comment that perhaps Dawn had a sugar daddy. Upon approach, Antonia saw that it was a nothing little house—small and one-storied with shingles darkened by the proximity to the salty ocean air, a tatty yard, and a driveway that needed a new shipment of gravel—whose land value was worth more than triple the house that perched upon it. The mailbox was beaten up and could have used a fresh coat of paint, but the front door was a cheery red with a coat of high gloss. There was a lime-green Toyota Land Cruiser parked in front with a vanity plate that said "SXYDWN," indicating Sexy Dawn was at home.

There was no need to ring the doorbell because when Antonia stepped on the front stoop, she could see clear through the windows to the backyard where Dawn Costa was lying on a lounge chair in a bikini, soaking up the rays. Antonia circumvented the house, made a right through the gate, and announced her arrival to her unwitting hostess.

"Hello, Dawn."

Dawn did not even stir. At first Antonia experienced a flash of panic that Dawn was dead (it seemed to be a trend these days), but when she drew closer, she saw that Dawn was wearing earbuds that were plugged into her phone and was transported away by some rock band in the cloud.

"Dawn!" said Antonia, poking her.

Dawn's eyes flew open, and she sat up abruptly, ripping the 'buds out of her ears. "What the hell?"

"Sorry to startle you."

Dawn's confusion turned to contempt when she realized who her interloper was. "What are you doing here?"

"I wanted to ask you some questions."

"I told you, I'm not talking to you without my lawyer."

"I know, I know, and I respect that. But there was just a pressing issue. Do you mind giving me your time for one second?"

Without an invitation, Antonia sat down on the lounge chair

next to Dawn and glanced around the yard. It was neatly kept, although there wasn't much to it. There was space for a pool but no pool, and room for a table set and a deck but neither of those. The two lounge chairs facing the yard were somehow begging for a focal point and Antonia knew once someone with money got their hands on this place there would be an oversized swimming pool and probably a swing set, hot tub, hammock, or other amenities. This was a budget situation.

Dawn swung her legs over the side of her lounge chair and stared at Antonia. Her gaze was unfriendly.

"You know, you really tend to butt in to things that have nothing to do with you."

"How do you even know why I'm here?"

"Okay, why are you here?"

The gauntlet had been thrown down by Dawn, and Antonia had to scurry to come up with a reason. Why was she here? The girl was not wrong to question it. She would start with honesty.

"I'm uncomfortable with this situation. You had booked a stay at my inn months ago and then you said you just booked it the other day. Why did you lie?"

"I must have forgotten."

"Forgotten? That seems weird."

"To be honest, I didn't book the inn. Lauren did."

"Lauren? Your stalker then not-stalker?"

Dawn nodded. "Yes. She booked it for me as a birthday present."

"That's a very nice present."

"She felt bad about what was going on."

"You mean her stalking you?"

"Right."

"Dawn, you realize how absurd this sounds."

"Whatever. Truth hurts."

"So she books you the inn and then ties you up in the inn? And leaves you fearing for your life? Then turns up at a murder scene, disoriented and claiming you were together?"

"Yeah, weird, right?" she asked insolently.

"Yes, very weird. And what about Gabriela Nesbo?"

"What about her?"

"It's another coincidence that you all worked together and she happens to live next door to Shane and Gary?"

"It's a small world."

"I doubt it's that small."

Dawn gazed down at her toes, which were coated with a chipped layer of purple lacquer, and bent down and ripped off a jagged nail. Antonia couldn't believe this girl was so relaxed when all evidence pointed to the fact that she was doing something criminal. At the very least, she had lied about Lauren tying her up, which was grounds for arrest for making fake claims to law enforcement. And at most, she was a murderer. Dawn finally glanced back up at Antonia.

"So, are we done here?"

"Done? We've barely begun. I don't think you realize how much trouble you're in."

"Oh, really? How much trouble am I in?"

"Well...when the police find out that you know Gabriela, and when they look more into your friendship with Lauren, they will find something."

"And what will they find?"

"They'll find...that the three of you conspired to kill Shane Boskin and Gary DiAngelo."

"Interesting. And how will they 'find' that out? How will they prove that? And by the way, why would we do that?"

It did not go unnoticed to Antonia that she had not instantly denied the accusation, rather she had clarified it.

"I think what happened was this: last summer, Shane and Gary, either one or both, tried to take advantage of you. It was traumatizing for you, but Lauren and Gabriela wouldn't back you up. Maybe they wouldn't go to the police or maybe they dismissed your accusations. So for a year, you plan to get back at all of them. In April you make a reservation for a room at the inn, giving yourself an alibi. Maybe you asked Lauren to do it for you as a gesture, whatever. Then you invite Lauren over and drug her and put her in the woods on Bull Path and then drug Shane and Gary and kill them. I think something is planned for Gabriela too, but I'm not sure what. But maybe you left evidence at her house. Any way you have it, you're framing them for the murder."

Dawn stared at Antonia for a minute. Then she slowly started clapping her hands together.

"Bravo! You nailed me. Wow, and I thought I was such a criminal mastermind. But all it took was one dumpy innkeeper to find out the truth." Dawn held out her hands to Antonia. "Why don't you just cuff me now? Are the police hiding in the bushes, waiting for my confession?"

"I'm certain I'm right."

"Of course you are! You got me! I plotted and planned a murder, then somehow gained superhuman strength to take on all of these big men like Shane and Gary and carry my friend Lauren, who has had one too many cheeseburgers in my opinion, into the woods and frame her. Wow. I'm awesome."

When she put it that way, Antonia couldn't deny her theory was flimsy. "Something like that."

"Something like that, right," said Dawn, nodding. "Now get the hell off my property before I call the police and accuse you of breaking and entering."

19

THE RESTAURANT WAS BOOKED TO CAPACITY, AND ANTONIA was busy with expediting the incoming dinner orders, so she really didn't have time to lament the fact that she had blown her chance with Dawn Costa. She did take time for brief mental recriminations with a note to self: have a plan. Sometimes it was not possible to wing it, she realized. One had to be at least, and at the *very* least, one or two steps ahead of a killer. Accusations and suppositions were one thing; proof was yet another. But without further ado, she returned to her priorities and assisted her very qualified team in the kitchen to await Nick Darrow's eight thirty reservation with feverish anticipation.

Antonia had to acknowledge that there was something very strange about being on the precipice of complete happiness. There is nothing more bizarre than having your dream come true, and being with Nick would really be a dream come true. When Antonia had pursued happiness, there had been a practical element to it all, a list of commands, a structure, and a map. And to be honest, always an elusive ending. But now that it was within reach, it opened an entirely different arena in her life, and she didn't know what to expect. It was an unsettling "be careful what you wish for" sensation that she tried to dismiss. She had thought herself an optimist, but with true love within her grasp, she felt the pessimism creep in. Was it because she had been burned before? Perhaps.

"He's here," said Glen with a secretive wink as he swept into the kitchen. Antonia had warned the staff earlier that he would be in attendance, and they had exchanged knowing looks, which she chose to ignore. *Let them think what they want*, she decided.

"Okay, thanks," she said, pushing a plate of brioche-crusted sea bass on the deck. She threw a parsley garnish on top of it and waited for the waiter to claim it.

Kendra sauntered over to where Antonia stood.

"Scram," she commanded.

"What do you mean?" asked Antonia.

"We all know you need to be out there to do your thing. Let us stay in here and do our thing."

Antonia was about to protest, but the look on Kendra's face told her it would be futile. Her eyes glided to Marty and Soyla's faces, as if searching for detraction, but their expressions confirmed that they were in accordance with their colleague. Instead of speaking, Antonia wiped her hand on her dish towel and threw it on her workstation. Wordlessly, she walked out of the kitchen to the mudroom where she hung up her apron, fluffed up her hair, reapplied her lipstick, and changed shoes before entering the dining room.

Nick Darrow was in a corner booth, languidly leaning against the cushion, resplendently turned out in a blazer and collared shirt. The glow that surrounded him was intensified, perhaps because his celebrity had set off a current among his fellow diners, or perhaps because the cobalt upholstery enhanced and electrified his blue eyes. Whatever it was, he was a point of light attracting all of the energy of the room, and when he raised his head to meet Antonia's gaze as she approached him, she couldn't deny the crackles of heat that she experienced. They call them "sparks" for a reason.

His smile was so genuinely happy that Antonia felt her heart drop to her feet.

"Hello, Chef."

"Hello there, um, patron?" She knew she had goofed.

Nick laughed. "That sounds strange. Just call me Nick."

"Okay, Nick."

She stood at the table staring down at him and felt at once awkward but at the same time excited.

"I once heard a story that the chef of this restaurant has a special guest she recites the menu to every evening. I wonder if I may be afforded the same privilege?"

He was referring to her ritual with Joseph. Almost every evening she would tell him what was for dinner and recommend what he should have. It wasn't always the most indulgent dishes on the menu—she had Joseph's heart and cholesterol level to think of—but it was always the dishes she knew he would enjoy. It had become a fun game between them, and she had confided the ritual to Nick. And now he wanted in on it.

"Of course, Nick, I can tell you what I would recommend. For appetizers there are a variety of dishes that you would enjoy. May I ask, are you a salad guy?"

"A salad guy? Why sure, Chef, but I prefer something hearty."

"We have a seared calamari with a spicy fennel arugula salad that always gets high marks."

"I'm sure everything gets high marks."

"I like to think so. In addition there is a delicious roasted yellow beet soup with tahini and pumpkin seeds. My personal favorite, though, is the trio of bruschettas—tomato and basil; burrata and local honey as well as olive tapenade. Then…"

"That sounds lovely but a bit too heavy for me."

Antonia turned around toward the voice behind her and couldn't believe what she saw. It was Melanie Wells, Nick's estranged wife.

She gave Antonia a small smile before she slid into the chair next to Nick, who appeared to be equally as stunned as Antonia.

"Melanie, what are—" before Nick could finish Melanie leaned over and gave him a peck on the cheek.

"What a coincidence, Nick; it truly makes one believe that great minds think alike."

Nick was angry. "What are you doing here?"

"I popped into town and decided I wanted a quaint local meal, after all those months of five-star dining on location, and this little inn came into my mind. I'm not sure why. I did remember we had a meal here once, although the meal itself was not so memorable. But that's what I want right now: ordinary. And I suppose that's what you want as well? Thus here we both are."

"Melanie! You're being very rude. I can't believe you have the nerve to show up here," hissed Nick.

"Why not?"

She lifted up the napkin at the place setting next to her (the one Antonia had told the staff to reserve for her) and thrust it in the air with gusto before placing it on her lap. There was amusement in her eyes as she took in Nick's astonished expression and when she looked upwards and gazed at Antonia, her retinas flickered with mirth. Evil mirth, Antonia might add.

"You were telling us the specials? Please do continue. I haven't yet heard anything I'm interested in eating."

Antonia noticed that Melanie was immaculately turned out in a tight rose-colored pantsuit, which enhanced her tanned, smooth skin. Her blond hair was blown out in a sexy Farrah Fawcett style that made her appear twenty years younger. She was close enough that Antonia noted that there was nary a wrinkle on Melanie's face, and if it was the work of plastic surgeons or dermatologists, then they all deserved the highest awards their professions offered because there was nothing artificial or pinched to suggest that they had ever touched Melanie's face. It took all of Antonia's might to compose herself. Her eyes widened, and she glanced at Nick, who turned and addressed his wife.

"Melanie, you were not invited, and you can't stay. I thought I had made everything clear."

"I'm just here for some food."

Nick was glowering.

Unfortunately a busboy took the inopportune moment to bring over the breadbasket and offer Nick and Melanie their choice of olive bread, Parker house rolls, whole-grain biscuits, or breadsticks. Of course, after much inquisition about gluten and sugar and all sorts of evil ingredients that might lurk in a breadbasket, Melanie selected the slimmest bread stick. Antonia was sure she would not even eat it; she merely wanted to prolong her presence at the table.

"And be a doll and bring me a glass of chardonnay," Melanie asked the busboy.

It was one of those times that Antonia regretted that she had not trained her support staff to say "I'll get your waiter," and she watched with dismay as the busboy hustled off to the bar to retrieve Melanie's beverage. All hands on deck was supposed to be a good thing. But in this case, it was not.

Nick attempted to stand up, but his position in the booth made it somewhat impossible with his wife to his right and his "girlfriend" standing to his left. He was left hunched over awkwardly. "Melanie, you're not staying."

She blinked several times before taking a sip of her water. "Don't make a scene, Nicholas."

"I'm not making a scene. I'm having dinner."

"And I'm joining you. Wouldn't it be odd if we were both at the same restaurant and not sitting together? The tabloids would be all over it. I thought we agreed to think of Finn."

Antonia could see the anger flooding Nick's cheeks. His breathing had intensified and he was using all of his patience to remain calm. "I am always thinking of our son. Don't even bring him into this."

"Wonderful. Then sit down and we will have dinner."

"I want you to go."

Melanie gave him a look that one gives a naughty child. "I will not leave. And you will sit down. People are beginning to stare."

"I don't care what people think," he replied with his voice raised.

Antonia glanced around the room. It was true, the two tables closest to Nick's had begun to eavesdrop, and one woman was shushing her husband so she wouldn't miss anything. No matter what was happening, no one wants this sort of scene at the inn.

"Yes, I do think it's best if you sit down," urged Antonia gently. "We have a delicious menu tonight, and there will be many more to come in the future. I'll send the waiter over with the menus."

With reluctance, and not before rolling his eyes at Melanie, Nick plopped back down. He was visibly irate; had he been a cartoon, steam would have been shooting out of both ears. Despite her anger and irritation, Antonia knew she had done the right thing to coax him to sit with his wife. Because, well, after all, she was his wife. Antonia moved to collect the waiter when Melanie held out her arm and stopped her.

"You were saying the specials. I'd like to hear them, please." Antonia paused and gazed down at her rival. Melanie's face was placid and she wore an innocent expression, but Antonia was now

aware that she was dealing with a formidable foe. She smiled beatif-
ically at the actress.

"Of course," she said, folding her hands demurely. "I must tell
you that the special ingredient we use in everything is butter. So
when I say that we have brioche-crusted snapper with wild rice,
please note that it is draped in butter sauce. We have a juicy filet
with an extra butter béchamel sauce. The grilled lobster tails are
glazed with butter and accompanied by creamed spinach and
butter-roasted potatoes. Lastly, we have an exquisite mushroom
risotto with butter-fried shiitake and portobello mushrooms
swirled with mascarpone. I do hope you will find something to
your liking on our butter menu."

Nick gave Antonia a crooked grin, and she could tell she had
scored a point in her invisible battle with Melanie. But Melanie
was not one to cower. She appraised Antonia from head to toe
before saying:

"Yes, it's quite obvious that you favor butter."

"Melanie!" said Nick harshly.

Melanie shrugged. "What? I'm talking about the menu."

Antonia had blushed but wouldn't be outdone. "Yes. I'm not
into anything artificial or fake. I'm all about warmth and comfort.
And I'll go get your waiter."

It was true it had been to her advantage that she was standing and able to make a quick exit before Melanie could retort, but
Antonia still chalked a win up for her team. That Melanie Wells
was a vicious little bitch. She was no doubt evil because she was
starving to death, and for what? To be as thin as a board? Clearly
Nick did not favor that type of woman. Antonia swung through
the kitchen door and marched toward the mudroom to put on
her apron.

"What, back so soon?" said Marty. But when he saw the expression on Antonia's face he softened. "You okay?"

"I'm fine," she replied, puffing out her cheeks. "It's just that we have a very unpleasant guest here. It's that horrible actress Melanie Wells!"

Marty made the connection at once. "Listen, Antonia. Don't forget, I'm a vet. I have no problem killing anyone you need whacked. I got your back, lady."

"Thanks."

"Antonia, if you want to hock a loogie in someone's food, we'll look the other way!" Kendra chimed in from her station.

"I hope I have not sunk that low, but I appreciate the support. I just can't believe that she showed up here."

"Cooking well is the best revenge!" Soyla said loudly, and everyone in the kitchen turned to face her. From a tiny woman who spoke softly all day long, it was a surprise to hear shouted fighting words. Everyone laughed and the tension was momentarily broken.

The dinner service felt interminable, and as it dragged on, it became more evident that Melanie Wells was not going down without a fight. She sent back every dish that she ordered, claiming it was either too cold or too hot or too spicy or underseasoned, and in the end her server reported that she didn't eat anything. Antonia had not wanted to sink to her level and avoided asking the waiter if he per chance happened to overhear what Nick and Melanie were talking about, but she did not have to anyway because Glen sauntered in and out of the kitchen with great frequency providing an update.

"He's answering her questions with yes or no," Glen reported on his first visit. "She's asked him if he got some repairs done on the house and he said yes and if he had told the house manager to call the pest control people about the stink bugs and he said no."

Antonia feigned indifference and did not want to pry further but secretly wished Marty, Kendra, and Soyla were more the gossipy type and attempted to interrogate Glen on every little detail, draining him for all that he knew. They did not, but Glen's loquaciousness proved useful tonight.

"She called him out on the monosyllabic answers and he said he had nothing more to say to her and she said, well, what about Finn—that's their son—I know that from *People* magazine—and he said he will answer questions if it has to do with their son, and so she keeps asking him things like, did he get Finn a new fleece and can he get Finn sneakers at Gubbins."

"Thanks for the update," Antonia said with feigned indifference.

Later in the evening, after Melanie had sent back her espresso (it was too cold) and Antonia was in a total and completely sour mood, Glen entered with uplifting news.

"He said she was behaving horribly and if she really cared about what the tabloids thought, she should stop being so difficult."

"Really?" Antonia asked, her interest piqued to the highest level of curiosity humanly possible. "What did she say to that?"

"She actually laughed—I think she knew I overheard—and then she put her hand out and pushed a piece of hair out of his face and said 'Oh, darling, you are too funny.'"

"What?"

Glen's eyebrows wiggled up and down. "I know. This tacky broad thinks she is so classy."

"You really think she's tacky?" Antonia blurted out, before returning to the cutting board in front of her and continuing to chop tarragon.

"Of course she's tacky. She's artificial. And she's not nice, which makes her tacky. I have met a lot of celebs in my life, a lot, and they can be really nice. They have no reason not to be; they owe their lives to us. They should be grateful. And I hate to say it, but especially the women, because when they hit forty, they are out the door. Their career is kaput."

"True," said Antonia, taking consolation in that fact. But in the back of her mind, Antonia knew she was wrong to be rooting against Melanie. She was Nick's wife after all, and they did share a child. They should be together, and it was probably time for Antonia to recuse herself and allow it. Although she did have to be honest, Nick himself said he was miserable. And it was hardly like he had left Melanie for Antonia, it was all just timing. Nick even said he was quite certain Melanie had a boyfriend. It was actually laughable for Antonia to think of herself as the other woman. For all she knew, she was just a cute fling for Nick, a small raft to help lead him out of the murky waters of his marriage, and once he got to shore, there was no telling that she would be useful anymore.

"They want to say goodbye," Glen announced after an hour.

"They do?"

"Well, she's in the bathroom, but he asked if you would come out."

"He did?"

"Yes."

"Go get him, Antonia," said Marty from behind the burner.

Antonia was about to fling off her apron and rush out of the kitchen when she stopped herself.

"No. I don't think that's a good idea. Please tell him good night for me."

Glen nodded. "Nice move," he said over his shoulder as he exited the kitchen.

She was not interested in playing games, but she didn't think it appropriate that she and Nick interact in the middle of her dining room in the middle of dinner service. They could talk tomorrow. She bent down and continued chopping, methodically and with increasing rapidity until the restaurant would have enough julienned basil to last a year.

"The risotto was fantastic."

Antonia looked up to see Nick smiling at her. Her staff immediately quieted and immersed themselves in their work, attempting to make themselves invisible so Antonia could have privacy.

"Thank you."

"I wish I could have eaten it with you."

"Yes…well." She wanted to say "another time" but decided not to. Perhaps there wouldn't be another time. Or perhaps there shouldn't.

"I'm really sorry about what happened."

Antonia waved her hand in the air as if she were swatting a fly. "Please, don't think anything of it."

"I have to drive Melanie home. She was dropped off here. Just like her to do this. Can we talk later?"

"Sure, anytime," said Antonia vaguely.

Nick leaned closer toward her. "Antonia, I'm really sorry about tonight. I had no idea Melanie was coming to town. I hate that she did this. I told you the woman is obsessed with playing games. It's inexcusable. I want to—"

He was about to whisper something, but he was interrupted. Larry Lipper banged open the door and stood on the threshold with his hands on his hips. He was perspiring heavily.

"Time to roll, Bingham," he commanded with Napoleonic authority. "We've got another body."

20

THUS ANTONIA FOUND HERSELF SITTING BESIDE LARRY LIPPER at ten o'clock at night, en route to yet another crime scene. She didn't feel guilty taking a quick leave of Nick.

"This is becoming a habit," said Antonia.

"Yeah, well, why did you have to change? Now we're late."

She looked at him incredulously. "Larry, the dead body's not going anywhere."

"Yeah, but I need to be the first one in. There are some wannabe crime reporters nipping at my heels, and I want to make sure to kick them away before they get the idea they can report on this crime."

"I'm sure you'll be the first one there. You said you heard it on the police radio?"

"Yeah."

"And why do you think it's connected to Shane and Gary's murders?"

"Duh, it's on the same street."

"Yes, I guess that means something. But I didn't come across the name 'Linda Mobley' at all in my investigation."

"Oh yeah, I was wrong about that. When you were busy braiding your hair or whatever you so desperately needed to do before you hustled into the car to solve crime, I heard another report on the scanner. The house was once owned by Linda Mobley, but she's already been in the ground for a couple of years, so it was actually her niece who was hacked tonight."

Suddenly, all of the pieces came together for Antonia, and she gasped. "You mean the victim was Gabriela?"

"Yeah, they said Gabriela, so probably."

"But that's Gabriela Nesbo, the one who worked with Lauren and Dawn. Oh, I don't believe it! I was just at her house. We had coffee together…"

Antonia was struck by how much sadness she felt. Gabriela Nesbo was dead? But she had wanted to be a decorator. She had plans. So sad.

"Wait a minute, you were investigating without me? What the hell, Bingham?"

"Before you get all pissy, don't forget you were AWOL today. What happened? Did you even look into the license plate that I sent you?"

Larry squirmed with discomfort. "Yeah, anyway, what can you tell me about this Gabriela Nesbo?"

Antonia gave Larry a quizzical look. "What happened?"

"All I know is she was found stabbed."

"I don't mean with Gabriela. I mean what happened to you with the license plate."

"Nothing. I think it may be a dead end. Or we let the police handle it."

Antonia's jaw dropped. She shifted in her seat so that she was completely facing Larry. He gave her a sidelong glance and quickly returned his attention to driving.

"This is not the Larry Lipper I know. 'Let the police handle it'? I have never heard that phrase come out of your mouth. Tell me now, Larry, or else. You know I can find out myself if I want to."

Larry banged his hands on the steering wheel. "Okay, okay! After you sent me the plate number I had my buddy run it down. It belongs to a guy named Eric Neiderhoffer. He lives in the city, but I scanned through Zillow and found out he has a place here near the old Bell Estate. I decided to make him a surprise visit. But you know, first I wanted to survey the scene, make sure I knew what we were dealing with. Next thing you know, this Eric calls the police and says I'm intruding. Wants to press charges and all that. It took a while to sort itself out."

"You mean you were arrested?"

"Not technically."

"But yes?"

"It's all because that jerk Deputy Kincaid was on duty. That guy has it out for me. Doesn't like the fact that he needs me to clean up crime in this town. None of my buddies were around, so he insisted on holding me in the pen. I had to get Burke down there to let me out. Jerk even gave me a court date."

She couldn't help but burst out laughing. Tears popped in her eyes. Larry gave her a disapproving look.

"Nice, Bingham. You think it's funny that I had to cool my heels in the clink?"

"Yes!" Antonia exclaimed giddily. She was heaving with chuckles. "I'm sorry, it's just the idea of you—little Larry Lipper—being locked up with some giant felons; I just can't get that hilarious image out of my head."

"There were no giant felons in there with me, just a guy who got a DUI and was sleeping it off."

"Okay, whatever. It's just too funny."

"I'm so glad you find it amusing," he said sarcastically.

There was a lot of police activity around Gabriela Nesbo's house and an officer was directing traffic. He motioned for Larry and Antonia to make a right, but Larry didn't budge, prompting the officer to approach. Larry rolled down the window and held up his press badge.

"Tell Lieutenant Gunn that Larry Lipper's here."

The young blond officer read Larry's press pass before recognition dawned in his eyes. "Ah yes, Mr. Lipper. I was specifically told not to allow you near the premises."

"What? That can't be right."

"That's from the chief. You're going to have to leave."

Larry was apoplectic. "What are you talking about?"

"Please turn your vehicle around."

"But…but we're not even going to the crime scene! We're heading to visit my friend Iris Maple."

"I can't let you through."

"Listen, Officer, Iris Maple is an elderly lady on the verge of death. The murder of her neighbor just may send her over the edge. Consider this a wellness call. You don't let me through? Blood on your hands and a cover line in the *Star* about how you hate old people. And don't think I won't be naming names."

The officer hesitated, and it was enough for Larry to roll up his window and press his foot on the accelerator toward Iris's house.

"That was cold, Larry. Bad karma."

"You gotta do what you gotta do."

There was no answer at Iris Maple's door, and for a split second, Antonia thought maybe Iris Maple really did need a wellness call, but then they were waved over by an older man on the edge of the driveway.

"Looking for Iris?" he asked helpfully. He was approximately in his late sixties and wore his Bermuda shorts hiked up and belted in the manner of a tourist.

"Yes, we wanted to check on her. All this murder going on in her neighborhood could cause that old ticker of hers to stop. Don't want the old biddy keeling over on us," said Larry.

The man chuckled, his fleshy lips quivering below his thick, white mustache. "Iris Maple will outlive us all, you can be certain of that. She is, however, not here."

"Do you have any idea where she might be?" asked Antonia, trying to be extra pleasant to make up for Larry's impertinence.

"Went with her nephew up island. Asked me to collect her newspapers while she's away."

"That's right, she mentioned she was leaving town," said Antonia.

"And how long will that be?" asked Larry.

"A couple of days." He gestured toward Gabriela's house and all of the police activity. "I'm glad Iris is somewhere safe. I'm starting to worry about living on this street. Shame about the girl."

Larry instantly donned his reporter cap and strolled up to the man. "I'm Larry Lipper, eminent crime reporter from the *East Hampton Star*. What's your name?"

"John Winchester."

"Mr. Winchester, did you know the victim, Gabriela Nesbo?"

"Didn't know her. Didn't even know her name until today. I saw her every now and then when I was driving by, but there was no socializing or anything. Not that kind of neighborhood. I've never even met my next-door neighbors; they only come a couple of weeks in July. I share my house with my brother's family: he gets June and July, I get August and September. We shut it up in the winter when the wife and I are down in Florida. It's funny, we didn't even know Iris lived on our street; the wife met her at a garden tour and made the connection. Might never have known."

"Did you hear anything suspicious last night?"

"I don't think so."

"What about any unusual or unfamiliar cars in the neighborhood? Did you see any? Maybe parked in Gabriela's driveway?"

"Yes, that I did."

"What?" Antonia and Larry exclaimed in unison. Larry whipped out his little brown book prepared to jot down notes.

"Yes, I was out walking my pooch and passed right by the house."

"Can you describe the car to me? Color and make?"

The man scratched his head idly. "Well, there were so many, it would be hard to remember... I think there was a blue one, and a white one—"

"Wait a minute, what do you mean?" Larry interrupted.

"Gabriela was having a party. There were about two dozen people there at the pool. The music was blasting, so no one heard anything. The cop told me Gabriela went inside to get more chips and when she never came out, her friend went looking for her and found her dead in her bathroom. The sliding doors in her bedroom were open so they think the killer went in or out through them. But it could have been someone at the party, although of course they all deny it. They took them all down to the station for questioning. Who knows? I'm just glad we have a German shepherd who would eat anyone alive if they tried that nonsense on me or the wife."

Something occurred to Antonia. "Mr. Winchester, did you happen to see a lime-green Toyota Cruiser with a vanity plate?"

His face brightened. "Why, yes, I did. Took me a second to figure out that it must say Sexy Dawn, because when I first saw the SX, my mind immediately went to baseball and I thought, good lord, we have a Red Sox fan in the neighborhood. I'm Yankees all the way. But then I got it. Was wondering if the person had a matching car with plates that said Sexy Sunset."

"Actually, Dawn is the name of the owner of the car," explained Antonia.

"Oh, I see. That explains it. I suppose she thinks very highly of herself."

"Yes, she definitely does," concurred Antonia.

"That's millennials for you."

Unable to get close to Gabriela's house, Larry and Antonia decided to head over to the police station and see what sort of activity was transpiring there. In particular they were interested to see who the police had detained, hoping that a "person of interest" would reveal themself and they would have further insight into what had happened. In any event, Antonia felt it was a good distraction from all of the upsetting events of the evening. From the fraught dinner with Nick and Melanie to the sad murder of Gabriela Nesbo, it had been an emotional roller coaster.

"I'm still in shock over Gabriela. I only just met her and now she's dead," lamented Antonia. "It's so sad. I even took her picture."

Antonia held up her phone to Larry, who barely glanced at it.

"Yeah, well, what can you do? Actually, what you can do is catch her murderer," advised Larry.

"All I know is that Dawn is somehow behind all of this. You know I never did show Gabriela's picture to Glen and Jesse to see if she was the one at the bar with Shane and Gary that night. I'm sure it was her. I bet Dawn enlisted her and Lauren to trap Shane and

Gary so she could kill them and put the blame on them. Now she's picking them off. I would be worried if I were Lauren. Actually, we should really find Lauren."

"I'm sure the police can deal with that."

"I wouldn't be so sure."

"I don't know, Antonia... While your amateur theory seems interesting, I have a really hard time buying that Dawn is some criminal mastermind."

"I know," said Antonia, biting her lip and nodding her head. "I agree. But that's why she messed up."

Larry and Antonia didn't dare enter police headquarters due to past cautions from the officers to stay out of police business, so instead they sat outside in the parking lot trying to scan the faces of the few people who were coming and going. It was difficult to make people out in the darkness. There were rows of white patrol cars lined up on one end of the structure. They reminded Antonia of sharks lying in wait for their prey. A few cops exited and entered the squat, white building through the doorways that were flanked with giant police shields, but other than that, it was quite mundane work. Larry grabbed a McDonald's bag from the back of his car and pulled out a quarter pounder with cheese from a Happy Meal box that had been shoved inside.

"Want some?" he asked Antonia, offering her the greasy bag.

She recoiled. "Larry, the closest McDonald's is in Southampton. When did you purchase this?"

He shrugged. "Yesterday."

"Vile."

"No, don't worry, McDonald's puts all sorts of stuff in their food so it can stay edible and fresh for months. Did you hear that they buried a guy with McDonald's french fries and like two years later, they had to exhume his body and the fries were still good?"

"I have absolutely no response to that. I can't imagine you can even hear what you are saying. And please do me a favor, never use the words 'fresh' and 'McDonald's' in the same sentence."

"Whatever," he said, taking a large bite of his burger. "Your loss."

"Why do you get the Happy Meal, may I ask? Are you escorting children around?"

"Duh, free toys."

Larry had a chocolate milk in his cup holder, and he flipped open the top with zest and glugged down half the bottle. Unable to watch this abomination, Antonia turned her focus toward the front door of the police station, which had opened and a man was exiting. She couldn't ascertain a clear view so she squinted and leaned forward in her seat to decipher the person swaggering out.

"You and me on another stakeout, Bingham," Larry said gleefully. "Just like old times…"

"Oh no!" whispered Antonia, her voice ripe with fear.

Larry leaned forward with excitement. "Who is it? You got an eyeball on our mass murderer?"

"It's Philip. My ex-husband."

"No way, that guy?"

They both watched in silence as Philip walked to the edge of the building and scanned the parking lot. As soon as he glanced in the direction of Larry's car, Antonia cowered down, afraid that he would see her. She peeked out, but it appeared that he wasn't interested in their car. He kept glancing at his cell phone.

"Want to tell me what he's doing here?"

She peeked through the window from her crouched position.

She was completely rattled. "He's back to make my life hell. Fortunately, the cops are on top of it. Genevieve had called me earlier to tell me that she had called the police on him, so I suppose they detained him."

Larry leaned back in his seat and gave Antonia a pensive look. "I'm surprised that guy is your type."

"Me too, I know. What do you mean?"

"You can tell by the way he walks that he thinks he's hot stuff. All macho and everything. I'm all about show don't tell."

"Yeah, well, he's definitely not. What's he doing now?"

Larry glanced out the window. "Just pacing around yelling into his phone."

"That sounds like him."

"What a loser that he can't take no for an answer."

"Yeah, it's true when you put it that way. He is a loser."

It was a good way to view Philip, as a loser. He would absolutely hate that assessment. He thought he was a winner in every way and that was why Antonia's departure was inconceivable to him. She was grateful that he had been brought to the police station. All she could hope for was that Sergeant Flanagan had told him to stay away from her. Fingers crossed.

"You going to stay down there?" asked Larry, motioning toward Antonia's contorted position between the glove compartment and the front seat.

"I don't want him to see me."

Larry looked out the window. "Well, well, what have we here?"

Antonia craned her neck to see. A woman had walked out of the police station and over to Philip. From Antonia's awkward position, it was difficult for her to be certain, but she thought it might be...

"It's Dawn."

"What?" yelped Antonia. She had forgotten that she was under the dashboard and popped up, hitting her head as she did so. "Ouch!"

As she rubbed her head, she sneaked a peek in time to watch Dawn walk up to Philip and say something. He shook his head and laughed, and then they continued talking.

"Um, does your ex-hubby know Dawn?"

"Not that I know of," said Antonia without confidence.

"They look awfully chummy."

It was true. They were chattering away easily.

"But wait...Dawn had the room next to Tomas Stefanowski at the inn. Maybe it really was Philip and they *are* in this together."

Dawn began rustling around her bag and pulled out a cigarette and lighter. Philip took the lighter from her and debonairly lit her cigarette.

"What a gentleman," Larry declared.

They watched in silence as Dawn sucked down her cancer stick and continued conversing. Antonia noted she looked fairly animated and happy considering her friend Gabriela had just been murdered. What was her connection to Philip? Was she in cahoots with him all along? If Philip was Tomas Stefanowski, then that meant that he and Dawn had connecting rooms at the inn. Had she helped him plant the surveillance cameras?

"They're on the move," Larry announced.

They watched as Philip and Dawn walked toward the row of cars out of their view. They heard an engine start up, and then a minute later, Dawn's lime-green Toyota pulled out of the lot with Philip in the driver's seat.

"Wow," said Antonia.

"Yeah, wow. Shall we follow her?"

Larry started his ignition.

"No. Please take me home. I'm tired."

Larry was about to say something but stopped. "You got it."

21

AFTER A HORRIBLE NIGHT'S SLEEP, ANTONIA WOKE EARLY FEELing as if she had a hangover. She took extra time applying a thick layer of wrinkle serum and face cream, attempting to keep creeping lines at bay. It brought her joy to think that her little effort might yield some fountain of youth results, but she knew it was a crapshoot. At the end of the day, you can lather, slather, and primp, but it all came down to good genes. Oh, and staying out of the sun, which wasn't such a problem for Antonia considering her workload at the inn and side job as a wannabe sleuth. She donned her "exercise" clothes (stretchy pants and long-sleeved T-shirt) and was about to set out for a walk on the beach when she stopped. Did she really want to face Nick this morning? Chances were high that he would be there with his dogs. Of course she had to discuss what had happened last night with Melanie, but she felt totally weary and had no energy to tackle sensitive topics with high emotional stakes. The events of the previous evening needed to percolate in her mind before she composed a plan. It would be a shame if she said anything premature or emotional, and she was fragile enough to do just that. She did, however, feel that it would do her good to walk and clear her head, so instead of heading to Georgica Beach, she drove to Egypt Beach and walked left toward Amagansett, where there would be no chance of running into Nick.

If someone had told her a year ago that she would be diverting her route in order to avoid a movie star with whom she was somewhat involved, she would not have believed it. *It was funny how so much could change so quickly*, she mused as she set out on her walk. The day was bright, splashy with sunlight, and only a small stream of clouds forming an arc, as if there was a distant smoker in the sky. It was as if no one told the gods that summer was over. There were several dog walkers and joggers along this stretch of the beach, but none that Antonia recognized. She walked briskly, taking the clear air into her lungs and trying to push any stressful thoughts out of her mind. When she returned to her car to shake the sand out of her shoes, she had a voicemail from Genevieve waiting. Antonia retrieved her message.

"Where have you been? I've been calling. Okay, well, we got the police to take Philip to jail or whatever, but they said they can only give him a stern warning, not arrest him. But don't worry, I'll stay on it! Also, I saw Joseph in town yesterday with a woman; she's…something else. Remind me to tell you about her. I hope he's not, like, dating her. TBD. Call me!"

Antonia knew she was correct not to trust Cheryl! That woman had slippery written all over her face. Antonia tried Genevieve back, but it went straight to voicemail. She'd call her when she returned home. In the meantime, she had to figure out how to tell Joseph. She didn't want him to think she wanted him all to herself and was sabotaging his chance for love. It must be dealt with delicately. Perhaps it was best to sweeten him up. She knew he liked the apple cider donuts made of chickpea flour from Jack's in Amagansett, so she decided to make a slight detour to the hipster coffee bar. It was a little piece of Brooklyn replete with bearded fedora wearers and girls in overalls.

The line was short and Antonia ordered two donuts and a cappuccino and stood to the side to wait for her drink to be ready. She tried Genevieve again, but there was still no answer. Antonia took a nibble of the donut while she waited. She had bought two for Joseph, but she remembered his cholesterol and knew he would be just as happy with one. She wandered over to the front where there was a stack of free local magazines and picked up a copy of *Hamptons*. Most of the publication consisted of party pictures taken at various charity benefits and horse shows that summer folk frequented, and Antonia knew very few of the featured guests. She did recognize some people who had dined at the inn, but other than that, it was pages and pages of well-groomed and tanned party people beaming from the two-dimensional world. She knew there was a part of the population that considered it a great accomplishment to have their picture displayed in a magazine, but Antonia couldn't understand what the fuss was about. Was it some sort of primal urge to document the fact that you existed or pure vanity?

Her name was called, and she was about to close the magazine and retrieve her coffee when something caught her eye. She opened the page as far as it would go and stared at the picture of the smiling blond woman next to the handsome man. It was Cindy Boskin (the real Cindy Boskin) and Paul DiAngelo, and if Antonia had any doubt, their names were in the caption below. At the top of the page it said, "Veuve Clicquot party at Baron's Cove." The date was August 10. That meant Cindy had been lying to her when she said she hadn't come out to the Hamptons this summer. She had most definitely been here, and with Paul DiAngelo to boot. Why hadn't they confessed that when she talked with them? In fact, Cindy had gone to great pains to say she wasn't out here this summer. And Paul had insisted he had "absolutely no idea" that her marriage was in a precarious state. Big fat liars, they were.

"Antonia?" the barista repeated, this time with more urgency as if Antonia had suddenly decided to abscond into a caffeine-less world and she was her only hope at salvation.

"I'm here!" she said, moving toward the counter and claiming her frothy beverage. She folded the copy of the magazine and tucked it under her arm as she walked out the swinging screen door. And right into Lauren Wayne.

After they both mumbled apologies, there was an awkward beat where they lingered in the doorway. Antonia knew this chance meeting was too great an opportunity to let pass without some sort of interrogation. Since she didn't have time to plan out her questions, she blurted out the first thing that came to her mind.

"Are you a killer?"

"What?" asked Lauren.

"Did you kill Gabriela?"

Lauren's face contorted from surprise to anger. "Are you crazy? I would never kill anyone. Gabriela is my friend. I'm devastated. I've been up all night crying since I heard the news."

Antonia gave her the hairy eyeball and indeed could confirm that Lauren's lids were red-rimmed and swollen and there were dark puffy bags hanging below. But she also knew that Lauren and her friend Dawn were sly as foxes, and she couldn't let her off that easily.

"Who did it then?" she demanded.

"How the hell do I know?" asked Lauren.

"Was it you and Dawn?"

"I'm not a killer."

"What about Dawn, is she?"

Lauren glanced down uneasily before lifting her head and meeting Antonia's gaze. "I don't know."

"You don't know?"

"I don't... I hope not."

"You hope not?" repeated Antonia. "That's not a very confident answer."

"Well, I'm not very confident she isn't. Someone is killing these people. And it's not me."

"Huh," Antonia retorted. She was desperately trying to think of more questions but before she could, Lauren pushed past her into the store.

"And if you will now excuse me, I am going to get some coffee," Lauren said on her way past.

"Oh, you do that," replied Antonia.

Joseph was in the parlor when Antonia got back to the inn. He was sitting by the window, sipping a cup of tea, a mass of newspapers spread out before him.

"Hi there!" Antonia bounced with extra gusto. She was worried that she would upset him once she told him about Cheryl, so she decided to overcompensate with unbridled enthusiasm.

"Hello, my dear," replied Joseph, giving her a warm smile.

"I brought you this," she said, handing him the paper bag.

"Thank you!"

He glanced inside, and his expression became quizzical. "A bag of crumbs?"

"Wait, what?" Antonia grabbed the bag back out of his hands and glanced inside. It was true. Except for a few meager dusts of sugar, there were no longer any donuts. Could it be that she had eaten both? She remembered absentmindedly chewing on them as she drove home pondering what to make of the newest revelation of Cindy and Paul. Was she seriously that gluttonous?

"I'm so sorry, Joseph. I think I got overexcited. I had picked up a donut for you from Jack's, and I'm so embarrassed but I ate it. Wow, epic fail."

"That's okay, as long as it was tasty."

"Yes, it actually was delicious, but I'll not dwell on that."

She sunk in the chair opposite him, a smile frozen on her face. Joseph arched an eyebrow.

"Don't look so guilty. I already had breakfast, my dear."

"It's not that."

"What is it then?"

Joseph's look became serious, and suddenly Antonia realized she could not be the one to say anything about Cheryl. Let someone else break his heart—aka the real person breaking his heart—Antonia was not going to be complicit. And besides, when she thought about it, the truth was she hadn't talked to Genevieve, so she technically did not know what Gen was alluding to when she said that Cheryl was something else. She could have meant that she was hilarious or brilliant. Although she did add that she hoped Joseph wasn't dating her. But that could be because she hoped Joseph wasn't dating her because she wanted to! Although that was impossible; Genevieve wouldn't want to date a woman. Bottom line was, until Antonia had concrete facts, she would remain mum. So instead of plying Joseph with donuts and bad news, Antonia took the time to fill him in on everything that had happened in the past twenty-four hours and ended with showing him the picture of Cindy Boskin and Paul DiAngelo from *Hamptons* magazine.

"I wonder why she would lie about not being here this summer when it could be so easily proven that she was here," Joseph commented.

"I know. Makes no sense."

"But is it your suggestion that she and this Paul are together? Did you sense that when you met them?"

"Not really. But they were both in shock, or pretending to be because they killed them."

"And from what I understand, she went to great pains to say that she and her husband were separated. Perhaps Paul wouldn't care that Cindy was with another man if he were with so many other women."

"Some men just can't let go. Even if they have other women on the side, they are still determined to act vengeful toward their wives."

Joseph knew who she was referring to, and his tone became gentle.

"When will Philip disappear?" Joseph mused. "That man does not want to take no for an answer."

"I know. Never did."

"I do hope he's not mixed up with the murders of these men and young women…although that said, it would be a good opportunity to put him in jail and throw away the key."

"Truth," replied Antonia, feeling very gangster. But inside she was tense. Where was Philip now? Had he left town, or should she expect to turn a corner and find him there?

"In regard to the murders of Shane and Gary, it always seems like there are more questions than answers when you get close to the end. I think you have two tasks: you need to further explore this man who was at the bar the night of the murders, the big fellow—"

"Eric Neiderhoffer."

"Yes, him. And give him a gold medal for locking up Larry Lipper."

"Ha, ha," laughed Antonia. She knew that Joseph was not a fan of Larry's.

"I jest, but in all seriousness, you need to ascertain if he is at all connected to this case. And you also have to locate Tomas Stefanowski and decipher if he is really Philip, and if not, then what his connection is to the events that unfolded."

"You're right."

"That said, I implore you not to put yourself in danger. Can I urge you to contact your friend Sergeant Flanagan and place him in charge of these inquiries?"

"You know I would love to in theory, but once I have a bee in my bonnet…"

Joseph sighed. "I know. You have a proclivity for danger."

"That's not true." Antonia began to protest but then stopped herself. "You're kind of right."

"Good. Now is there any way I can assist you?"

"I'm sure we can think of something."

Antonia spent a few hours in her office following up on all the real work that she was supposed to do every day—that is, clerical. There were communications from travel agents with whom she had been forging relationships in an effort to coax them into recommending the Windmill Inn to travelers. She had to write up a little spin on why her inn was better than every other in town and what she could offer tourists from around the globe. In addition she had to review the onslaught of bills that her accountant had sent over, which always put her in a chipper mood (not), as well as a stack of estimates for a new heating system that needed to be assessed. There were the usual solicitations from local charities for use of the inn for their benefits that required an answer. The list was endless. It was Antonia's least favorite part of owning an inn.

Connie popped in to say that Sergeant Flanagan would stop by this afternoon at around three p.m. At first Antonia bristled—his visits always made her feel as if she were a child sent to the principal's office for bad behavior—but then she relaxed. Maybe she should download absolutely everything she knew and let him finish out the investigation. There was no shame in letting it go and returning to focus on the real issues in her life. Especially now that she had a romantic life.

Speaking of which, Nick had left her a message that he wanted to talk with her. She hadn't purposely screened his call. She was on the phone with a travel agent in England when she saw a blocked number try her cell, and she knew it must be him, but she was glad that she both had a valid excuse for not picking up as well as a chance to hear what he had to say before speaking to him directly. Unfortunately, all he had said was that it was Nick and to call him back. She listened to the recording several times attempting to gauge his tone. (Was he desperate for her to call him back? Was he resigned to the fact she might not? Did this classify as life or death for him?) Sadly there were no inflections in his voice that revealed his emotional state. Thus she had no choice but to call him back, yet, again, she wanted to take her time. She had never thought of herself as one of those gals who plays coy, but perhaps she was growing up.

Glen popped his head in her office around lunchtime. Antonia had just returned from preparing herself a healthy lunch: avocado toast with a poached egg. She felt very au courant squeezing the lemon, dappling it with sea salt and freshly ground pepper, and flaking it with chia seeds. Perhaps this was the fall she would get healthy! She instantly had visions of herself strolling on the beach in a bikini with washboard abs, preaching to the masses on the joys

of all that healthy eating. It was all fun and good, but the problem
was she finished the toast in less than two minutes and was instantly
hungry again five minutes later. This after having ingested not one
but two donuts for breakfast. There was a reason food trends like
avocado toast were merely food trends: they didn't sate you. Give
her a gooey cheese plate any damn day of the week.

"I think it's her," said Glen.

Antonia was pulling out an emergency pack of Nutella with
pretzel sticks when he came bursting into her office.

"Who?"

"That girl that was killed. Gabriela something. I think she was
the one here that night with the dead hedge funders."

Antonia swiveled her chair around. "Are you sure?"

"Am I one hundred percent sure? No. But I was looking at the
pic you sent me and I pulled up her social media stuff, and yeah.
She looks right. She had dressed really plain though. Like on pur-
pose, I kind of think. Not sure. But she had those bushy eyebrows
that I didn't remember until I saw Gabriela's pictures."

"Wow, okay, thanks for letting me know."

"No prob. And listen, where do you want me to put the movie
star tonight? Table three?"

"What movie star?"

"Melanie Wells. She must have loved the food last night 'cause
she booked again."

The color drained from Antonia's face. "There must be some
mistake."

"I don't think so. Her manager called and asked for a table for
two. Said she couldn't wait to come back."

Antonia gulped.

"I'll put her up front so people can see her? Get the crowd excited?"

"No. Put her in the back. Table sixteen."

"By the bathroom?"

"Sure. She'll love the privacy."

Glen gave her a curious look before leaving. Antonia knew she was being immature, but she was also certain Melanie was up to something. She hadn't eaten a bite of her food and relished sending it back. There was no way she was returning for the cuisine. But the question was, who was her dinner partner? She had booked a table for two. Was Nick accompanying her? That would be cruel. Why would he do that to her? She had known he was complicated, but this was plain diabolical. Antonia's blood began to boil. Just as she picked up the phone to call him and give him a piece of her mind, her cell rang. She glanced at the screen, saw that it was a blocked call and knew Nick must have beaten her to the punch. She couldn't wait to give him a piece of her mind.

"Listen," she began into the phone, without even greeting him. "I don't know what sort of sick game you're playing. But this is too complicated and I am not interested in getting in the middle of your marital drama. You told me it was over, but clearly Melanie does not agree with you. It was never my intention to be the other woman. I would never break up a marriage. I think we should not see each other until you figure out what you want."

There was a pause, and she could hear Nick breathing. Then he spoke. Only it wasn't Nick's voice, it was Philip's.

"Well, well, Antonia, baby, it seems that you are screwing up yet another person's life. I'm on Team Melanie on this one."

Antonia's heartbeat quickened. "Philip? What do you want? You know you're not allowed to contact me."

"That's no way to say hello to your husband."

"*Ex*-husband," Antonia corrected.

"Semantics. But let's not argue, shall we? Too much arguing! You have to stop all this now. I am getting very angry at your attacks on me. Very angry. Rein in your attack dogs, tell them to leave me the hell alone, and listen very carefully. You and I are bound together forever. It's our destiny. We're entwined. And one way or another, I'm going to make you realize that. There is no you without me."

There was no doubting he was insane. Antonia didn't know what to say. "There is no you and me. I'm going to keep having you thrown in jail every time you come near me or contact me. Do you understand?"

"Now listen here," he hissed. "You understand something. You're mine. If I see you again with another man or putting on white lacy underpants with the intention of shacking up with another man, you're done for. I'm a patient guy, but my patience is wearing thin. This will be over soon."

Antonia hung up on him. How did he know about her underwear? She shivered and sat back in her seat, glaring at her phone as if it were responsible for her misery. She prayed it wouldn't ring again. Philip sounded even crazier and more threatening than usual. She was truly scared. As soon as Sergeant Flanagan came by, she would tell him everything and come up with a plan. There had to be something the law could do, right?

She leapt out of her chair and fled her office to head to the kitchen to make herself a cup of tea. Or perhaps something stronger. She needed to be around people right now, gather her thoughts, come up with a plan.

22

"Ah, Antonia, we were just coming to find you. Ruth and Penny wanted to talk with you," said Jonathan.

Antonia had literally almost bumped into them when she turned the corner in the front hall. Jonathan instantly sensed her distress.

"Is everything okay?" he asked with concern.

"Yes, yes," she answered with no confidence in her voice. He put his arm on her shoulder and leaned in to say something but before he could the two ladies pushed past him, brimming with gossip.

"Antonia we have to talk to you!" remarked Ruth.

"We have some hot news about—" Penny glanced around to make sure no one was listening and then dropped her voice to a whisper. "About the murders!"

"Which ones?" asked Antonia wearily.

"Are there more?" squealed Penny.

Ruth practically rubbed her hands together. "Has a killer struck again?"

"I'm not sure… Who are you referring to?" asked Antonia.

"We're talking about the Wall Street gentlemen. Shane and Gary," said Penny.

"As per your instructions, we followed the couple that came to tea at the inn," said Ruth with great pride.

"Wait, what? I didn't ask you to follow them," said Antonia, suddenly worried. "Let's go in here."

She took Ruth and Penny by the arm and led them into the library.

"Do you want me to come?" asked Jonathan.

"No, it's fine. We just have to clear some things up," said Antonia, making one of those gestures to imply that she had it all under control.

"We're solving crimes!" trilled Penny. "You are not going to believe what we discovered about the murders!"

Antonia closed the double doors, catching the eye of two guests standing at reception who gave her puzzled looks when they heard the word "murder." She gave them a wink and fake smile as if it were all a big joke and pressed the doors tightly. She motioned for Penny and Ruth to sit down. They did so reluctantly, twitching with excitement.

Antonia sat down in the upholstered wing chair across from them. "So what's up?"

"After Paul and Cindy left the inn, we decided to tail them," offered Ruth.

"Cagney and Lacey style," interjected Penny.

Ruth turned to her and frowned. "I'd like to think more like Starsky and Hutch."

"Good point," agreed Penny.

"We hopped in our car and followed them out of the parking lot. Now here's where it gets interesting. We assumed that they would be heading back to New York. Our plan was to follow them as far as the Seafood Shop in Wainscott, then we would do a U-ey and get back in time for our bridge game. But *quelle surprise,* they did not make a westbound turn! Instead they made a left and drove to the parking lot where the Domaine Franey wine store is located."

"Did you know there was once a Gristedes grocery store there? Long ago," mused Penny.

"Not important," retorted Ruth, irritated by the interruption. "Well, Penny and I had no idea what was going on. We thought perhaps they wanted to grab a bottle of wine for the road, which seemed a little silly, particularly since why go to this specific wine store that was out of the way? There were plenty on the way to the city…"

"But then we thought maybe there was a specific wine that this store had that they wanted for the road," interjected Penny.

"Yes, because not everyone carries every wine, and there is a very nice selection at Domaine Franey," said Ruth. "Well, we all pull into the parking lot, and don't you worry, Antonia, we were the epitome of discretion, and then we wait for them to get out of their car, but they don't."

"They just sit there," said Penny with a nod.

"At this point, we are not sure what is going on. But we knew that you had asked us to keep an eye on this couple."

"That's not what I meant," said Antonia, but her voice was drowned out by Ruth.

"And we wanted to fulfill our promise to you. So we are sitting for about ten minutes…"

"Maybe fifteen," Penny corrected.

"Could be fifteen. Yes. And then another car pulls into the lot. A white car with Pennsylvania plates."

"I wrote down the number!"

Antonia's interest was piqued, and she sat erect in her chair. "I know whose car it is."

"It was an Asian woman," said Ruth firmly, ignoring Antonia. "I'd say midthirties…"

"Yes, I've met her," inserted Antonia.

"Well then, do you know what happened?" asked Ruth.

"Her name is Gloria. She was Shane Boskin's girlfriend, and she pretended to be his wife, Cindy. She's been driving around to funeral homes trying to find his body. She said the real Cindy Boskin won't tell her where he is being held, and she was demanding to be informed. She said his marriage was over. It's a very tense situation," said Antonia. She was pleased to be one step ahead of them.

Ruth's eyebrows shot up, and she and Penny exchanged amused looks.

"Didn't look tense to us," said Ruth.

"No, they looked pretty friendly," added Penny.

"What do you mean?" asked Antonia.

"Let us tell our story without interruptions and you will find out," said Ruth in a snippy tone.

"Sure."

"They all gathered together in the parking lot—Cindy, Paul, and the Asian woman."

"Gloria."

"Gloria, right. Penny and I walked over to where we were within earshot but not conspicuous. We pretended to be dotty old ladies, looking for our keys and our shopping lists, searching through our bags, but in reality we were snooping on them. We thought it very interesting that Cindy Boskin thanked this woman for 'taking care of her husband.' She said now both of their lives could move forward. Then they exchanged numbers, and Cindy asked her to stay in touch, said she wanted to know her whereabouts at all times. Then the woman said she would like to know where Shane's body was, and Cindy said she didn't think it was wise for her to show up at the funeral or funeral home, seeing as everything that's happened, she should lay low and remain discreet. She handed her an envelope and said it was nice doing business with her. That's a direct quote also, I wrote it down immediately in my little day planner."

"She did," confirmed Penny.

Antonia was astonished. "Are you implying that you think Cindy had this woman kill Shane and Gary?"

"I most certainly think that is what she was implying," said Ruth with a firm nod of her head.

"But why would they have Gary killed? What did Paul say to all this?"

"Paul said it was a tragedy, and he apologized to that woman on behalf of his brother and said he was sorry that Gary had not treated her better. Then Gloria went on a bit of a rant as to how unsupportive Gary was, how he never liked her, and frankly he got what he deserved," said Ruth.

"Then Paul said, that's harsh and tried to calm her down, but he again said sorry about his brother's behavior," Penny added.

"This is wild," said Antonia. Her head was spinning. Was it all a conspiracy between Cindy, Gloria, and Paul? So that Cindy and Paul could be together? It didn't make sense.

"So I must have seen Gloria at the funeral home after this happened. She was angry with Cindy and said she was trying to find Shane's body. She didn't seem to have very happy thoughts about Cindy," said Antonia.

"I imagine it's hard to do a group killing," said Ruth. "Someone always turns on the other person. Don't you watch crime shows on television?"

"What happened after? How did they all leave it?" asked Antonia.

"They got in their separate cars and drove away. We followed Paul and Cindy for a while; we couldn't go as far as Wainscott because we were short on time, but we followed them to the gas station on Toilsome Lane and then left. It was enough excitement for one day," said Ruth.

"Why did you wait to tell me?" asked Antonia.

"My sciatica was acting up after our stakeout, and that kept me in bed," said Ruth. "We wanted the pleasure of telling you in person, so I made Penny wait."

"It was terribly difficult, but we must await orders from our chief. What would you like us to do next?" asked Penny, excitement flashing in her eyes.

"I think we need to go straight to the police," said Antonia.

"Boring!" Ruth boomed. "We want in on solving the case. Once we tell them, we are out of it."

"And it's so much fun! We haven't been this exhilarated since they tossed Bambi Brooks out of the Garden Club," said Penny.

"I understand, ladies, but this is serious stuff. We need to let the police handle it."

Ruth's eyes became narrow. "I'm sorry, Antonia, but I'm going to call you out on ageism. We know for a fact that you never allow the police to handle investigations and you conduct your own. The only reason we can surmise that you would not include us is because we are old ladies. Now we ask you, who better to snoop around than old ladies? No one ever suspects old ladies! We can be the Miss Marples of East Hampton!"

Antonia did not want to say that she considered *herself* the Miss Marple of East Hampton. She stared into the eager eyes of her friends and clients and decided to acquiesce.

"Okay, let me think of our next move."

They clapped their hands together with mirth. Antonia stared at the ceiling, wondering what task she could assign them that wouldn't lead them into the path of danger. Perhaps she could reassign them to investigate something else. She'd let them think it was regarding this case...

"Ladies, there's a woman named Cheryl Cooke who is in town. I need to know everything there is about her."

"Is she a suspect?" asked Penny, eyes wild with glee.

"Well, let's just say that I suspect her of something."

"We are on it! Give us all the details."

——————— ———————

After escorting her sleuthing team out of the inn, Antonia felt a headache coming on, so she went to her apartment to procure Advil. Her place was as she had left it, no boogeymen hovering behind the doors or in the closets, thank goodness (she did take the time to check). But it still sadly appeared as if an intruder had ransacked the place. The bed was sloppily made; there were dishes in the sink; the throw pillows were untidily thrown off the sofa, and her clothes were draped all over the bedroom. She realized with dismay that she hadn't had time to clean up the mess that she made when she threw apart her place in search of surveillance cameras and listening devices.

Antonia opened the medicine cabinet in her bathroom and retrieved the pills, which she washed down with a cup of tap water. When she closed the door, she stared at her reflection in the mirror and noticed that her eyes appeared tired and there were tiny wrinkles in the corners, caused by anxiety. Her English skin, which she inherited from her father, was basically a road map alerting everyone to whatever was going on in her life. If she imbibed red wine or tomato sauce, she had rosacea; if she'd been in the sun, she had red cheeks; if she was stressed, her face looked like Edward Scissorhands had used her as a human pumpkin and carved out some new lines to make a jack-o'-lantern. Why couldn't she have gotten her mother's Italian skin? It always appeared tan and healthy, even if she hadn't been in the sun, and was as smooth and unblemished as a marble statue.

Antonia made her way into her bedroom and began picking clothing up off the floor and putting it in the hamper. On the slipper chair that she used as a giant clothes rack, she retrieved the lacy white bra that she had foolishly worn on her date with Nick. That had been an embarrassment of optimism! As *if* he would see her undergarments. She chucked them into the hamper, making a mental note that she'd have to do an entire laundry cycle for delicates. Suddenly something dawned on her and a chill ran down her spine. What was it that Philip had said on the phone? He had remarked about her "putting on white lacy underpants" for another man. Not only that, he had said, "If I *see* you putting on white lacy underpants." Which meant one thing: he had seen her.

Antonia cautiously glanced around her room, frozen in place, moving only her eyes from as far left to as far right as possible without turning her head. How had Philip seen her? Hadn't the cops done a scan of her apartment and found nothing? Not leaving anything to chance, she had conducted her own search as well after they had left, which yielded nothing. But they had to have missed something if he knew about the lacy underwear. She never wore lacy underwear when they were married (he didn't deserve them). Finally summoning up courage, she did a one-eighty in slow motion, moving her body around in tiny movements like the Bionic Woman "running" on the old TV series of her youth. Her room was not abundantly furnished; there were not many nooks and crannies to rummage around in and hide surveillance equipment. She had already conducted a thorough search of all the lampshades and anywhere else that someone might have tucked away a miniscule camera.

The bedroom window shades were closed; Antonia had been sure to close them after she found the telescope upstairs aimed at her window. She tried to remember if her shades had been open when Genevieve was there, thinking perhaps Philip had peered through the window. But no; there was no way she would have been naked in front of her window. What if guests of the inn had been strolling through the garden? But still. She walked over to the window, ripped open the curtains, flipped up the shade. If she had expected a camera to fall out, she was disappointed. She ran her hand along the windowsill and through the folds of the curtains, but there was nothing. She opened it, peered into the garden, and fumbled her hand up and out of the window, sliding it across the exterior. Her reward was a few chipped white paint flecks that would need to be touched up. She yanked her hand inside. What was she missing? One more scan of the room again resulted in perplexity. Perhaps the closet? She flung open the closet door and peered in. The meager clothing that remained after Genevieve's visit hung in silent clumps in the darkened storage unit. It was as if there had been a bargain basement sale and the rejects were all that remained. She slammed the door shut, and faced her own perplexed reflection in the full-length mirror.

The mirror. She moved toward it and ran her hand around the entire edge. Would Philip really have had time to remove the mirror, put a device behind it, and replace it? Yes, probably, considering she would often leave her apartment for eight hours or more at time. She had a faint memory of the man in the hardware store from so many years ago warning her that surveillance devices can be hard to detect behind a mirror, which was possibly why the police missed it. Her hand groped along the bottom of the mirror and she found a spot where the glue was loose. She pulled at the mirror, trying to slide it off the door. There was a small slit at the bottom, enough to alarm Antonia. She wiggled her fingers through, and it partially became unsealed. She tried harder, but the rest was stubbornly held together by something stronger than Krazy Glue. With Herculean strength (the kind that only rears its head in life-or-death situations), she pulled at the mirror.

"Come on," she coaxed herself, as she panted with effort.

She pulled at the glass, scratching her nails underneath it so that they almost tore off. She could hear the soft suction of the glass separating from the door. Her impatience got the best of her and she yanked, cracking off a small portion below. She glanced down at her hands and realized she had cut herself; a small stream of blood was trickling down her palm. She lifted her eyes to reassess the mirror and her strategy and once again caught her reflection in it. It suddenly occurred to her that Philip could be watching her now, laughing at her, and the thought of it enraged her. She stormed into her living room and opened the front hall closet. On the top shelf was an old, Easter-egg-blue Tiffany box that had once housed a cachepot that a friend had gifted her for a noteworthy birthday. It currently held a jumble of household necessities such as a hammer, nails, a screwdriver, wall hangers, duct tape, and, weirdly, a lint brush. She pulled it down, took out the hammer, and marched back to her room.

Adrenaline was rushing in her veins as she hoisted the hammer behind her head and with full force smashed the mirror. It cracked but still held on to the wall. She lifted the hammer again and bashed the middle. It was liberating. She felt as if she were hammering

Philip in the head. The noise was deafening. She kept at it, hacking away like a Weedwacker in a field. The shards of glass floated to the floor in chunks and slivers. She stared at her fractured visage in the mirror and took the hammer to it again. Finally the entire mirror chinked down with a loud bang. She peered closely. Hanging behind it was a small camera that had been recording her every move. She ripped it off and stomped on it.

"What the hell is going on?"

Sergeant Flanagan was standing on the threshold of her doorway with his gun drawn, his alert eyes darting around the room. Behind him was Jonathan, his face awash in concern, his forehead glistening with sweat, and his fear palpable. Antonia turned toward them and realized she must look like a crazy person. She was standing in a pool of fissured glass with blood streaming down her hands, her eyes wild and her hair wonky. She had played right into Philip's hands.

23

By this point in their relationship, Antonia had surmised that Sergeant Flanagan must be an incredibly deft card player. He had that extraordinary ability to conceal his true feelings and assume a poker face. Perhaps he should chuck the whole crime-solving business and head to Vegas to make some real money, she thought. But then, at the end of the day, solving crimes was possibly more addictive than gambling for those who had it in their blood, so why fix what ain't broke?

He had taken great care to once again listen to her account of Philip's continuing campaign of terror. They sat in her living room after she bandaged her hand (thankfully no one thought she needed stitches), and he took copious notes, called his colleagues to keep them abreast of the situation and on the lookout, and made sure they reported to Philip's police officer buddies back in California what was really going on. Antonia was gratified when he said he was totally impatient with the way everything about Philip was handled and would no longer accept Philip's "get out of jail free" card. Antonia signed a document officially pressing charges against Philip for the surveillance.

After they had covered everything regarding her ex-husband, Antonia felt compelled by Sergeant Flanagan's compassion to apprise him of everything she had learned about Shane, Gary, and Gabriela's murders. In his customary fashion, Sergeant Flanagan didn't indicate that he already knew what Antonia had told him, but she had the impression that she had not uncovered any groundbreaking revelations. His interest was somewhat piqued when she mentioned Paul and Cindy Boskin's picture in *Hamptons* magazine after Cindy's insistence that she hadn't been there all summer, and he asked for Antonia to show it to him.

"I left it with Joseph, but I'll grab it back from him on your way out," she said.

"Thank you," replied Sergeant Flanagan. He was still sitting on the armchair in her apartment taking down her statement.

"So they must have told you also that they weren't here this summer, huh?" she asked eagerly. "Cindy Boskin?"

He gave Antonia a look, which betrayed nothing. "I'm not at liberty to say."

"Okay, right, right. How about you blink once if I'm right, and twice if not?"

He was not amused. "Can't do it."

"No fair! All right, well, I guess I will conjecture that she had said the same to you and that's why you want the magazine."

He continued writing and didn't look at her, so she kept babbling.

"It just doesn't make sense. On the one hand you have Cindy and Paul. And maybe they were in cahoots with fake Cindy. I can see why they might want to kill Shane, but why Gary? And then what about Lauren and Dawn and Gabriela? Glen thinks it was Gabriela that was there with Shane and Gary that night. So how do they play into it? Why would Gabriela end up dead?"

"Miss Bingham," said Sergeant Flanagan glancing up at her. "I think it best to let me do my job and let you do your job. And first and foremost, you need to vacuum up that mirror to avoid further harm."

"Okay, yes, I will."

"Seriously," he said staring her in the eye. "Haven't you had enough danger for one week? One year?"

"True."

She escorted the officer to the front hall and had him wait by reception while she ran up to Joseph's apartment to obtain the magazine. In a total déjà vu, when he opened the door, she found Cheryl seated again in his living quarters.

"Me again, sorry to barge in," said Antonia.

"No problem, my dear."

"Hi, Cheryl!" she said, waving through the doorway at Joseph's new friend.

"Hey, Antonia! We've got to stop meeting like this! Let's the three of us have dinner one night soon?"

"Sounds lovely," Antonia lied. She noticed that Cheryl was wearing a silk blouse that was unbuttoned a little too far down for her taste. Hussy.

"Do you want to come in?" offered Joseph.

"I can't stay. Sergeant Flanagan is waiting for me downstairs. I just wanted to show him the copy of *Hamptons* magazine with a photo of Cindy and Paul."

Joseph's face fell. "I meant to talk with you about that."

He went inside and retrieved the magazine, opening it to the party picture page where Cindy Boskin was featured. He pulled on his reading glasses from around his neck and pointed to the headline.

"I studied this again and happened to notice the date. This picture was taken a year ago."

"What?"

"Yes, I believe it's one of those promotional ads. I'm often fooled by them as well. I'm terribly sorry I didn't tell you sooner."

Antonia sighed with disappointment. "Bummer. I feel stupid now."

"You shouldn't, Antonia!" boomed Cheryl from her seat. "Joseph told me all about what a good detective you are. Seems like there're a lot of crimes that wouldn't have been solved without you."

Antonia gave her a smile without showing her teeth. "He's too kind."

"Oh, that he is," said Cheryl, smiling flirtatiously at Joseph. "But I do think he's sincere."

"Yes," said Antonia, hoping to escape as quickly as possible. "Gotta jam, Sergeant Flanagan awaits. Thanks, Joseph."

"Hopefully see you tonight!" said Cheryl cheerfully. "We're planning on coming downstairs for dinner."

"Wonderful."

Antonia returned downstairs to Sergeant Flanagan.

"False alarm," she announced. She filled him in on the mix-up with the date. He took it better than she did, nodding and not exhibiting any desire to scream cry, as she did.

"Don't worry, Miss Bingham. There are always a lot of dead ends. That's part of being a detective. You can't have a gem every time."

"I guess."

"Trust me, I've been doing this a lot longer."

"Well, I suppose that removes Cindy Boskin from the suspect list?"

Antonia tried to read his face, but he said nothing.

"I think you need to stick to innkeeping, and I'll take care of the rest."

Chastened, Antonia decided for once to follow orders and went to the kitchen to prep dinner. She still had not returned Nick's call, which she knew made her appear coy, but the truth was that she didn't know what to say, and it wasn't something she wanted to deal with right now. That meant that she was running the risk of having to address it if he showed up with Melanie for dinner, but what could she do? Well, she could just hide out in the kitchen. It was not only a good idea, but productive. That way she would also avoid Joseph and Cheryl having their cozy little dinner à deux. Yuck.

Cooking was generally a relaxing exercise for Antonia, but her stomach was in knots due to Melanie's impending arrival. It was a shame, because she truly believed that the chef's emotions could be felt in the food that they created, and basically, right now she was sending out plates full of anxiety to all of her guests. She wouldn't be surprised if she received a call from the health inspector the next day telling her she had poisoned all of her customers. Normally composing a wispy little side salad to accompany a pork loin was no problem, but tonight Antonia felt as if she were asked to translate the Bible into Chinese. Every time the kitchen door swung open, she was prepared for Glen to announce that Melanie was there with Nick and they were feeding each other spaghetti like the dogs in *Lady and the Tramp*. It was almost a relief when she was finally alerted to Melanie's presence in an offhand way.

"What does this mean, *VIP halibut*?" asked Marty with confusion. He had snatched the dinner ticket off the line and was staring at it with scorn on his face.

The waiter answered him in a low tone. "It's for that actress."

Antonia's ears pricked up.

"Which actress?" snapped Marty.

"I don't know her name… She was in some movie my mother likes."

"Melanie Wells?" asked Antonia with faux innocence.

"Um, yeah, I think so."

Antonia was secretly gratified that the young waiter had no idea who her nemesis was. Glen had said that actresses are considered dinosaurs in Hollywood once they reach the age of forty, so perhaps there was some justice in the world.

"What, that crazy bitch is here again?" asked Marty. "She makes our life hell. Why doesn't she stay home to not eat?"

The young waiter shrugged. "Beats me. But I know famous people like to be seen. Makes them feel important. Insecure childhoods, all that stuff."

"Are you a psychologist now?" asked Marty.

The young waiter straightened up. "Why, yes, I'm studying—"

"I was asking rhetorically," Marty interrupted. "Now get out of here. I need to make Miss Golden Globe some VIP halibut. Maybe I'll just coat it in truffles and caviar and send it out to her, would that be good enough? Or shall I dust it with diamonds?"

When the waiter finally left, Antonia's curiosity got the best of her. She sidled over to Marty's station and glanced down at the dinner ticket. "So, um, what else did Melanie's table order?"

"A block of gold," he said, throwing a filet on the fire.

Antonia took a look at the ticket. "Noodles with butter?"

"If that's what it says."

"That seems weird. So she doesn't want any butter or fat to touch her fish but she wants a bowl of straight carbs?"

"Maybe it's for her dining companion."

That gave Antonia pause. Was Nick playing some sort of trick on her? How cruel to come to her restaurant and request noodles.

Had this all been some evil joke? Incensed, Antonia threw down her apron and banged her way out of the kitchen. She made a beeline for the worst table in the restaurant where she had sat Melanie. It was time they had a little tête-à-tête. She strode with absolute confidence toward the back, passing customers enjoying the bounty of her delicious food. See? Hundreds, if not thousands, of foodies relished her fine cuisine.

She spotted Melanie and quickened her speed. Melanie of course looked gorgeous, her hair all flowy and backlit by the soft lighting. She was midsentence but ceased speaking, as if sensing Antonia's oncoming presence. She turned and stared at her as she approached. Their eyes locked and narrowed into slits. This was war. Antonia took a second to flit her eyes over to Melanie's dinner companion and...stopped. She literally stopped so abruptly that a busboy carrying a tray of drinks almost collided with her.

She didn't expect this. Melanie was not dining with Nick. She was not dining with some manager or agent or fellow celebrity. She was dining with a young boy, a child, who Antonia had to assume was her son, Finn. It took the wind out of Antonia's sails. Round one, Melanie.

Before Antonia spun around, she had just enough time to see Melanie's lips curl into a satisfied smile. Antonia paused in the middle of the dining room to take a deep breath. She had to gather her thoughts. It took her a moment to realize that she no longer felt anger, no longer felt rage. Everything evaporated at once, all the animosity. She felt sad. Here Melanie was, fighting for her family, and here Antonia was, standing in the way. It was something she couldn't justify; no matter how much she wanted Nick, she wouldn't be the woman who came between him and the mother of his child. Maybe they still had a chance to be a family and she would be forever guilty if she sensed that she had been an obstacle.

"Antonia, come at once!" commanded Glen. He took her by the arm and led her to the front of the room.

"What's going on?"

"That man is in the bar. You know the big guy who was here the night Shane and Gary were? The one who became enraged when his chair was knocked?"

"Eric Neiderhoffer?"

Glen looked confused. "I'm not sure his name, but the big guy?"

"Yes, yes, let's go!"

Eric Neiderhoffer was indeed a "big guy." He stood about six foot three or four inches tall, and he had a head of thick, uncombed, curly dark hair, which added another inch. He was not unattractive; his features were quite strong with big blue eyes and a large, straight nose that matched his face. He probably carried an extra twenty pounds, though, which diminished the clarity of his features. Had his chin been chiseled and his cheeks not flabby, he might have been quite a looker.

They found him sitting at the bar, a female companion next to him who he appeared to be totally fixated on. He kept touching her thigh, and she would daintily swat his hand away. She was cute—Southeast Asian, with a tiny figure and liquid brown eyes—and didn't seem to be as captivated with him as he was with her, or perhaps she equated disapproval with flirtatiousness. Her skirt was certainly short enough to indicate that she was interested, Antonia noted with a hint of censure.

"What do we do?" asked Antonia. "You think I just up and ask him about that night?"

"Dunno," said Glen. "I think maybe you call your cop friend. I don't want anything to do with this situation, just wanted to let you know."

With that, Glen returned to his maître d' station to greet incoming guests. Sometimes it was difficult for Antonia to remember that not everyone wanted to be her partner in crime. Well, what can you do? She ascertained that she definitely had the home court advantage. She waltzed up to Eric Neiderhoffer and his date and introduced herself as the innkeeper.

"I just wanted to make sure you had everything you needed and were enjoying yourselves?" she asked demurely.

"Yes, thanks," said Eric, before abruptly turning his back to her and returning his attention to his companion.

"That's great," said Antonia, a bit disconcerted.

"Actually..." said the companion.

"Yes?" Antonia asked eagerly, like a child called up onstage by a star.

"We could use more nuts," said the companion.

Antonia deflated. "Of course. I'm sorry, I didn't catch your name?"

"Janet."

"Yes, Janet. I will definitely get you more nuts."

Antonia motioned to Jesse, who was behind the bar, and made her own version of a sign language motion for nuts, which looked more like a teenage boy squeezing a girl's breast. Jesse was undoubtedly confused and came over to Antonia.

"What did you want?"

"Nuts! We need nuts!"

He nodded his head and said, "Sure thing, Antonia."

Antonia beamed at her guests, who were no longer interested in her. Not one to be deterred, she tapped Eric on the shoulder.

"Yes?"

"I understand you were here the other night, and I'm flattered that you have chosen to come here two nights this week."

"Um, you're welcome."

"What with so many other options in town…"

"Yeah." Again, Eric made it clear that he had no interest in talking with her by literally turning his back on her again. Well, Antonia had no choice but to take the bull by the horns.

"Listen, Eric, last time you were here, you became quite irate at a fellow customer. I want to know what your relationship was to Shane Boskin and Gary DiAngelo?"

He swiveled around in his chair, and his voice became tense. "What are you talking about?"

"Oh, you know, Mister," insisted Antonia.

"No, I do not know," he said in a furious voice.

"Antonia! You are needed over here."

Antonia turned around to see Larry Lipper fast approaching. He was shaking his head as if warning her.

"What?"

"Come with me," he said, taking her firmly by the arm and yanking her away.

"Hey, I know you—" said Eric.

Larry put up his hand first as a stop sign but then made a show of dividing his fingers into a peace sign. "Yo, bro, got no beef with you. Happen to be chilling at the same resty. Talk at ya later."

He pulled Antonia across the bar.

"What was that about?" she asked with confusion.

"It's not him. I don't want you to waste your time accusing him and sussing him out when I can say with absolute authority that he is not our killer. And the reason I pulled you away is he is a very litigious person and not one you want to cross."

"How do you know it's not him?"

"I dumpster dove into his garbage. I know; I'm shameless. But there is beauty in acknowledging what you are. Incidentally, I found receipts for the night of the murder. He was at Stop and Shop buying groceries. I discovered a receipt from twelve oh four a.m. and I went there and asked them about him, you know, just to confirm, and apparently he made quite an impression. The guy is OCD, with a capital OCD—that's why he freaked out when someone knocked into him here. He's not our guy."

"But what about how he said 'Bull' on the night of the murder? He was planning on going to Bull Path."

Larry shook his head. "I think he was just saying 'bullshit.' He says it a lot."

Antonia glanced over at Eric, who was still chatting up his lady friend, and nodded. It was a pity; he was obnoxious enough to incite great pleasure in those who arrested him, and it would be a loss not to relish his apprehension. But you can't arrest an innocent man, no matter how annoying he is.

"Any other leads?" Antonia inquired in a defeated tone.

"I've been trying you all day. Where have you been?"

Nick Darrow somehow appeared at Antonia's elbow and put his arm on her shoulder. She jerked away, instinctively irritated, until she realized who it was. She gaped into his stormy eyes, which were a particularly attractive shade of blue this evening.

"What?"

"I said I've been trying to get in touch with you all day. Where were you?"

"I haven't had a chance to return your calls, sorry. Been busy," she said with defiance.

"Antonia, look, can I talk to you in private for a second?"

He glanced at Larry, who shrugged.

"For a second."

They moved over to a quiet corner of the bar.

"You look great."

"Thanks."

"But I can tell you're pissed, and you have every right to be. Melanie is playing games. The fact that she brought my son here is ludicrous. She should be prosecuted. I hate to say this, but she's a terrible mother. She's only ever used our son as a prop. You know this; I've told you all this. And she doesn't care one bit about me— it's only about image. She thinks that two celebrities together are a power couple, which helps her fame to endure. She just wants to be relevant; she doesn't really want me."

His eyes were pleading, but Antonia was steadfast. "Don't we all want to be relevant?"

"Of course we do. But she's a mean bitch. I hate to say this about the mother of my child, but it's true. She is vain. She is opportunistic."

"Seems like she just wants her family to stay together."

Nick became frustrated. "You know how you don't listen to your parents when they tell you not to do something? How you think you know better? Well, my parents told me not to marry her. They said she was incapable of love, that she only cared about herself. My dad, who was not the most intellectual person you ever met, called her a narcissist. But no, I was young and in love, really not in love in retrospect but enamored, and I thought my parents were provincial and low class and didn't understand anything. But they were right. Melanie is manipulative. Melanie only loves herself. I can only hope with every fiber in my body that she loves Finn, and I would only say this to you, but I doubt it. She only loves him because he is a reflection of her. Do you know how awful it is to see him approach her and try and engage her, and when she is not on camera or in public, she rejects him? This is not a good person we're talking about, Antonia. I don't ever want you to think you are getting in the way of me and Mary Poppins. Not that you are getting in the way—it's all been over. Please, Antonia. I beg you. Don't give up on me. You are what gets me out of bed in the morning. I think of you, and it all feels good, whenever everything else is going bad. I know, it's corny, but it's like, you're the end of the rainbow and I feel like I have slogged through the muck, lost a few leprechauns on the way, and I am finally close to the pot of gold."

He didn't wait for her answer and pulled her toward him and kissed her. She was at first conscious of everyone else in the room, but as the kiss lingered became only aware of him. She would never again doubt the phrase "he swept me off my feet." He'd definitely done it. He'd had her at "hello." "Frankly, my dear," she *did* give a damn. She'd deny her father and refute her name if it came to that.

But there was a tiny, funny thing. When she pulled away from him and caught Larry Lipper staring at her, his face...well, for the first time, she couldn't make out Larry's face. What did that expression mean? She was suddenly very conscious of where she was and what she was doing, and she wiped her mouth with embarrassment and pulled away from Nick.

"Let's talk tomorrow," she said softly.

"Promise?"

"Yes."

"Promise?"

"Yes," she laughed.

He left reluctantly, hanging on to her hand in a long, drawn-out goodbye before disappearing out the side door.

She felt everyone's eyes on her when she returned to Larry. He was not amused.

"Is your Harlequin Romance moment over, Bingham? Can we finally get back to work? We do need to find a murderer, after all."

"Yes," answered Antonia giddily. The kiss had drained her. It had literally sucked out all of her adrenaline from top to bottom and left her a quavering blob.

"Thank you for your renewed attention. We don't have much time. We have to get to Lauren Wayne's house."

"Lauren Wayne?" asked Antonia with surprise. "Really?"

24

LAUREN WAYNE'S HOUSE WAS IN SPRINGS. EVERY TIME ANTONIA heard someone call it "the Springs," she had a visceral reaction. Yes, the sign to Springs said "Welcome to *the* Springs" but no native called it that. It was Springs School, not *the* Springs School. You would have to search far and wide to find a Bonacker (aka a local; so named because of proximity to Accabonac Harbor) who called it "*the* Springs." It was the hipsters who had newly discovered the region who used the article "the." Just another example of their pretentious behavior.

Antonia and Larry pulled into Lauren's driveway and parked behind a small sedan. The house was modest but well kept. They could see a light on in the living room, which illuminated their path to the front door. They knocked, and Lauren Wayne invited them in. She didn't offer them a beverage or anything else that suggested she wanted them to stay, but she did immediately launch into her story, during which they were held captive by her unabbreviated diatribe. The only interruptions were by her roommate, who would walk in and out of the room, spooning miniscule drops of Greek yogurt into her mouth. She'd pause, listen, and then retreat, then do the same all over again. The yogurt cup was apparently bottomless, and her fatuous expression did not in any way reveal her impression of the course of events.

"It's all Dawn," began Lauren as she paced in front of her shiny, black-tiled gas fireplace. A fake log was throwing some light into the room, its glints reflected in the crystal dream catchers that were hanging in the windows.

"What do you mean?" Larry pressed.

Lauren was twisting her hands in knots, simultaneously picking at her fingernails and ripping dead skin off her cuticles. If Antonia were her teacher, she would have recommended a large dosage of Ritalin and sent her to the nurse's office.

"I mean, she was furious. At us…at those guys… I never wanted to be involved, okay? I'm like, a reluctant participant. You know what that means? I'm not guilty."

"Okay, Lauren, we get that it wasn't your idea," said Larry in his best attempt at a soothing voice. "But whose idea was it? And what exactly did you do?"

Lauren stared at her thumb as if she were a baby in a crib just realizing she had opposable thumbs, before pushing her eyeteeth forward to rip off a patch of dead skin. "I guess I should start at the beginning."

"A very good place to start," trilled Antonia, quoting Julie Andrews from *The Sound of Music*.

"Last summer we were all working together, as you know. It was fun, we'd work, then sometimes there were cute guys and we'd go out with them after. A lot of them had money and wanted to have fun, and that was cool with me. I wanted to have fun. So one night we go out with these guys Shane and Gary. They seemed nice. I mean, Shane was not my type at all. He was a real loud-mouth, needed to be center of attention and all that. I like the more subtle types, quiet guys. Gary was more like that. Anyway, we all head over to Dawn's house. And you know, we're hanging, drinking, and you know, you know."

"Sorry, we don't know," said Antonia. "You're going to have to fill us in on the blanks."

Lauren rolled her eyes. "Well, Shane was aggressive toward Dawn. I can confirm that she did kind of lead him on, but when she realized he was married (he'd been hiding his wedding ring) she kind of flipped out. But it had already gone too far, they were in a bedroom and kinda naked and the lights were out, and they were both drunk. But at the end of the day, no means no, right? And he wouldn't back off. She apparently yelled for help, and Gabriela and I were outside, so we didn't hear, but Gary had gone in to use the bathroom. He came into the room but did nothing to help her. Dawn freaked out. Rightly so, but it became an obsession with her. She wanted to destroy Shane's life. She called his wife and told her everything. She followed him around for weeks, telling other women he was talking to what a scumbag he was. She tried to ruin his life. Then she came up with a plan…"

Lauren's voice trailed off. Antonia could tell she needed a little more prompting, but before she was able to say anything, Larry jumped in.

"Get to it, what was the plan?"

Lauren bit her lower lip. "She wanted to set them up. She had Gabriela go with them to the inn, pretend everything was all hunky-dory now, had me come over to hang out. The plan was that she would take incriminating photographs and then blackmail them. You have to understand, I wasn't going to do it; she was the one who would benefit. I just said that I'd go along with them and party. But this is where things took a turn. It was supposed to be that we all partied and then she got the pictures and left. The plan to stay at the Windmill Inn for free was perfect because Shane and Gary knew where she lived and in case they came after her to get the incriminating pictures, she had a hideout…"

"I hardly offered for her to stay at the Windmill Inn for free. She totally exploited us." Antonia sniffed.

"Don't interrupt, Antonia," warned Larry. "How did it take a turn, Lauren? What went wrong?"

Lauren shook her head. "I don't know. I promise you; I never knew she would kill them. It was never the plan. And now Gabriela? I can't believe she killed her too."

"What did the police say?" Larry asked.

"Are you crazy? I can't go to the police! They'd arrest me for extortion."

"But if you were a witness to murder, surely they won't?" asked Antonia.

"That's the thing. I didn't actually *see* her murder them. What I told the police was true; I did go to her house and watch a movie. We were going to head out after the movie, you know, late night, and we were just waiting for Gabriela to call and say they'd left the bar. But then I don't know what happened. I woke up that next day in the woods. I think Dawn drugged me, drove to Shane and Gary's, and left me there somewhere. I think she wanted insurance. She wanted it to look like I committed the murders; that's why she told you and the police that I had tied her up in the Windmill Inn. Gabriela and I both were set up. And now Gabriela's dead. Dawn is a psychopath."

"How was Dawn able to kill those guys?" asked Antonia.

"Gabriela slipped them something at the bar. By the time they all returned to the house, they should have already been kind of out of it."

"According to the neighbor, they were making a lot of noise."

"Well, like I said: I don't remember anything from their house. All I know is that Dawn denies killing them. Says Gabriela must have done it. Or me," said Lauren.

"Did Gabriela kill them?" asked Larry. "Maybe she was the one?"

Lauren shook her head. "No, I don't think so. Gabriela was really freaked out. She lives nearby, and her role was to get them drugged and get them in the hot tub with her, and then she would make a mess to make it look like they had attacked her. I was supposed to be in the hot tub as well. But Gabriela didn't really remember anything either. She remembered Dawn arriving, and they each had a drink while the guys called to them from outside. She said she never saw me there. Then, Gabriela started to feel woozy too. She remembered waking up in her bed. She didn't know what happened. We both thought Dawn framed us. And now Gabriela's gone." A sob escaped Lauren's mouth, and she covered her face with trembling hands.

"Why would Dawn kill Gabriela?" asked Antonia.

"It's actually *your* fault," said Lauren accusatorily, flinging her hands away from her face and pointing at Antonia in anger. "*You* kept showing up and hounding us and Gabriela got scared and wanted to go to the police. Dawn must have killed her to shut her up."

"What does Dawn say?"

"She denies it all. Says there's another killer out there. But let me tell you something, Dawn is very, very smart, no matter what you think. She never felt we had her back, and now she's inflicted revenge on all of us."

"What is Dawn's connection to Philip?" asked Antonia.

Lauren looked confused. "Philip?"

"My ex-husband. Also known as Tomas Stefanowski, I believe."

"Oh, I think he's the dude she met through her blog. He was fan-guying her. Liked her articles or something on *Best and Worst Places to Stay in the Hamptons* and they agreed to meet up when he came to town. He actually booked the rooms at the inn, said that he was a gentleman and would book two, so no pressure."

Of course, thought Antonia. Philip was devious like that, scary enough to cyberstalk and figure out how to get to Antonia. If only "no pressure" extended to her. Antonia was fed up.

"Lauren, you have to go to the police," said Antonia.

"No. You have blood on your hands now that Gabriela's dead! You have to prove Dawn did it. Once you do, I will tell my story. Until then, I'm disappearing."

Larry and Antonia drove through the darkened streets to Dawn's house. Antonia's mood was gloomy. Had she really been responsible for Gabriela's death? That was horrible. Too unbearable to think about. And Philip's tentacles extending across the country to connect with locals in an effort to add more problems to Antonia's life was infuriating. Larry remained unruffled. He chattered on as if he had just been told to pick up some takeout, not that he was indirectly responsible for the death of a young woman. Antonia was waiting for him to pull out an old McDonald's bag.

They pulled just past Dawn's driveway, so that their car was obscured, and Larry killed the lights and motor.

"How are we going to get her to confess?" asked Antonia.

"We'll think of something."

When they approached the house, they could see through the side window courtesy of a desk lamp. Larry put his fingers to his lips and motioned for Antonia to follow. At this point, she was in so deep that it didn't matter if she trespassed. Besides the fact that Dawn had warned her that if she ever came by again, she would call the police on her for trespassing, so what was the difference?

The lights in the bedroom were on, and the shades wide open, affording an uninhibited view of Dawn's boudoir. On top of the large queen-size bed was an open suitcase, with piles of clothes tucked inside. Larry gave Antonia a look by wiggling his eyebrows. Suddenly, Dawn walked into the room. Larry and Antonia immediately ducked down and squatted, their heads leaning against the shingles. They heard Dawn talking on her phone.

"Yeah, I'm heading out tonight. I'm pretty freaked out. I wish I had never met…"

She wandered out of the door before they could hear who she was talking about, but Antonia didn't need to hear, she knew.

"Philip. I bet she regrets ever doing anything with him," she whispered.

Larry nodded. Antonia glanced around and realized she was standing in a pile of deer droppings. She grimaced.

Dawn came back in. "Psychotic. I'm not kidding. I didn't know what I was dealing with. Certifiable. I have to leave town and go under the radar. Yeah, I have an aunt in Florida. I think I'll go there first, but I'm not kidding, I may need to go far away."

Antonia could feel the deer poop squishing into her shoe. She made a move to lift her foot and fell with a thud onto the ground. The noise was louder than she wished.

Dawn's voice suddenly went silent. Antonia and Larry pressed their bodies closer against the house. They could hear Dawn's footsteps come closer to the window then literally could hear her breathing. The window was abruptly slammed shut and the shade pulled down.

Larry gave Antonia a withering look. They waited a few more

breathless moments before sliding along the house and then dashing to their car. After pausing long enough to ensure the coast was
clear, they turned on the motor and pulled away.

"What the hell, Bingham, you smell like crap."

"It's deer poop."

"Inside my car? I can't believe you! Throw those out."

"I won't. I'm wearing my favorite Crocs. Don't you have some
napkins with your candy in the glove compartment?"

"I don't. Why would I need napkins in my car? Am I a mom?"

Antonia was holding up her shoe, looking in the back for something to wipe it with, when Larry snatched it out of her hand and
threw it out the window.

"Hey!"

"My car, my rules."

Antonia sulked. "I loved those shoes."

"And you can head to Kmart tomorrow and buy a new pair."

They both took a moment to relax. Finally Antonia spoke.

"So what do we think? Head to the cops?"

"Are you kidding? No way. We need to figure out how to nail Dawn."

"But it looks like she's heading out of town."

"Then we only have a few hours."

"Okay, so what do you suggest we do?"

"Thinking." Larry cranked up his stereo and began drumming
on the steering wheel along with Bon Jovi.

Antonia stabbed the dial into silence.

They drove on, not talking, their minds reeling. Finally
Antonia spoke.

"I have an idea."

25

THE INN WAS COMPLETELY QUIET AND SHROUDED IN DARKNESS. Antonia sat in the dimly lit dining room that was illuminated by candlelight. The only noise keeping her company was the soft hum of the small refrigerator behind the bar. That and the impatient, nervous tapping sound that her fingers were making on the table. Thinking of Larry's odious car drumming, she willed her hands still.

Antonia checked the clock on her phone for the tenth time. It was just after two a.m. and Lauren had said she would be there by now. Antonia hoped Lauren wouldn't run too late because she had asked Dawn to join her there at two fifteen, and if Lauren bumped into Dawn in the parking lot, she might be too scared to enter. The plan was definitely flawed, but it was the best they could come up with in haste. It also hinged on several factors, like whether or not Larry would be able to convince their special guest to come along. Or whether or not their special guest was even home. And lastly, whether or not the special guest would put aside her hatred of Larry to come. Antonia could only wish.

"I don't understand why we couldn't just meet back at my house," said Lauren, as she strolled into the dining room. "It's pretty freaky coming here at night. And why don't you have any lights on?"

"We needed a neutral spot," said Antonia, avoiding the question about the dim lighting.

Lauren plopped her heavy leather handbag onto the table,

the hardware clanking upon the table. She sat down in the chair opposite Antonia, who had purposely chosen a table without a banquette. She wanted everyone to have easy access in and out of their designated seats.

"I don't think this is going to work," sighed Lauren.

"We can hope." Antonia stood firm.

"Do you have a gun? Because Dawn may freak out and then come after us like she did Gabriela and Shane and Gary."

"I don't have a gun. But I do have a very sharp Japanese ceramic knife. I taped it under the table, reachable at any point."

"Ceramic? I hope that's enough."

"Trust me, it is," said Antonia.

Five or so tense minutes later, Antonia and Lauren heard the outside door squeak open, followed by the sound of footsteps. Suddenly Dawn appeared on the threshold of the inn's dining room. Antonia could swear the candlelight flickering across her face made her appear more sinister than usual.

"What is this?" Dawn asked, her eyes flitting from Antonia to Lauren.

"An intervention," joked Lauren.

"No, seriously," said Dawn. "What's going on?"

Antonia folded her hands on the table. "You thought you were here to meet someone else, right?"

"Yes."

"Tomas Stefanowski?" asked Antonia.

Dawn briefly hesitated before nodding. "Yeah."

"Well, I am Tomas Stefanowski," announced Antonia.

"What?" asked Dawn in confusion.

"I mean, tonight I am," Antonia clarified. "I went on your blog and read through that adorable little correspondence between you and him on the message board. How cute that he loved your article bashing my inn! How darling that you both agreed to come here and stay and then eviscerate my inn on your website. You used and exploited me, stayed here for free, lied about Lauren tying you up, and then framed her for murder! And now you were coming to meet him again?"

"Wait! That's not what happened!" insisted Dawn. "I had nothing to do with their murders. Lauren is the killer!"

"What?" gasped Lauren. "Why would you say that, Dawn? You know I had nothing to do with this. You wanted revenge on Shane and Gary. And you drugged me!"

The rage and anger on Dawn's face was evident. She walked toward them, seething. "You have to stop lying, Lauren. I had nothing to do with those guys. You told everyone that Shane went too far with *me*, but it was *you* he attacked. It was *you* who wanted revenge on those guys. You drugged Gabriela after I dropped you off! And you drugged yourself! Then you waited a few days and killed Gabriela too!"

"You're insane," said Lauren, shaking her head.

"I'm insane? *I'm* insane? That's a joke. Hilarious. You're *such* a liar, Lauren. *Such* a liar."

Lauren turned toward Antonia and gave her a pleading look. "See what I'm dealing with? She's a maniac. Repeating herself..."

Dawn bristled. "You're the maniac! I should have told someone about your plan. I never knew you would *kill* those guys...and now Gabriela. What did she ever do to you?"

"Me kill them? Me?"

Lauren stood up. Antonia could see the vein on her neck throbbing. She and Dawn were now face-to-face, so close that Antonia surmised they could feel each other's breath.

"Yes, you," said Dawn. "You knew I'd be staying at the inn later that night, so you had Gabriela bring the guys here earlier to frame me."

"Absurd."

"Lauren, you are seriously sick."

"And you are a serious killer, Dawn."

"You are!"

Just as it appeared that Lauren and Dawn were about to start rolling around the floor scratching each other's eyes out and pulling each other's hair, Larry Lipper and Iris Maple entered the dining room. Larry flipped on the overhead lights, and the harsh, sudden illumination made Lauren and Dawn freeze.

"What's going on?" asked Larry.

Behind him stood Iris Maple. Despite the fact that it was the middle of the night and she had no doubt been roused from her bed, Iris appeared very awake and quite put together. She had on a neat little jacket over a tailored pantsuit and nary a hair on her head was out of place.

Antonia stood up and motioned for them to come and sit down. "Iris, so sorry to wake you. I'm so grateful that you would come."

"It's no problem, Antonia. My only hesitation was the messenger," she snidely gestured toward Larry. "But I'm happy to help. Larry said you had an idea who murdered the hedge funders and Gabriela?"

"Yes," said Antonia, nodding. She glanced at Dawn and Lauren, who had ceased their fighting and were staring at her inquisitively. "Do you recognize this woman?"

"Yeah. She's the woman whose house I went to after I was in the woods," said Lauren.

"How are you feeling, dear?" asked Iris.

"Not great right now," confessed Lauren.

"I don't understand. Who is this woman? What is she doing

here?" demanded Dawn. "In fact, what are any of us doing here? Where's Tomas?"

"We wanted a front row seat at a female boxing match," said Larry, pulling up a chair to face the ladies.

Dawn gave him a scathing look. "I'm not staying. I don't want to be around this psychopath."

She began to leave, but Antonia stopped her. "You can't leave. Iris Maple lives on Bull Path and knew all the victims. And I'm pretty sure she knew the killer. You can't leave before you hear what Iris has to say."

"What does she have to say?" asked Dawn impatiently.

Iris gave a quizzical look. "Yes, what do I have to say?"

"You know," prompted Antonia. "How you know who the murderer is?"

"I know who the murderer is?" repeated Iris, a confused look on her face.

"Why don't you sit down, Iris. Here, you can have my seat."

Iris settled into the chair and pulled it up to the table. "Thank you."

"So, Iris, you were telling me about the murderer," Antonia prompted. She winked at Iris, who caught her drift.

"Of course. You ladies murdered those partiers. And I know this because of my close proximity to their house."

Iris turned and winked at Antonia.

Dawn rolled her eyes again. "This is a joke. Did you really think this would work? It's pathetic. You're wasting your time."

"Yes, Antonia," added Lauren. "It's clear you're trying to use this old hag to get Dawn to fess up. I thought you'd come up with a real plan. It's just a time suck. Lame." She lifted her purse off the table and made to leave.

Iris stiffened. "Now, see here, young lady. You should respect your elders! You and your dastardly friends should stop ruining my quality of life. Spend less time partying and making noise and guzzling alcohol and do something useful in the world!"

Lauren's eyes squinted, and an evil expression passed over her face. "Not even going to comment," said Lauren. "You'll be dead soon."

"She's threatening to kill me too!" Iris yelped.

"Not gonna kill you. I just mean you're old and irrelevant. It's people like you who ruin fun," said Lauren.

Dawn stared at Lauren then turned back to Antonia. "See? Lauren's not all nice. She has everyone fooled. She set this all up and now plays the victim. I'm out of here."

There was nothing Antonia could do to stop Dawn from leaving. She banged the door on the way out. Lauren followed quickly after, only waiting long enough to hear Dawn's car engine start and take off.

Antonia, Larry, and Iris were left sitting around the table. The plan had gone horribly wrong, and Antonia was embarrassed. She should have left it all to Sergeant Flanagan after all. Now he'd have to be called in to clean up her mess; Dawn and Lauren could be halfway to Rio by morning.

"So, what's my lead?" asked Larry, tipping back in his chair as he reached into his pocket and withdrew a couple of linty Twizzlers.

"Oh, I don't know, Larry. It's not all about your stupid byline, you know!" snapped Antonia. "Oh, Iris, I am so sorry to have awakened you to bring you into this." She reached her hand across the table toward Iris in supplication.

"It's quite all right, Antonia. Now that the neighborhood has been cleared of revelers, I will be able to sleep well soon enough." Iris gave Antonia a small smile and patted her hand.

Antonia put her other hand on top of Iris's and patted back. She felt something and glanced down. She hadn't noticed before, but Iris's sleeve had rolled up a bit and scratches along Iris's arm were visible.

"What happened?"

Iris glanced down. "Oh, I was gardening. You know, sometimes you forget that roses have thorns."

"Right," said Antonia.

Iris stood abruptly. "If that's all you need of me, I would love to return home. Larry, I assume you will be driving me back?"

Larry stood as well. "Sure thing."

Antonia remained seated. She was reviewing the murders in her mind. Something was bothering her. She remembered something Gabriela had said.

"Iris? Did you ever complain about Gabriela's music or noise?"

"Oh, I don't remember, my dear. Let bygones be bygones. So sad that she died."

Iris's face was immobile, but there was something in her eyes that gave Antonia pause.

"You used the word 'dastardly' earlier. I remember when I first went to talk to Gabriela I mentioned her neighbor, and she started to say something about her neighbor calling something dastardly..."

"Oh, I may have. Her music could be frightfully loud," said Iris as she edged toward the door. "Come on, Larry."

Antonia stood up. "And she was having a party when she was murdered. Just like Shane and Gary... What are those scratches on your arm, Iris?"

"I told you. Roses."

"But I went in your garden. You don't have rosebushes..."

Iris's eyes flashed. Larry turned in Iris's direction, his mouth slightly agape.

"What are you suggesting, Bingham?" he asked almost with amusement.

"How much did the noise bother you?" asked Antonia, walking toward Iris.

"This is nuts, Bingham. They found giant shoe prints at the murder scene."

"And Iris had giant shoes in her house. Remember, Larry? When you wore them? Your feet were swimming in them."

"I wouldn't say that," he retorted defensively.

"This is foolish, Antonia. Why in the world would I kill them?" asked Iris.

"You were fed up with the noise and the partying. You had the opportunity. Enough was enough."

Antonia was now a foot away from Iris Maple and staring her down. Iris met her gaze but then suddenly grabbed Antonia, hooked her arm around her neck, and held a knife to her throat. It was the knife Antonia had placed under the table in case Lauren and Dawn had become homicidal! Iris held it to Antonia's neck.

"Don't anyone make a move!" she said softly.

Antonia was not about to make a move. She knew how sharp that ceramic blade was. She had just sharpened it herself an hour ago. She could debone an entire cow with it, no problem.

Larry put up his hands. "Listen, Iris, don't worry. We can work this out. Antonia just runs her mouth off. We all know she's full of crap. Just drop the knife and we'll forget this ever happened."

"Not likely," snapped Iris. She was squeezing Antonia so hard that she was cutting off her circulation. Antonia thought she might faint. For someone so petite, Iris was strong. Probably from carrying armloads of books for all those years.

"Please," choked Antonia.

"Why did you have to interfere? It was a *good* thing I was doing. I was restoring peace to our village! If we removed all the partiers and revelers, it would return to the quaint place where I was born and raised. Those people had no regard for anyone but themselves! They were selfish and destructive!"

Larry was trying to signal something to Antonia, but her vision was becoming blurry.

"Iris, come on," he said, stepping toward her.

"Don't come any closer!" she snapped.

"You don't have to do this!" pleaded Larry.

"No. She doesn't."

Antonia's eyes darted to the doorway. Sergeant Flanagan stood on the threshold, his gun drawn. Before she fainted, Antonia knew she had never been so happy to see someone in her life.

26

Iris Maple had remained silent as she was led away in handcuffs. Antonia and Larry were separated as they gave their statements to the police. When everyone had finally left, Antonia went behind the bar, pulled out a bottle of tequila, and poured two shots. She handed one to Larry.

"Tequila? I think we should be drinking something more 'police procedural,' like scotch."

"Yeah, well, I don't drink hard liquor, only the occasional margarita, so this will have to do. Cheers."

They clinked glasses and downed their shots.

"Hit me again," said Larry.

Antonia poured him another shot, and one for herself. The liquid burned down her throat, but it felt good to have some sort of sensation to cut through the shock and exhaustion. "Nice."

"You know," said Larry, leaning back in his chair and putting his hands behind his head. "I will never underestimate little old ladies again."

"Or librarians!"

"Yeah. I should have remembered from grade school that they're forces to be reckoned with."

"I'm glad the killer's behind bars."

"Yeah. Thanks to us again."

Antonia nodded. It was true. They'd solved another crime. "I still think the Lauren and Dawn situation was bizarre."

"I think they each truly thought the other had committed the murder. Funny though, seems like it *was* Lauren who wanted to set the guys up. I always thought Dawn was the bad guy. But she just wanted a free hotel room."

"Yeah, 'bad guys' come in every shape and form these days."

The golden September sun was peeking through the windows. Larry looked at his watch before standing. "I'm beat. I know you want me to spend the night, Bingham, but I've got to head home and file the report for the paper."

"It's a weekly, Larry."

"Yeah, but they update the website every day. Rain check?"

Antonia nodded with a smile. "Rain check. Go get some rest."

"You too."

Antonia was bone-tired but high on adrenaline. There was no way she could sleep now. It was only an hour or so before her usual walk on the beach, and maybe Nick would be there.

As she was washing out the shot glasses in the kitchen, the door swung open.

"I just heard," said Genevieve. "Are you okay?"

Genevieve was dressed in a short, black-feathered cocktail dress and ten-inch heels. It appeared she had not yet gone to bed either.

"I'm fine. Geez, word travels fast."

"I was on a date with a cop. I met him the other day when I called the fuzz on Philip. Very cute. His divorce will be final in three months."

"Oh boy."

Genevieve walked over and hugged Antonia. "I'm so glad you caught the killer. I would tell you to stop fighting crime, but you're super good at it. Even my cop beau says so."

"I'll take that as a compliment."

"Yeah, he says his boss—Sergeant Flanagan?—likes you. Thinks you're smart. He says he's going to run Philip out of town. They'll make his life hell if he comes back."

"That's some consolation."

"Do you have anything to eat? I'm famished."

Antonia made them a big breakfast of western omelets and toast, with fruit on the side, as well as a strong pot of coffee. They hadn't caught up in a while, and it was nice to banter. Antonia loved hearing Genevieve tell all about her frenetic love life. It was a nice distraction from murder. Suddenly she remembered something.

"Genevieve, the other day you left me a message about the woman Joseph was seeing. What did you mean that she was something else and you hoped he wasn't dating her?"

"I said that?"

"Yes, what did you mean? It's important."

"Oh, yeah. Her. First of all, she's too young for him."

"I agree!"

"She's not classy."

"Totally."

"And I think she's a gold digger."

"Me too."

Antonia felt slightly guilty bashing Cheryl but was thrilled that her instincts were correct.

"Trashy."

"I hope it's a passing phase. She's only here on weekends."

"Really? I see her during the week."

"When?" Antonia shot up in her seat.

Genevieve shrugged. "I mean, all the time. She's always here."

"But she said she's rarely in the Hamptons."

"Well, she's a liar."

"Wow." Antonia was unsure how she would break the news to Joseph. It would devastate him.

"I mean, she definitely works in the liquor store on Tuesdays and Wednesdays because that's when I usually pop in for my—"

"Wait, what?"

"I said she works in the liquor store—"

"Cheryl?"

"Who's Cheryl?"

"Isn't that who we are talking about?"

"I'm talking about Gwendolyn. The girl who works in the liquor store. I saw her running after Joseph on Main Street the other day then flirting her ass off with him. He then accompanied her to the store. I think he totally fell for her routine."

Antonia felt stupid. "She was recommending some sherry for him. That's all. I was talking about Cheryl this whole time."

"Who's Cheryl?"

Antonia shook her head. "It's not important. I think sometimes I'm better off minding my own business."

"Speaking of which, did you see the gossip mags? Oh, wait, I know the answer to that. I can't believe I buried the lead; I got so distracted with you and the homicidal librarian! Anyway, there are pictures of Melanie Wells and Jackson Abrams!"

"Who's Jackson Abrams?"

"He's an actor, on that show *Menace*. Apparently, they've been having an affair for a year! She's totally been stepping out on your man. No wonder Nick moved on to greener pastures. And this way, the divorce will be quick and easy."

Antonia's heart was beating quickly. "Are you sure?"

"Of course. I saw the pictures of them kissing with my own eyes."

"I need to go. Like, now."

Nick was down by the ocean's edge, his pants rolled up and his feet wet. He was throwing the tennis ball to his dogs, who were eagerly retrieving it. Antonia paused for a minute to watch him. He was so handsome with his hair blowing in the wind, surrounded by his dogs in his happy place. He turned and met her gaze, before breaking into a big smile and waving. Antonia ran down to meet him.

About the Author

Photo by Tanya Malott

A fan of mystery and crime novels, a cooking enthusiast, a former employee of Ina Garten's Barefoot Contessa store, and a generally nosy person, Carrie Doyle combined all of her interests to create Antonia Bingham, the foodie innkeeper and reluctant detective who stars in the Hamptons Murder Mystery series. Carrie is the author of several novels and five optioned screenplays (one of which was produced and screened at the Sundance Festival). She was the founding editor-in-chief of the Russian edition of *Marie Claire* magazine and has written for several magazines. She is currently a contributing editor at *Hamptons* magazine. Visit Carrie's author site at carriedoyleauthor.com.

IT TAKES TWO TO MANGO

Trouble in Paradise!

Dive into a brand new cozy mystery series from Carrie Doyle!

After Plum Lockhart's job as a travel magazine editor is eliminated in corporate cuts, she decides she's sick of cold winters in NYC and fruitless swiping on dating apps—what she needs is a dramatic change of scenery. On a whim, she accepts a job as a villa broker and moves to a beautiful Caribbean island.

However, paradise isn't as perfect as it seems: the slow pace of island life, the language barrier, and a cutthroat office rival make Plum question leaving her old life behind. But when a client is found dead in the jacuzzi of Casa Mango—a property Plum manages—she knows she's really in a jam. With a killer loose on the island, Plum will have to deal with a stonewalling police chief, a string of baffling clues, and a handsome Director of Security to solve this deadly case!

For more Carrie Doyle, visit:

sourcebooks.com

Also by Carrie Doyle

Hamptons Murder Mysteries
Death on Windmill Way
Death on Lily Pond Lane
Death on West End Road

Writing as Carrie Karasyov
The Infidelity Pact

Writing as Carrie Karasyov with Jill Kargman
The Right Address
Wolves in Chic Clothing
Bittersweet Sixteen
Summer Intern
Jet Set